BEST BOOK OF FUN AND NONSENSE

BEST BOOK
OF
FUN AND
NONSENSE

Edited by
PAULINE RUSH EVANS

Illustrated by
GEORGE WILDE

Doubleday & Company, Inc., Garden City, New York

ACKNOWLEDGMENTS

Thanks are due to the following authors, publishers, publications and agents for permission to use the material indicated.

Brandt & Brandt for "The New Pup" from PENROD, His Complete Story by Booth Tarkington, published by Doubleday & Company, Inc. Copyright, 1929, by Booth Tarkington. Reprinted by permission. The Cresset Press, Ltd. for "A Meal With a Magician" from MY FRIEND MR. LEAKEY by J. B. S. Haldane. Reprinted by permission of the publishers. Dodd, Mead & Company, Inc. for "What Do You Do with a Moose?" from HONK: THE MOOSE by Phil Stong. Copyright © 1935 by Phil Stong. Reprinted by permission of the publishers. J. M. Dent Ltd. for "The Emperor's New Clothes" by Hans Christian Andersen translated by Mrs. Alice Lucas. Doubleday & Company, Inc. for "How the Rhinoceros Got His Skin" from JUST SO STORIES by Rudyard Kipling. Reprinted by permission of Mrs. George Bambridge, The Macmillan Company of Canada and Doubleday & Company, Inc.; "The Ransom of Red Chief" from WHIRLIGIGS, by O. Henry. Copyright 1907 by Doubleday & Company, Inc. Reprinted by permission of the publishers. Greenberg: Publisher for "The Last of the Dragons" from FIVE OF US—AND MADELINE by E. Nesbit, 1932. Reprinted by permission of the publishers. Harcourt, Brace and Company, Inc. for "Clever Manka" from THE SHOEMAKER'S APRON, copyright, 1920, by Parker Fillmore, renewed, 1948, by Louise Fillmore; "The Middle Bear" from THE MIDDLE MOFFAT by Eleanor Estes, copyright, 1942, by Harcourt, Brace and Company, Inc.; "How Hot Balloons and His Pigeon Daughters Crossed Over into the Rootabaga Country" from ROOTABAGA PIGEONS by Carl Sandburg, copyright, 1923, by Harcourt, Brace and Company, Inc.; renewed, 1951, by Carl Sandburg. Reprinted by permission of the publishers. Harper & Brothers for "How Tom Won the Bible Prize" from THE ADVENTURES OF TOM SAWYER by Mark Twain; "The Talking Cat" from THE TALKING CAT by Natalie Savage Carlson. Copyright, 1952, by Natalie Savage Carlson. Reprinted by permission of the publishers. Houghton Mifflin Company for "Jack and the Robbers" from THE JACK TALES by Richard Chase, copyright 1943, and reprinted by permission of and arranged with Houghton Mifflin Company, the authorized publishers. Alfred A. Knopf, Inc. for "Herbert's Remarkable Improvement" from HERBERT by Hazel Wilson. Copyright 1942, 1943, 1944, 1945, 1946, 1948, 1950 by Hazel Wilson; "Freddy Solves Some Mysteries" from FREDDY THE DETECTIVE by Walter R. Brooks. Copyright 1932 by Walter R. Brooks. Reprinted by permission of the publishers. J. B. Lippincott Company for "Oranges and Lemons" from ITALIAN PEEP-SHOW by Eleanor Farjeon. Copyright 1927, 1945 by Eleanor Farjeon. Reprinted by permission of the publishers and Ann Watkins, Inc. Little, Brown & Company for "The Lama" by Ogden Nash. Copyright 1931, by Ogden Nash; "Penguin's Promenade" and "In the Barbershop" from MR. POPPER'S PENGUINS by

Introduction

HUMOR, as lots of people have said, is a funny thing.

It's also a dangerous thing. The moment you say that you think something is funny, somebody will appear from nowhere and say, "What! You think *that* is funny?" Nobody knows what makes people insist that what you think is funny really isn't. But they do. You can test it yourself. Call your younger brother in and tell him a funny story. And see what happens.

For some reason everybody is sure that *he* has a good sense of humor—and is equally doubtful about his friends'. I know lots of people who admit that they have no ear for music, that they are terrible at mathematics, or that they have a poor color sense. But I have never heard a person say, "I have a poor sense of humor."

Perhaps you think that after collecting the stories for a book like this, one should stand up in the introduction and say, "These are all very funny," and then explain why. But I can't do that. All I can say is that here is a book of the things I like best—and they are at least good stories.

It's a big book filled with all sorts of characters that I think you'll like—Penrod and Pecos Bill, Pippi the Superchild, Mr. Thurber's grandfather and Uncle Remus, Tom Sawyer and Alice, Mr. Popper's penguin, a kindly old dragon, a rhinoceros with a crumb under his skin, and a detective-pig. Who can explain creatures like that? Nobody should try to.

The only thing to do is to enjoy them.

Danbury, Conn.   P.R.E.

Contents

MR. POPPER'S PENGUINS 13
PENGUIN'S PROMENADE
IN THE BARBERSHOP
  by Richard and Florence Atwater

A JUST SO STORY:
HOW THE RHINOCEROS GOT HIS SKIN 20
  by Rudyard Kipling

THE LAMA 23
  by Ogden Nash

THE SQUIRE'S BRIDE 24

THE EMPEROR'S NEW CLOTHES 29
  by Hans Christian Andersen

UNCLE REMUS 35
THE WONDERFUL TAR-BABY STORY
HOW BRER RABBIT WAS TOO SHARP FOR BRER FOX
BRER RABBIT GROSSLY DECEIVES BRER FOX
  by Joel Chandler Harris

THE PALACE ON THE ROCK 46
  by Richard Hughes

HERBERT'S REMARKABLE IMPROVEMENT 51
  by Hazel Wilson

KING O'TOOLE AND HIS GOOSE   61

THE DUCK AND THE KANGAROO   66
    by Edward Lear

PECOS BILL INVENTS MODERN COWPUNCHING   70
    by James C. Bowman

THE PRINCESS WHOM NOBODY COULD SILENCE   82

LITTLE EDDIE GOES TO TOWN   86
    by Carolyn Haywood

THE NIGHT THE GHOST GOT IN   94
    by James Thurber

THE MIDDLE MOFFAT   100
    THE MIDDLE BEAR
    by Eleanor Estes

CLEVER MANKA   112
    by Parker Fillmore

FREDDY THE DETECTIVE   119
    FREDDY SOLVES SOME MYSTERIES
    by Walter R. Brooks

THE WALLOPING WINDOW-BLIND   138
    by Charles Edward Carryl

ORANGES AND LEMONS   141
    by Eleanor Farjeon

ALICE IN WONDERLAND   148
    HUMPTY DUMPTY
    by Lewis Carroll

ALICE'S EVIDENCE   159
    by Lewis Carroll

CONAL AND DONAL AND TAIG 160
by Seumas MacManus

HONK: THE MOOSE 167
WHAT DO YOU DO WITH A MOOSE?
CITY COUNCIL
by Phil Stong

LIMERICKS 177
by Edward Lear

JACK AND THE ROBBERS 180
by Richard C. Chase

THE LAST OF THE DRAGONS 187
by E. Nesbit

A CENTIPEDE 196

THE ADVENTURES OF TOM SAWYER 197
HOW TOM WON THE BIBLE PRIZE
by Mark Twain

PIPPI LONGSTOCKING 208
PIPPI PLAYS TAG WITH SOME POLICEMEN
by Astrid Lindgren

THE TALKING CAT 214
by Natalie Savage Carlson

YOUNG SAMMY WATKINS 223

A PENROD STORY: THE NEW PUP 224
by Booth Tarkington

THE 13TH IS MAGIC 245
MRS. WALLABY-JONES
by Joan Howard

A ROOTABAGA STORY: HOW HOT BALLOONS
AND HIS PIGEON DAUGHTERS CROSSED OVER
INTO THE ROOTABAGA COUNTRY   254
   by Carl Sandburg

A MEAL WITH A MAGICIAN   259
   by J. B. S. Haldane

THE DUEL   273
   by Eugene Field

THE RANSOM OF RED CHIEF   275
   by O. Henry

FROM

Mr. Popper's Penguins

RICHARD AND FLORENCE ATWATER

---

*Captain Cook is a penguin that has been sent as a present
to Mr. Popper by an Antarctic explorer. Mr. Popper provides
a nice cool home for the bird in the refrigerator. And the
bird provides the Popper family with many unusual and
hilarious adventures.*

Penguin's Promenade

Mr. Popper soon found that it was not so easy to take a
penguin for a stroll.

Captain Cook did not care at first for the idea of being put on
a leash. However, Mr. Popper was firm. He tied one end of the
clothesline to the penguin's fat throat and the other to his own
wrist.

"*Ork!*" said Captain Cook indignantly. Still, he was a very
reasonable sort of bird, and when he saw that protesting did him
no good, he recovered his customary dignity and decided to let
Mr. Popper lead him.

Mr. Popper put on his best Sunday derby and opened the front
door with Captain Cook waddling graciously beside him.

"*Gaw,*" said the penguin, stopping at the edge of the porch to
look down at the steps.

Mr. Popper gave him plenty of clothesline leash.

"*Gook!*" said Captain Cook, and raising his flippers, he leaned
forward bravely and tobogganed down the steps on his stomach.

Mr. Popper followed, though not in the same way. Captain
Cook quickly got up on his feet again and strutted to the street

ahead of Mr. Popper with many quick turns of his head and pleased comments on the new scene.

Down Proudfoot Avenue came a neighbor of the Poppers, Mrs. Callahan, with her arms full of groceries. She stared in astonishment when she saw Captain Cook and Mr. Popper, looking like a larger penguin himself in his black tailcoat.

"Heavens have mercy on us!" she exclaimed as the bird began to investigate the striped stockings under her house dress. "It isn't an owl and it isn't a goose."

"It isn't," said Mr. Popper, tipping his Sunday derby. "It's an Antarctic penguin, Mrs. Callahan."

"Get away from me," said Mrs. Callahan to Captain Cook. "An anteater, is it?"

"Not anteater," explained Mr. Popper. "Antarctic. It was sent to me from the South Pole."

"Take your South Pole goose away from me at once," said Mrs. Callahan.

Mr. Popper pulled obediently at the clothesline, while Captain Cook took a parting peck at Mrs. Callahan's striped stockings.

"Heaven preserve us!" said Mrs. Callahan. "I must stop in and see Mrs. Popper at once. I would never have believed it. I will be going now."

"So will I," said Mr. Popper as Captain Cook dragged him off down the street.

Their next stop was at the drugstore at the corner of Proudfoot Avenue and Main Street. Here Captain Cook insisted on looking over the window display, which consisted of several open packages of shiny white boric crystals. These he evidently mistook for polar snow, for he began to peck at the window vigorously.

Suddenly a car wheeled to the near-by curb with a shriek of its brakes, and two young men sprang out, one of them bearing a camera.

"This must be it," said the first young man to the other.

"It's them, all right," said the second young man.

The cameraman set up his tripod on the sidewalk. By this time a small crowd had gathered around, and two men in white coats had even come out of the drugstore to watch. Captain Cook,

however, was still too much interested in the window exhibits to bother to turn around.

"You're Mr. Popper of 432 Proudfoot Avenue, aren't you?" asked the second young man, pulling a notebook out of his pocket.

"Yes," said Mr. Popper, realizing that his picture was about to be taken for the newspaper. The two young men had, as a matter of fact, heard about the strange bird from the policeman, and had been on their way to the Popper house, to get an interview, when they saw Captain Cook.

"Hey, pelican, turn around and see the pretty birdie," said the photographer.

"That's no pelican," said the other, who was a reporter. "Pelicans have a pouch in their bills."

"I'd think it was a dodo, only dodos are extinct. This will make an elegant picture, if I can ever get her to turn around."

"It's a penguin," said Mr. Popper proudly. "Its name is Captain Cook."

"*Gook!*" said the penguin, turning around, now that they were talking about him. Spying the camera tripod, he walked over and examined it.

"Probably thinks it's a three-legged stork," said the photographer.

"This bird of yours—" said the reporter. "Is it a he or a she? The public will want to know."

Mr. Popper hesitated. "Well, I call it Captain Cook."

"That makes it a he," said the reporter, writing rapidly in his notebook.

Still curious, Captain Cook started walking round and round the tripod, till the clothesline, the penguin, Mr. Popper and the tripod were all tangled up. At the advice of one of the bystanders, the tangle was finally straightened out by Mr. Popper's walking around the tripod three times in the opposite direction. At last, Captain Cook, standing still beside Mr. Popper, consented to pose.

Mr. Popper straightened his tie, and the cameraman snapped the picture. Captain Cook shut his eyes, and this is the way his picture appeared later in all the newspapers.

"One last question," said the reporter. "Where did you get your strange pet?"

"From Admiral Drake, the South Pole explorer. He sent him to me for a present."

"Yeah," said the reporter. "Anyway, it's a good story."

The two young men jumped into their car. Mr. Popper and Captain Cook continued their walk, with quite a crowd following and asking questions. The crowd was getting so thick that, in order to escape, Mr. Popper led Captain Cook into a barbershop.

The man who kept the barbershop had, up to this time, been a very good friend of Mr. Popper's.

In the Barbershop

It was very quiet in the barbershop. The barber was shaving an elderly gentleman.

Captain Cook found this spectacle very interesting, and in order to get a better view, he jumped up on the mirror ledge.

"Good night!" said the barber.

The gentleman in the barber's chair, his face already white with lather, half-lifted his head to see what had happened.

"*Gook!*" said the penguin, flapping his flippers and reaching out his long beak toward the lather on the gentleman's face.

With a yell and a leap, the gentleman rose from his reclining position, left the barber's chair, and fled into the street, not even stopping for his coat and hat.

"*Gaw!*" said Captain.

"Hey," said the barber to Mr. Popper. "Take that thing out of my shop. This is no zoo. What's the idea?"

"Do you mind if I take him out your back door?" asked Mr. Popper.

"Any door," said the barber, "as long as it's quick. Now it's biting the teeth off my combs."

Mr. Popper took Captain Cook in his arms, and amid cries of "*Quork?*" "*Gawk!*" and "*Ork!*" made his way out of the shop and its back room and out a door into an alley.

Captain Cook now discovered his first back stairway.

Mr. Popper discovered that when a penguin has found steps going up somewhere, it is absolutely impossible to keep him from climbing them.

"All right," said Mr. Popper, panting up the steps behind Captain Cook. "I suppose, being a bird, and one that can't fly, you have to go up in the air somehow, so you like to climb stairs. Well, it's a good thing this building has only three stories. Come on. Let's see what you can do."

Slowly but unwearyingly, Captain Cook lifted one pink foot after another from one step to the next, followed by Mr. Popper at the other end of the clothesline.

At last they came to the top landing.

"Now what?" inquired Mr. Popper of Captain Cook.

Finding there were no more steps to climb, Captain Cook turned around and surveyed the steps that now went down.

Then he raised his flippers and leaned forward.

Mr. Popper, who was still panting for breath, had not supposed the determined bird would plunge so quickly. He should have remembered that penguins will toboggan whenever they get a chance.

Perhaps he had been unwise in tying one end of the clothesline to his own wrist.

At any rate, this time Mr. Popper found himself suddenly sliding, on his own white-clad stomach, down the three flights of steps. This delighted the penguin, who was enjoying his own slide just ahead of Mr. Popper.

When they reached the bottom, Captain Cook was so eager to go up again that Mr. Popper had to call a taxi, to distract him.

"432 Proudfoot Avenue," said Mr. Popper to the driver.

The driver, who was a kind and polite man, did not laugh at his oddly assorted passengers until he had been paid.

"Oh dear!" said Mrs. Popper, when she opened the door to her husband. "You looked so neat and handsome when you started for your walk. And now look at the front of you!"

"I am sorry, my love," said Mr. Popper in a humble tone, "but you can't always tell what a penguin will do next."

So saying, he went to lie down, for he was quite exhausted from all the unusual exercise, while Captain Cook had a shower and took a nap in the icebox.

How the Rhinoceros Got His Skin

RUDYARD KIPLING

ONCE upon a time, on an uninhabited island on the shores of the Red Sea, there lived a Parsee from whose hat the rays of the sun were reflected in more-than-oriental splendour. And the Parsee lived by the Red Sea with nothing but his hat and his knife and a cooking stove of the kind that you must particularly never touch. And one day he took flour and water and currants and plums and sugar and things, and made himself one cake which was two feet across and three feet thick. It was indeed a Superior Comestible (*that's* magic), and he put it on the stove because *he* was allowed to cook on that stove, and he baked it and he baked it till it was all done brown and smelt most sentimental. But just as he was going to eat it there came down to the beach from the Altogether Uninhabited Interior one Rhinoceros with a horn on his nose, two piggy eyes, and few manners. In those days the Rhinoceros's skin fitted him quite tight. There were no wrinkles in it anywhere. He looked exactly like a Noah's Ark Rhinoceros, but of course much bigger. All the same, he had no manners then, and he has no manners now, and he never will have any manners. He said, "How!" and the Parsee left that cake and climbed to the top of a palm-tree with nothing on but his hat, from which the rays of the sun were always reflected in more-than-oriental splendour. And the Rhinoceros upset the oil-stove with his nose, and the cake rolled on the sand, and he spiked that cake on the horn of his nose, and he ate it, and he went away, waving his tail, to the desolate and Exclusively Uninhabited Interior which abuts on the islands of Mazanderan,

Socotra, and the Promontories of the Larger Equinox. Then the Parsee came down from his palm-tree and put the stove on its legs and recited the following *Sloka*, which, as you have not heard, I will now proceed to relate:

> *Them that takes cakes*
> *Which the Parsee-man bakes*
> *Makes dreadful mistakes.*

And there was a great deal more in that than you would think.

Because, five weeks later, there was a heat-wave in the Red Sea, and everybody took off all the clothes they had. The Parsee took off his hat; but the Rhinoceros took off his skin and carried it over his shoulder as he came down to the beach to bathe. In those days it buttoned underneath with three buttons and looked like a waterproof. He said nothing whatever about the Parsee's cake, because he had eaten it all; and he never had any manners, then, since, or henceforward. He waddled straight into the water and blew bubbles through his nose, leaving his skin on the beach.

Presently the Parsee came by and found the skin, and he smiled one smile that ran all round his face two times. Then he danced three times round the skin and rubbed his hands. Then he went to his camp and filled his hat with cake-crumbs, for the Parsee never ate anything but cake, and never swept out his camp. He took that skin, and he shook that skin, and he scrubbed that skin, and he rubbed that skin just as full of old, dry, stale, tickly cake-crumbs and some burned currants as ever it could *possibly* hold. Then he climbed to the top of his palm-tree and waited for the Rhinoceros to come out of the water and put it on.

And the Rhinoceros did. He buttoned it up with the three buttons, and it tickled like cake-crumbs in bed. Then he wanted to scratch, but that made it worse; and then he lay down on the sands and rolled and rolled and rolled, and every time he rolled the cake-crumbs tickled him worse and worse and worse. Then he ran to the palm-tree and rubbed and rubbed and rubbed himself against it. He rubbed so much and so hard that he rubbed his skin into a great fold over his shoulders, and another fold underneath, where the buttons used to be (but he rubbed the buttons

off), and he rubbed some more folds over his legs. And it spoiled his temper, but it didn't make the least difference to the cake-crumbs. They were inside his skin and they tickled. So he went home, very angry indeed and horribly scratchy; and from that day to this every rhinoceros has great folds in his skin and a very bad temper, all on account of the cake-crumbs inside.

But the Parsee came down from his palm-tree, wearing his hat, from which the rays of the sun were reflected in more-than-oriental splendour, packed up his cooking stove, and went away in the direction of Orotavo, Amygdala, the Upland Meadows of Anantarivo and the Marshes of Sonaput.

The Lama

OGDEN NASH

The one-l lama,
He's a priest,
The two-l llama,
He's a beast.
And I will bet
A silk pyjama
There isn't any
Three-l lllama.

The Squire's Bride

ONCE upon a time there was a rich squire who owned a large farm, and had plenty of silver at the bottom of his chest and money in the bank besides; but he felt there was something wanting, for he was a widower.

One day the daughter of a neighboring farmer was working for him in the hayfield. The squire saw her and liked her very much, and as she was the child of poor parents, he thought if he only hinted that he wanted her she would be ready to marry him at once.

So he told her he had been thinking of getting married again.

"Ay! one may think of many things," said the girl, laughing slyly. In her opinion the old fellow ought to be thinking of something that behoved him better than getting married.

"Well, you see, I thought that you should be my wife!"

"No, thank you all the same," said she; "that's not at all likely."

The squire was not accustomed to be gainsaid, and the more she refused him the more determined he was to get her.

But as he made no progress in her favor he sent for her father and told him that if he could arrange the matter with his daughter he would forgive him the money he had lent him, and he would also give him the piece of land which lay close to his meadow into the bargain.

"Yes, you may be sure I'll bring my daughter to her senses," said the father. "She is only a child, and she doesn't know what's best for her." But all his coaxing and talking did not help mat-

ters. She would not have the squire, she said, if he sat buried in gold up to his ears.

The squire waited day after day, but at last he became so angry and impatient that he told the father, if he expected him to stand by his promise, he would have to put his foot down now, for he would not wait any longer.

The man knew no other way out of it but to let the squire get everything ready for the wedding; and when the parson and the wedding guests had arrived the squire should send for the girl as if she were wanted for some work on the farm. When she arrived she would have to be married right away, so that she would have no time to think it over.

The squire thought this was well and good, and so he began brewing and baking and getting ready for the wedding in grand style. When the guests had arrived the squire called one of his farm lads and told him to run down to his neighbor and ask him to send him what he had promised.

"But if you are not back in a twinkling," he said, shaking his fist at him, "I'll—"

He did not say more, for the lad ran off as if he had been shot at.

"My master has sent me to ask for that you promised him," said the lad, when he got to the neighbor, "but there is no time to be lost, for he is terribly busy today."

"Yes, yes! Run down into the meadow and take her with you. There she goes!" answered the neighbor.

The lad ran off and when he came to the meadow he found the daughter there raking the hay.

"I am to fetch what your father has promised my master," said the lad.

"Ah, ha!" thought she. "Is that what they are up to?"

"Ah, indeed!" she said. "I suppose it's that little bay mare of ours. You had better go and take her. She stands there tethered on the other side of the pea field," said the girl.

The boy jumped on the back of the bay mare and rode home at full gallop.

"Have you got her with you?" asked the squire.

"She is down at the door," said the lad.

"Take her up to the room my mother had," said the squire.

"But, master, how can that be managed?" said the lad.

"You must just do as I tell you," said the squire. "If you cannot manage her alone you must get the men to help you," for he thought the girl might turn obstreperous.

When the lad saw his master's face he knew it would be no use to gainsay him. So he went and got all the farm-tenants who were there to help him. Some pulled at the head and the forelegs of the mare and others pushed from behind, and at last they got her up the stairs and into the room. There lay all the wedding finery ready.

"Now, that's done, master!" said the lad; "but it was a terrible job. It was the worst I have ever had here on the farm."

"Never mind, you shall not have done it for nothing," said his master. "Now send the women up to dress her."

"But I say, master—!" said the lad.

"None of your talk!" said the squire. "Tell them they must dress her and mind and not forget either wreath or crown."

The lad ran into the kitchen.

"Look here, lasses," he said; "you must go upstairs and dress up the bay mare as a bride. I expect the master wants to give the guests a laugh."

The women dressed the bay mare in everything that was there, and then the lad went and told his master that now she was ready dressed, with wreath and crown and all.

"Very well then, bring her down!" said the squire. "I will receive her myself at the door," said he.

There was a terrible clatter on the stairs; for that bride, you know, had no silken shoes on.

When the door opened and the squire's bride entered the parlor, you can imagine there was a good deal of tittering and grinning.

And as for the squire, you may be sure he had had enough of that bride, and they say he never went courting again.

From *Fairy Tales from the Far North*, edited by P. C. Asbjörnsen and Jörgen Moe.

The Emperor's New Clothes

HANS CHRISTIAN ANDERSEN

Many years ago there was an Emperor who was so excessively fond of new clothes that he spent all his money on them. He cared nothing about his soldiers, nor for the theater, nor for driving in the woods, except for the sake of showing off his new clothes. He had a costume for every hour in the day, and instead of saying as one does about any other King or Emperor, "He is in his council chamber," here one always said, "The Emperor is in his dressing room."

Life was very gay in the great town where he lived; hosts of strangers came to visit it every day, and among them one day two swindlers. They gave themselves out as weavers, and said that they knew how to weave the most beautiful stuffs imaginable. Not only were the colors and patterns unusually fine, but the clothes that were made of the stuffs had the peculiar quality of becoming invisible to every person who was not fit for the office he held, or if he was impossibly dull.

"Those must be splendid clothes," thought the Emperor. "By wearing them I shall be able to discover which men in my kingdom are unfitted for their posts. I shall distinguish the wise men from the fools. Yes, I certainly must order some of that stuff to be woven for me."

He paid the two swindlers a lot of money in advance so that they might begin their work at once. They did put up two looms and pretended to weave, but they had nothing whatever upon their shuttles. At the outset they asked for a quantity of the purest gold thread, all of which they put into their own bags while they worked away at the empty looms far into the night.

"I should like to know how those weavers are getting on with the stuff," thought the Emperor; but he felt a little queer when he reflected that anyone who was stupid or unfit for his post would not be able to see it. He certainly thought he need have no fears for himself, but still he thought he would send somebody else first to see how it was getting on. Everybody in the town knew what wonderful power the stuff possessed, and everyone was anxious to see how stupid his neighbor was.

"I will send my faithful old minister to the weavers," thought the Emperor. "He will be best able to see how the stuff looks, for he is a clever man and no one fulfills his duties better than he does!"

So the good old minister went into the room where the two swindlers sat working at the empty loom.

"Heaven preserve us!" thought the old minister, opening his eyes very wide. "Why, I can't see a thing!" But he took care not to say so.

Both the swindlers begged him to be good enough to step a little nearer, and asked if he did not think it a good pattern and beautiful coloring. They pointed to the empty loom, and the poor old minister stared as hard as he could but he could not see anything, for of course there was nothing to see.

"Good heavens!" thought he, "is it possible that I am a fool? I have never thought so and nobody must know it. Am I not fit for my post? It will never do to say that I cannot see the stuffs."

"Well, sir, you don't say anything about the stuff," said the one who was pretending to weave.

"Oh, it is beautiful! quite charming!" said the old minister, looking through his spectacles; "this pattern and these colors! I will certainly tell the Emperor that the stuff pleases me very much."

"We are delighted to hear you say so," said the swindlers, and then they named all the colors and described the peculiar pattern. The old minister paid great attention to what they said, so as to be able to repeat it when he got home to the Emperor.

Then the swindlers went on to demand more money, more silk, and more gold to be able to proceed with the weaving; but they put it all into their own pockets—not a single strand was ever put into the loom, but they went on as before weaving at the empty loom.

The Emperor soon sent another faithful official to see how the stuff was getting on, and if it would soon be ready. The same thing happened to him as to the minister; he looked and looked, but as there was only the empty loom, he could see nothing at all.

"Is not this a beautiful piece of stuff?" said both the swindlers, showing the beautiful pattern and colors which were not there to be seen.

"I know I am not a fool!" thought the man, "so it must be that I am unfit for my good post! It is very strange though! However, one must not let it appear!" So he praised the stuff he did not see, and assured them of his delight in the beautiful colors and the originality of the design. "It is absolutely charming!" he said to the Emperor. Everybody was talking about the splendid stuff.

Now the Emperor thought he would like to see it while it was still on the loom. So, accompanied by a number of selected courtiers, among whom were the two faithful officials who had already seen the imaginary stuff, he went to visit the crafty impostors, who were working away as hard as ever they could at the empty loom.

"It is magnificent!" said both the honest officials. "Only see, your Majesty, what a design! What colors!" And they pointed to the empty loom, for they thought no doubt the others could see the stuff.

"What!" thought the Emperor; "I see nothing at all! This is terrible! Am I a fool? Am I not fit to be Emperor? Why, nothing worse could happen to me!"

"Oh, it is beautiful!" said the Emperor. "It has my highest approval!" and he nodded his satisfaction as he gazed at the empty loom. Nothing would induce him to say that he could not see anything.

The whole suite gazed and gazed, but saw nothing more than all the others. However, they all exclaimed with his Majesty, "It is very beautiful!" and they advised him to wear a suit made of this wonderful cloth on the occasion of a great procession which was just about to take place. "It is magnificent! gorgeous! excellent!" went from mouth to mouth; they were all equally delighted with it.

The Emperor gave each of the rogues an order of knighthood to be worn in their buttonholes and the title of "Gentlemen weavers."

The swindlers sat up the whole night before the day on which the procession was to take place, burning sixteen candles, so that people might see how anxious they were to get the Emperor's new clothes ready. They pretended to take the stuff off the loom. They cut it out in the air with a huge pair of scissors, and they stitched away with needles without any thread in them. At last they said: "Now the Emperor's new clothes are ready!"

The Emperor, with his grandest courtiers, went to them himself, and both the swindlers raised one arm in the air, as if they were holding something, and said: "See, these are the trousers, this is the coat, here is the mantle!" and so on. "It is as light as a spider's web. One might think one had nothing on, but that is the very beauty of it!"

"Yes!" said all the courtiers, but they could not see anything, for there was nothing to see.

"Will your Imperial Majesty be graciously pleased to take off your clothes," said the impostors, "so that we may put on the new ones, along here before the great mirror?"

The Emperor took off all his clothes, and the impostors pretended to give him one article of dress after the other, of the new ones which they had pretended to make. They pretended to fasten something round his waist and to tie on something; this was the train, and the Emperor turned round and round in front of the mirror.

"How well his Majesty looks in the new clothes! How becoming they are!" cried all the people round. "What a design, and what colors! They are most gorgeous robes!"

"The canopy is waiting outside which is to be carried over your Majesty in the procession," said the master of the ceremonies.

"Well, I am quite ready," said the Emperor. "Don't the clothes fit well?" and then he turned round again in front of the mirror, so that he should seem to be looking at his grand things.

The chamberlains who were to carry the train stooped and pretended to lift it from the ground with both hands, and they walked along with their hands in the air. They dared not let it appear that they could not see anything.

Then the Emperor walked along in the procession under the gorgeous canopy, and everybody in the streets and at the windows exclaimed, "How beautiful the Emperor's new clothes are! What a splendid train! And they fit to perfection!" Nobody would let it appear that he could see nothing, for then he would not be fit for his post, or else he was a fool.

None of the Emperor's clothes had been so successful before.

"But he has got nothing on," said a little child.

"Oh, listen to the innocent," said its father; and one person whispered to the other what the child had said. "He has nothing on; a child says he has nothing on!"

"But he has nothing on!" at last cried all the people.

The Emperor writhed, for he knew it was true, but he thought, "The procession must go on now," so he held himself stiffer than ever, and the chamberlains held up the invisible train.

FROM
Uncle Remus

JOEL CHANDLER HARRIS

When Joel Chandler Harris was a child, he heard the Negroes on the Georgia plantation where he lived tell wonderful folk tales of the goings on in the animal world. Harris retold these old stories through the character of Uncle Remus, a kindly old Negro retainer who spins his yarns for a little boy who visits him in his cabin in the quiet of the evening. Uncle Remus is surely one of the best loved of all American story tellers, but today the dialect in which he speaks is hard for most people to read. That's a pity, for the stories are much too good to miss. Here, then—with the dialect greatly simplified—are three of Uncle Remus' best yarns about smart and sassy Brer Rabbit, who's the hero of many of the tales, and his old enemy, wily Brer Fox.

The Wonderful Tar-Baby Story

DIDN'T the fox *ever* catch the rabbit, Uncle Remus?" the little boy asked the old man one evening.

"He come mighty near it, honey, sure as you're born. One day after Brer Rabbit had fooled him so many times, Brer Fox went to work an' got him some tar, and then he mixed it with some turpentine and fixed up a contraption that he called a *Tar-Baby*. He took this here Tar-Baby and set him down right smack in the big road and then went and lay down in the bushes and watched for to see what was goin' to happen.

"Brer Fox didn't have to wait long either. Pretty soon Brer Rabbit come prancin' down the road lippity-clippity, clippity-lippity, just as sassy as a jay-bird. Brer Fox, he just lay low. Brer Rabbit kept prancin' right along 'til he spied the Tar-Baby settin' there, and then he fetched up on his hind legs lookin' mighty astonished. The Tar-Baby just set there doin' nothin', and Brer Fox, he kept on layin' low in the bushes.

" 'Mornin'!' says Brer Rabbit. 'Nice weather this mornin',' he says.

"Tar-Baby ain't sayin' nothin', and Brer Fox, he lay low in the bushes.

" 'How is the state of your health at present?' says Brer Rabbit to Tar-Baby.

"Brer Fox, he wink his eye slow and lay low, and Tar-Baby still ain't sayin' nothin'.

" 'How are you gettin' along?' says Brer Rabbit. And when there ain't no answer, he says, 'Is you deaf?' he says, 'Because if you is, I can holler louder.'

"Tar-Baby just kept on settin' there, and Brer Fox just keep on watchin' from the bushes.

" 'You're mighty stuck up, that's what you is,' says Brer Rabbit. 'And I'm goin' to cure you, that's what I'm goin' to do,' he says.

"Brer Fox, he sorta chuckle in his stomach, he did, but Tar-Baby ain't sayin' nothin'.

" 'I'm goin' to learn you how to talk to respectable folks if it's the last thing I do,' says Brer Rabbit. 'If you don't take off that old hat and say howdy-do to me, I'm goin' to bust you wide open,' says he.

"Tar-Baby stay still and Brer Fox lay low just like before.

"Brer Rabbit kept on askin' him to say howdy-do, and Tar-Baby kept on sayin' nothin' at all, 'til finally Brer Rabbit draw back his fist and—*blip*—he hit Tar-Baby right smack on the side of the head. And right there's where Brer Rabbit made his big mistake. His fist stuck fast, and he couldn't pull loose. The tar held him tight. But Tar-Baby just set still. And Brer Fox, he kept on layin' low.

" 'If you don't let me loose, I'll knock you again,' says Brer Rabbit, and with that he fetched Tar-Baby a swipe with the other hand. And *that* stuck.

" 'Turn me loose,' hollers Brer Rabbit. 'Turn me loose now, before I kick the natural stuffin' out of you,' he says. But Tar-Baby ain't sayin' nothin'—just keeps on holdin' fast. Well, then Brer Rabbit he commenced to kick, and the next thing he know his feet are stuck fast too. Brer Rabbit squalled out that if Tar-Baby didn't turn him loose, he'd butt with his head. Well, of course Tar-Baby *didn't* turn him loose, and Brer Rabbit butted, and then he got his head stuck, too.

"Well sir, just about that time old Brer Fox, he sauntered out of the bushes, lookin' just as innocent as a mockin' bird.

" 'Howdy, Brer Rabbit,' says Brer Fox, says he. 'You look sort a stuck up this mornin',' he says, and then he rolled on the ground and he laughed and he laughed 'til he couldn't laugh no more. 'I reckon you're goin' to have dinner with me this time, Brer Rabbit,' he says. 'I've laid in a heap o' nice vegetables and things, and I ain't goin' to take no excuse from you,' says Brer Fox."

Here Uncle Remus paused and raked a huge sweet potato out of the ashes on the hearth.

"Did the fox eat the rabbit, Uncle Remus?" asked the little boy.

"Well, now, that's as far as the tale goes," replied the old man. "Maybe he did—and then again, maybe he didn't. Some people say that Judge B'ar come along and turned him loose. And some say he didn't. . . . But ain't that Miss Sally I hear callin' you? You better run along now."

How Brer Rabbit Was Too Sharp for Brer Fox

"Uncle Remus," said the little boy one evening when he found the old man with little or nothing to do, "Uncle Remus, *did* the fox kill and eat the rabbit when he caught him with the Tar-Baby?"

"Law, honey, ain't I tell you about that?" replied the old man, chuckling slyly. "I declare to gracious, now, I ought to told you that. But old man Nod was ridin' on my eyelids so heavy that a little more and I'd a disremembered my own name. And on top o' that, just then your mammy come callin' you for to go to bed.

"What was it I tell you when I first begin? I tell you that Brer Rabbit was a monstrous clever creature—leastways, that's what I laid out for to tell you. Well, then, honey, don't you go and make no other calculations. 'Cause in them days when anything was goin' on, Brer Rabbit and his family was right at the head of the gang—and there they stayed. Before you sheds any tears about Brer Rabbit, you just wait and see whereabouts Brer Rabbit ends up.

"When old Brer Fox find Brer Rabbit all mixed up with that Tar-Baby, he feel mighty good. He just roll on the ground and laugh. By and by he up and says, says he:

"'Well, I 'spect I got you this time,' says he. 'Maybe I ain't, but I reckon I has. You been runnin' round here sassin' me a mighty long time. But now I 'spect you done come to the end of the row. You been cuttin' up your capers and bouncin' round in this neighborhood 'til you come to believe that you're the boss of the whole gang.'

"'And besides that, you're always gettin' in somewheres where

you don't have no business,' says Brer Fox, says he. 'Who asked
you to come and strike up an acquaintance with this here Tar-
Baby? And who got you all stuck up there the way you is? Nobody in the whole round world but yourself. You just took and
jam yourself on that Tar-Baby without waitin' for any invite,'
says Brer Fox.

"'Well, there you is,' says Brer Fox, 'and there you'll stay 'til I
fixes up a brush-pile and fires her up,' he says, ''cause I'm goin' to
barbecue you this day, sure,' says Brer Fox, says he.

"Then Brer Rabbit he begin to talk mighty humble, he did.

"'I don't care what you do with me, Brer Fox,' says he, 'just so
you don't fling me in that brier patch. Roast me, Brer Fox,' says
he, 'but don't fling me in that brier patch.'

"'Well, it's so much trouble for to kindle a fire,' says Brer Fox,
says he, 'that I 'spect maybe I'll have to hang you instead,' he
says.

"'Hang me just as high as you please, Brer Fox,' says Brer Rabbit, 'but for the Lord's sake don't fling me in that brier patch,'
says he.

"'I ain't got no string,' says Brer Fox. 'I 'spect I'll just have to
drown you,' says he.

"'Drown me just as deep as you please, Brer Fox,' says Brer
Rabbit, says he, 'but don't fling me in that there brier patch,'
he says.

"'There ain't no water nigh here,' says Brer Fox, 'so I 'spect
maybe I'll just have to skin you instead,' he says.

"'Skin me, Brer Fox,' says Brer Rabbit, says he, 'snatch out
my eyes, tear out my ears by the roots, and cut off my legs,' he
says, 'but please, Brer Fox, please don't fling me in that brier
patch,' says he.

"Brer Fox he want to hurt Brer Rabbit just as bad as he can,
of course, so he catch him by the hind legs and he slung him
right spang in the middle of the brier patch. There was a considerable flutter when Brer Rabbit land in the bushes, and Brer
Fox he sorta hang 'round for to see what goin' to happen. By
and by he hear somebody call him, and he look and 'way up on
the hill he see Brer Rabbit settin' cross-legged on a log, combin'

the tar out of his hair with a chip. Then Brer Fox know he been tricked—tricked mighty bad. And Brer Rabbit he couldn't help but fling back some of his sass, and he holler out from the hill:

"'Why, I was bred and born in a brier patch, Brer Fox—bred and born in a brier patch!'

"And with that he skip out o' there just as lively as a cricket in the embers."

Brer Rabbit Grossly Deceives Brer Fox

One evening when the little boy, whose nights with Uncle Remus were as entertaining as those Arabian Nights of blessed memory, had finished supper and hurried out to sit with his venerable patron, he found the old man in great glee. Indeed, Uncle Remus was talking and laughing to himself at such a rate that the little boy was afraid that he had company. The truth is, Uncle Remus had heard the child coming and, when the rosy-cheeked little chap put his head in at the door, was engaged in a monologue, the burden of which seemed to be:

"Ole Molly Har'
W'at you doin' dar
Settin' in de cornder
Smokin' yo' seegar?"

Whatever this vague allusion meant, it somehow reminded the little boy that the wicked Fox was still in pursuit of the Rabbit, and his curiosity immediately took the shape of a question.

"Uncle Remus, did the Rabbit have to go clean away when he got loose from the Tar-Baby?"

"Bless gracious, honey, that he didn't. Who? Him? Well, you don't know nothin' at all about Brer Rabbit if that's the way you puttin' him down. What he goin' 'way for? He maybe stayed sorta close 'til the tar rub off his hair some. But it wasn't many days before he was lopin' up and down the neighborhood the same as ever—and I don't know if he wasn't more sassier than before.

"But somehow it seem that the tale about how he got mixed up with the Tar-Baby got 'round amongst the neighbors. Leastways, Miss Meadows and the gals got wind of it, and the next time Brer Rabbit paid them a visit Miss Meadows tackled him 'bout it. The gals set up a monstrous gigglement, but Brer Rabbit he set up just as cool as a cucumber, he did, and let 'em run on."

"Who was Miss Meadows, Uncle Remus?" inquired the little boy.

"Well, don't ask me, honey. They was just in the tale, Miss Meadows and the gals was, and I tell the tale to you just the way it was give to me. . . . Well, then, Brer Rabbit just set there sorta like a lamb, he did, and then by and by he cross his legs, and he lean back and wink his eye slow. Then he up and say, says he:

" 'Ladies, Brer Fox was my daddy's ridin' horse for thirty year —maybe more, but for thirty year that I knows about,' says he. Then he paid the ladies his respects, and he tip his hat, he did. And off he march, just as stiff and stuck up as a stick.

"Next day, Brer Fox he come a'callin' on the ladies, and when he begin to laugh about Brer Rabbit, Miss Meadows and the gals

they ups and tells him about what Brer Rabbit say. Well, Brer
Fox he grit his teeth, he did sure enough, and he look mighty
grumpy. But when he stood up for to go, he up and he say, says
he:

"'Ladies, I ain't disputin' what you say—but I tell you this:
I'll make Brer Rabbit chew up his words and spit 'em right here
where you can see 'em,' says he. And with that, off went Brer
Fox.

"As soon as he got to the bit road, Brer Fox shook the dew
off his tail and made a straight shoot for Brer Rabbit's house.
Brer Rabbit was expectin' him, of course, and when he got there,
the door was shut fast. Brer Fox knock. Nobody ain't answer.
Brer Fox knock again. Still nobody answer. Brer Fox keep on
knockin'—blam, blam! And then Brer Rabbit holler out, but
mighty weak.

"'Is that you, Brer Fox? I want you to run and fetch the doctor. Somethin' I et this mornin' is killin' me. Please, Brer Fox,
run quick for the doctor,' says Brer Rabbit, says he.

"'Why, I just come to fetch you, Brer Rabbit,' says Brer Fox.
'There's goin' to be a party up at Miss Meadows's,' says he. 'All
the gals goin' to be there, and I promise that I'd fetch you. The
gals they all said that it wouldn't be no party exceptin' I fetch
you,' says Brer Fox, says he.

"Brer Rabbit say he was too sick to go. Brer Fox say he wasn't
—and then they had it up and down, disputin' and contendin'.
Brer Rabbit say he can't walk. Brer Fox say he carry him. Brer
Rabbit say how? Brer Fox say in his arms. Brer Rabbit say he
'fraid he drop him. Brer Fox he promise he won't.

"By and by Brer Rabbit say he go if Brer Fox tote him on his
back. Brer Fox say he do that. But Brer Rabbit say he can't ride
without a saddle. Brer Fox say he get a saddle. Brer Rabbit say
he can't set in the saddle unless he have a bridle for to hold on to.
Brer Fox say he get the bridle. But Brer Rabbit say he can't ride
without blinders on the bridle, 'cause maybe Brer Fox shy at
stumps along the way and fling him off. Brer Fox he say he get a
blind bridle.

"Then Brer Rabbit say he go. And Brer Fox say he ride Brer

Rabbit most up to Miss Meadows's, but then he let him get down and walk the rest of the way. Brer Rabbit agree and Brer Fox hustle off after the saddle and the bridle.

"Of course, all along Brer Rabbit know the game that Brer Fox was fixin' for to play, and he determine to outdo him. Well, by the time he comb his hair, and twist his mustache, and sorta spruce himself up, why here come Brer Fox with the saddle and bridle on, lookin' as perky as a circus pony. He trot right up to the door and stand there pawin' the ground and chompin' the bit like a sure enough horse. Brer Rabbit he mount, he did, and they amble off.

"Brer Fox he can't see behind because of the blind bridle he wearin', but by and by he feel Brer Rabbit raise one of his feet.

" 'What you doin', Brer Rabbit?' says he.

" 'Shortenin' the left stirrup, Brer Fox,' says he.

"By and by Brer Rabbit raise up the other foot.

" 'What you doin' now, Brer Rabbit?' says he.

" 'Pullin' down my pants, Brer Fox,' says he.

"But all this time, bless gracious, honey, Brer Rabbit was puttin' on his spurs. When they got close to Miss Meadows's where Brer Rabbit was to git off, Brer Fox made a motion for to stop. Then Brer Rabbit he slap the spurs into Brer Fox' flanks—and you better believe that Brer Fox begin to cover the ground. When they got to the house, Miss Meadows and all the gals was settin' on the piazza. Instead of stoppin' at the gate, Brer Rabbit rode right on by, he did, and then came gallopin' back down the road and up to the horse-rack, which he hitch Brer Fox at, and then he sauntered into the house, he did, and shake hands with the gals, and set there smokin' his seegar same as a town man. By and by he draw in a long puff and let it out in a cloud. Then he square himself back and holler out, he did:

" 'Ladies, ain't I done tell you Brer Fox was the ridin' horse for our family? He sorta losin' his gait now, but I reckon I can fetch him 'round in a month or so,' says he.

"Then Brer Rabbit sorta grin, he did, and the gals giggle, and Miss Meadows, she praise up the pony. And there was Brer Fox hitched fast to the rack, and couldn't help himself."

"Is that all, Uncle Remus?" asked the little boy as the old man paused.

"Well, that ain't exactly all, honey—but it wouldn't do to give out too much cloth for to make one pair of pants," replied the old man sententiously.

The Palace on the Rock

RICHARD HUGHES

THERE was once a King who lived in a one-roomed palace. It was on the top of a steep rock right in the middle of the town he governed. The top of the rock was so small that the palace covered it all, though the palace had only one room; and the sides of the rock were so steep that the only way to get up to the palace was to climb a rope.

Now this was all very well when the King was young; but as he got older he and the Queen had more and more children; and so, living together in one room like that, they began to feel rather crowded. The Queen was always telling the King he ought to build on other rooms to the palace. But when she said that the King always asked her what she thought he was to build them on, seeing the palace already covered the whole of the rock.

But all the same the King thought there must be some way of doing it, so he sent for his Prime Minister. The Prime Minister was an old man with a long white beard, and did not much like scrambling up a rope to the palace, but when the King told him to, he had to, of course. So up he came.

"Look!" said the King. "I've got sixteen children, and the Queen and I and all sixteen have to live together in one room. Just look what it's like!"

And indeed the room was in a terrible mess. The King sat on his throne in the middle with two of the older boys running clockwork trains between his legs. One of the little princesses was sitting in the coal-scuttle because there were no empty chairs left to sit on. The Queen had cleverly sewn the bottoms of two of the curtains to the tops, in order to make bags, and two more

children were sitting in them. The eldest prince shot at them with a water pistol if they put their heads out. Two other children had climbed on to the King's desk, and were busy emptying his inkpot into the milk jug. Far more children were sitting on the Queen's knees than there was room for, and the youngest of all, the baby, was asleep in the King's crown, which had been hung upside down from a hook in the ceiling.

The Prime Minister looked, and he agreed that something would have to be done about it; but the difficulty was to know what. So he told the King he would think it over.

"All right," said the King, "but think it over fairly quickly; and if you haven't thought what is to be done in a week it will be the worse for you."

So the Prime Minister slid down the rope again, and began to think. But he couldn't think of anything. Then he remembered he had heard that down by the seaside a long way off there lived a wise old man. And he thought perhaps that wise old man could help him. So the Prime Minister took his bicycle and began to bicycle to the sea. It was a long way, and there were many hills to go up and many hills to go down, and he was tired and out of breath when at last he came to the seaside.

There by the sea sat an old man mending some very large lobster pots (which are traps for catching lobsters in). The old man did not look very wise, but the Prime Minister told him what the trouble was, and asked him what to do.

"How much money have you got with you?" said the old man.

"I've got sixteen pounds," said the Prime Minister.

"That will be just enough," said the old man, "to buy from me these sixteen lobster pots. And if you buy them I will give you sixteen big iron hooks as a present."

"Why should I want your lobster pots?" said the Prime Minister crossly. "What use are they to me?"

"Think!" said the old man. "After all, you *are* Prime Minister, you ought to be able to think out a simple thing like that! How many windows has the one-roomed palace got?"

"Sixteen," said the Prime Minister.

"Well, then," said the old man, "that is just right. Hurry up, pay your money and take them away."

So the Prime Minister paid for the pots and tied them all over his bicycle. Then he hung the iron hooks round his neck where they dangled and jangled, and started to ride back to the town. It had been difficult enough riding down to the sea, and it was far harder and more tiring riding back to the town with all those pots and iron hooks. The Prime Minister was tired and dusty and thirsty and wanting tea and buttered toast more than ever he had in his life before, when at last he got back to his home. But all the same he only made a hurried tea, and then climbed up the rope to the palace with all his pots and hooks.

When he got there, things were worse than ever before. If the children had been naughty before they were twice as naughty now, and the King and Queen were nearly distracted.

"If you have got a really good idea," said the King, "I will give you ten sacks full of treasure."

"Right," said the Prime Minister, "I have." And he put all the pots down on the floor. He then put a bag of candy in each pot. Then he went away as if he had forgotten the pots and began leaning out of the windows, fixing an iron hook outside to the windowstill of each one.

Now it was not long before the children caught sight of the candy in the lobster pots, because lobster pots are made of a sort of open basketwork that you can easily see into. Each lobster pot has a hole, of course, for the lobster to get in by. And once they saw the candy inside it was not long before the children were wriggling through the holes after it, one into each pot. Now, though lobster pots are easy to get into, the whole cleverness in making them lies in the fact that they are not nearly so easy to get out of. Once the children were inside them, there they were. They squawked a little and asked to be taken out.

"Not a bit of it," said the Prime Minister. "That's where you stay!" And taking all the lobster pots one by one he hung them on the hooks outside each of the windows.

"There!" he said to the King and Queen. "Now you can have the whole room to yourselves, and a little peace at last! And yet the children will be quite handy to give their suppers to—if you remember to give them suppers, that is to say.

"If they squawk too much you can just shut the windows," he added.

The King and Queen were delighted, and thought they had the cleverest Prime Minister that any King ever had (and indeed there are not many prime ministers today who can manage the same trouble so neatly). So the King gave him his sacks of treasure gladly, and the Prime Minister went home to have a second tea; and as he was eating it he looked out of his own window up at the palace, and thought how pretty the lobster pots looked, swinging from all the windowsills, each with one of the pretty little royal children inside it.

Herbert's Remarkable Improvement

HAZEL WILSON

IT ALL began with his mother's worrying about his ears. There was nothing unusual about Herbert's ears. They stuck out a little and were a nuisance to wash, but they were perfectly good ears. Not a thing in the world was the matter with them, until one day Mrs. Yadon noticed that Herbert was getting deaf.

"I ask him and ask him to empty the wastebasket and he doesn't hear me," Mrs. Yadon complained to Mr. Yadon. "Can the boy be getting deaf?"

"His great-aunt on my father's side of the family went deaf at the age of eighty-nine," said Mr. Yadon. "Deafness may run in the family."

"Oh, dear, I'm so worried about Herbert," said Mrs. Yadon, "for, besides getting deaf, he is growing more and more forgetful. Yesterday I sent him to the store for a pound of spinach and he came back with a big bag of potato chips instead, and today I sent him for vinegar and he brought back maple sirup. And there's another thing: have you noticed how hard it is lately to get Herbert up in the morning? He used to wake with the birds, but now I have hard work to get him out of bed by seven thirty especially on school days. I'm really worried about Herbert's health."

"Then why," asked Mr. Yadon, "don't you take him to a doctor?"

"That is just what I am going to do," said Mrs. Yadon.

"Good," said Mr. Yadon. Then he added thoughtfully, "It might be well to take Herbert to two doctors, for if one doctor

can do him good, it stands to reason that two doctors would do
him twice as much good."

"Then I suppose three doctors would do him three times as
much good," said Mrs. Yadon. "Do you think three doctors will
be enough?" she asked anxiously, for she always wanted to do
what was best for Herbert.

"Herbert might get too tired if he went to more than three
doctors," said Mr. Yadon.

So on Wednesday afternoon Herbert had an appointment with
Dr. Brown at two o'clock, with Dr. White at three, and with Dr.
Gray at four.

Dr. Brown was a sad, thin man who rubbed his nose with his
bony forefinger. He looked ready to cry when he heard about
Herbert's deafness, his forgetfulness, and how he hated to get
up in the morning, especially on school days.

"Too bad! Too bad!" he kept murmuring.

"What do you think is the matter with Herbert?" Mrs. Yadon
asked anxiously.

Dr. Brown looked very sad. "I'm afraid there is a good deal the
matter with Herbert," he sighed. "Now I suggest that you try
giving him capsules containing vitamins A, B, C, D, E, F, G,
and sometimes Y and Z. It may be too late for anything to do
him any good," he said gloomily. "If he gets worse let me know."
And he went to rubbing his nose again, though it was already red
on that side.

Mrs. Yadon now felt more worried about Herbert's health
than ever. She worried steadily until it was time to visit Dr.
White.

Dr. White was a fat, cheerful man. He was bald on top and
looked as if he liked nearly everything. He poked Herbert in the
ribs with a fat finger, which made Herbert laugh, for he was
quite ticklish.

"What do you think can be the matter with Herbert?" asked
Mrs. Yadon, when she had finished describing his symptoms.

"Nothing serious at all," said Dr. White cheerfully. "Nothing
at all serious."

He went to a shelf and took down a box containing large pink
pills. "These pills contain iron, zinc, copper, tin, sulphur, soda,

gold, silver, platinum, and seven other rare and costly minerals. Give Herbert one before every meal, and I feel sure you'll see a remarkable improvement. Why, he'll be hungry enough to eat a dog. Lucky if he doesn't eat you out of house and home," he joked, and gave Herbert another poke on the ribs with a fat finger.

"Hee, hee!" laughed Herbert.

"Ha, ha!" chuckled jolly, fat Dr. White.

Dr. White made Mrs. Yadon feel less worried about Herbert, but they still had to keep their appointment with Dr. Gray.

Dr. Gray was neither fat nor thin. His hair and his clothes all matched his name and he wore large spectacles. He now proceeded to look at Herbert over his spectacles. He listened without interrupting while Mrs. Yadon described Herbert's ailments.

"In a case like Herbert's," he then said thoughtfully, "I prescribe my own remedy, made according to my own secret formula." He opened a large drawer that contained a great many bottles and boxes and began to read the labels. "Remedy for chilblains. No, that's not it. Cure for falling hair. How is Herbert's hair, Mrs. Yadon? Doesn't he need a good hair tonic?"

"I don't think so, Doctor Gray," said Mrs. Yadon. "Herbert's hair grows so fast now that he has to have it cut every other Tuesday."

Dr. Gray went on looking. "Cure for sprains. Any sprains?" he asked Herbert. "I thought not. Ah, here's just what I was looking for, my own secret formula for the improvement of memory, muscle, hearing, headache, appetite, and aspiration." He unscrewed a large jar filled with yellow stuff that looked like butter. "One teaspoonful of this spread on bread, crackers, or even on cookies, eaten with meals three times a day, will do something for Herbert. I shall, in fact, look to see Herbert improve by leaps and bounds."

Both Mrs. Yadon and Herbert were glad that Dr. Gray was the last doctor they had to visit, for by that time they were tired of going to doctors.

That night at supper Herbert started all three remedies. He took the capsules containing the vitamins A, B, C, D, E, F, G, and, sometimes, Y and Z. And he tried to swallow the large pink pill containing iron, zinc, copper, tin, sulphur, soda, gold, silver, platinum, and several other rare and costly minerals, but it stuck in his throat and he had to dissolve it in orange juice before he could get it down. Then he did not like the taste of Dr. Gray's secret formula for the improvement of memory, muscle, hearing, headache, appetite, and aspiration. When spread on bread it did not taste like butter at all. Herbert declared it tasted like axle grease flavored with glue, and he refused to eat it until his mother sprinkled it so thickly with powdered sugar that if he ate it without much chewing he could only taste the sugar. Herbert was very fond of powdered sugar.

Tired of so much doctoring, Herbert went to bed early. He did not hear his mother tell him to open his window, though she asked him to fourteen times. And he forgot and left his light on. It was plain to be seen that Herbert badly needed to improve.

His improvement began before dawn. Instead of sleeping till he was late for breakfast, Herbert was out of bed by five. And he awoke feeling so full of life and high spirits that he sang the Marine hymn through twelve times without stopping, and he had a very large voice for his age.

"Oh, dear," groaned Mrs. Yadon. "I did want to sleep till seven and it's hardly five o'clock. I do wish Herbert had slept longer this morning."

"I thought you wanted me to wake up early," yelled Herbert. He had heard his mother's voice through two doors and a hall, though she had hardly spoken above a whisper.

Mrs. Yadon suddenly realized that Herbert must have begun to improve, and she was so pleased that she woke up Mr. Yadon to tell him about it. "Herbert has already begun to improve," she said happily.

Half an hour later when she called Herbert to breakfast, he came sliding down the banisters so fast that he was at the dining room table in ten seconds.

At breakfast it was evident that Herbert was greatly improved. His eyes were bright and his color excellent, also his appetite. He ate hot cereal, three soft-boiled eggs, and five pieces of toast. He also took the vitamin capsules, two of them, the large pink pill containing the many minerals, and a teaspoonful of Dr. Gray's secret formula, spread on toast and sprinkled thickly with powdered sugar.

After breakfast Herbert showed even further improvement. He heard his mother the first time when she asked him to empty the wastebasket, but he went with it so fast that he stubbed his toe and spilled half of the trash on the back steps. His mother, however, was so glad he had begun to improve that she did not scold him.

As days went by, Herbert improved more and more. In fact, by the end of the week his parents did not see how they could stand it if he improved any more. He ran and he jumped. He sang and he shouted. Dr. Gray had certainly known what he was talking about when he said that Herbert would improve by leaps and bounds, for he went leaping and bounding all over the neighborhood. The neighbors on the right complained of the noise; so did the neighbors on the left. The old lady who lived across the street would have been disturbed if she had not been deaf as a post.

Soon Herbert was able to hear a whisper a block away. He could even hear a fly walk. And he was never tired and seemed to require less and less sleep and was often racing about the house at midnight, only to be up fresh as a daisy before dawn. It became more and more difficult for his parents to get a good night's sleep—to say nothing of the neighbors.

Yet it was Herbert's steadily increasing appetite that worried his parents most. The bill at the grocery store grew so big that Mrs. Yadon felt she could not afford to send out her weekly wash. It began to look as if jolly Dr. White had not been joking when he had said that Herbert might eat his family out of house and home.

Ten days after beginning the remedies prescribed by the three doctors, this was what Herbert ate for his dinner:

three pounds of lamb chops (large loin chops),
one large roast chicken with chestnut dressing,
one half a halibut (a middle-sized one weighing 89 pounds),
one peck of new potatoes,

*two cans of peas (he didn't like peas very well, but he had to have a
  green vegetable),*
three loaves of bread,
one dozen and a half chocolate eclairs,
one gallon of floating-island pudding.

He also sucked so many lollipops he had enough sticks to
make a model log cabin. His mother let him eat candy between
meals in order to spoil his appetite for the next meal. She hated
to stint him, but the kitchen range was not large enough to cook
one of his meals, and the grocery store did not have enough sup-
plies on hand to fill her orders, even if she had had money enough
to pay for them.

One morning after Herbert had gone leaping and bounding to
school, his parents had a long talk. They realized that something
had to be done to keep Herbert from improving any more; in
fact, he had already improved far too much. His poor parents
did not know what to do.

"Let's send for Uncle Horace," said Mr. Yadon, "for Uncle
Horace always knows what to do about everything."

The situation was so urgent that Uncle Horace came by airplane. He arrived none too soon, for the day before, Herbert had
not realized his strength and had pulled up a large elm tree on the
school grounds, with one hand and not half trying, and Miss
Jenkins, the school principal, said that one more mistake like
that and Herbert would be expelled. And the grocery store refused to charge any more groceries. And there was not a whole
chair in the house, for Herbert had sat down so hard in them all
that he had broken the seats.

When Uncle Horace opened the Yadons' front door, Herbert
had just jumped from the third floor to the first and landed on
his feet. He was just sliding swiftly up the banisters when he
caught sight of Uncle Horace. "Look who's here!" he shouted
joyfully, but so loudly that he actually did raise the roof a full
inch.

Uncle Horace heard all about the remedies the three doctors
had given Herbert.

"They have all done him good," sighed his mother. "They've

all done him too much good. He's improved so much we can't stand it." And the poor woman burst into tears.

Uncle Horace patted her shoulder kindly. "Ahem. Just what seemed to be the matter with Herbert before you took him to the doctors?" he asked.

Mrs. Yadon explained. "But," she declared, "now I wouldn't care if I had to speak a hundred times before he heard me. Or if I sent him to the store after salt and he came home with an ice-cream cone. I'd rather he'd oversleep till noon than go on improving."

"There, there," said Uncle Horace soothingly. "It shouldn't be hard to stop Herbert's remarkable improvement. We'll just discontinue all three remedies. But not all at once. Herbert's un-improvement must be gradual."

Following Uncle Horace's advice, Herbert stopped taking the capsules containing the vitamins A, B, C, D, E, F, G, and sometimes Y and Z that very day. The next day he omitted the large pink pill containing iron, zinc, copper, tin, sulphur, soda, gold, silver, platinum, and seven other rare and costly minerals. And on the third day he discontinued Dr. Gray's secret formula for the improvement of memory, muscle, hearing, headache, appetite, and aspiration. There was still a lot of the three remedies left, so Herbert buried them in the garden under a grapevine that needed improvement.

Herbert's parents watched from the back porch, while Uncle Horace helped with the burial. "Maybe the stuff will make the grapevine grow," said Uncle Horace, and even as he spoke, the grapevine did begin to grow. The remedies had already begun to take effect.

Plants usually grow so slowly that you cannot see them grow any more than you can see the hour hand of a clock move, but this grapevine grew so fast that you not only could see it but could hear it grow. It sounded something like the noise of ocean waves, a little like a vacuum cleaner, and a good deal like an electric fan. The leaves grew as big as umbrellas, and the small green bunches of grapes turned purple and became as big as bathtubs.

"Say, maybe it will grow so high that I can climb to the sky and visit the giant, like Jack and the beanstalk," cried Herbert.

But even as he spoke, the grapevine stopped growing.

"The roots took in all the good of the remedies at once," explained Uncle Horace. "It probably won't grow much more, but I doubt if there is another grapevine a tenth of its size in the whole United States."

Herbert was a little disappointed that the grapevine had not grown taller than a skyscraper, but he decided that it was big enough so that he could charge admission to see it. And that is what he did all the rest of the afternoon. One cent or ten pins to see the giant grapevine. As many as fifty children came, and one bunch of grapes made refreshments enough for all.

The circus was coming to town the following Friday and Uncle Horace promised to take Herbert if he was a good boy all the week. Herbert did try to be good, and on Friday afternoon he got his reward. He had a wonderful time at the circus. Of course all week he had been unimproving a little each day, but he was still much too strong for a boy of his age. Herbert was glad of that, though, for he was even stronger than the strong man at the circus. Herbert could lift more weight. He could even lift the strong man himself with one hand. After he had snapped a steel bar with one twist, the manager asked Herbert to join the circus. Herbert wanted to, but he knew his mother would not like it. Also, he realized that the effects of the three wonderful remedies would continue to wear off. So Herbert said, "Thank you very much, but I'll not join the circus just now." Then he shook hands so hard with both the circus manager and the strong man that they both said, "Ow!"

Herbert was no longer nearly as hungry as he had been a week before. Six ice-cream cones and two hot dogs and a bag of potato chips were all he wanted. He spent a most enjoyable afternoon. His balloons did not even break on the way home. He got home just in time for supper.

"Wash your hands before you come to the table," his mother told him, but he showed no sign of having heard her. And although she asked him twelve times to hang up his cap, he left it on the kitchen floor.

"He's right back where he was before I took him to those three doctors," sighed Mrs. Yadon.

Uncle Horace, right from the first, had had his suspicions about what made Herbert's hearing so bad, why he forgot, and why he hated to get up in the morning, especially on school days.

"The doctors improved Herbert too much, but I think I know how to improve him just enough," said Uncle Horace. And he took Herbert right over his knee and spanked him good. "Now, ask Herbert to wash his hands," he told Mrs. Yadon, and when she did, Herbert heard her, though she spoke in a low voice.

"All that Herbert needed was a little of the old-fashioned remedy of a spanking," said Uncle Horace.

From that time on, Herbert was better about hearing and remembering. He still hated to get up in the morning, especially on school days, but he did not dare stay in bed too long after his mother had called him. He remembered the old-fashioned medicine that Uncle Horace had recommended to be repeated as necessary. A spanking, he thought, was worse to take than Dr. Gray's secret formula that did not taste at all like butter.

The grapevine stopped bearing giant grapes and went back to producing bunches of its usual size. But it was still the largest grapevine in the United States. And Herbert could still run the fastest and jump the highest of any boy in his school. Just that trace of the wonderful remedies lingered.

King O'Toole
and His Goose

Och, I thought all the world, far and near, had heerd of King O'Toole—well, well, but the darkness of mankind is untollable! Well, sir, you must know, as you didn't hear it afore, that there was a king, called King O'Toole, who was a fine old king in the old ancient times, long ago; and it was he that owned the churches in the early days. The king, you see, was the right sort; he was the real boy, and loved sport as he loved his life, and hunting in particular; and from the rising o' the sun, up he got and away he went over the mountains after the deer; and fine times they were.

Well, it was all mighty good, as long as the king had his health; but, you see, in the course of time the king grew old, by raison he was stiff in his limbs, and when he got stricken in years, his heart failed him, and he was lost entirely for want o' diversion, because he couldn't go a-hunting no longer; and, by dad, the poor king was obliged at last to get a goose to divert him. Oh, you may laugh, if you like, but it's truth I'm telling you; and the way the goose diverted him was this-a-way: You see, the goose used to swim across the lake, and go diving for trout and catch fish on a Friday for the king, and flew every other day round about the lake, diverting the poor king. All went on mighty well until, by dad, the goose got stricken in years like her master, and couldn't divert him no longer; and then it was that the poor king was lost entirely. The king was walkin' one mornin' by the edge of the lake, lamentin' his cruel fate, and thinking of drowning himself, that could get no diversion in life, when all of a sudden, turning round the corner, whom should he meet but a mighty decent young man coming up to him.

"God save you," says the king to the young man.

"God save you kindly, King O'Toole," says the young man.

"True for you," says the king. "I am King O'Toole," says he, "prince and plennypennytinchery of these parts," says he; "but how came ye to know that?" says he.

"Oh, never mind," says Saint Kavin.

You see it was Saint Kavin, sure enough—the saint himself in disguise and nobody else. "Oh, never mind," says he, "I know more than that. May I make bold to ask how is your goose, King O'Toole?" says he.

"Blur-an-agers, how came ye to know about my goose?" says the king.

"Oh, no matter; I was given to understand it," says Saint Kavin.

After some more talk the king says, "What are you?"

"I'm an honest man," says Saint Kavin.

"Well, honest man," says the king, "and how is it you make your money so aisy?"

"By makin' old things as good as new," says Saint Kavin.

"Is it a tinker you are?" says the king.

"No," says the saint; "I'm no tinker by trade, King O'Toole; I've a better trade than a tinker," says he—"What would you say," says he, "if I made your old goose as good as new?"

My dear, at the word of making his goose as good as new, you'd think the poor old king's eyes were ready to jump out of his head. With that the king whistled, and down came the poor goose, just like a hound, waddling up to the poor cripple, her master, and as like him as two peas. The minute the saint clapt his eyes on the goose, "I'll do the job for you," says he, "King O'Toole."

"By Jaminee!" says King O'Toole, "if you do, I'll say you're the cleverest fellow in the seven parishes."

"Oh, by dad," says Saint Kavin, "you must say more nor that— my horn's not so soft all out," says he, "as to repair your old goose for nothing; what'll you gi' me if I do the job for you?— that's the chat," says Saint Kavin.

"I'll give you whatever you ask," says the king; "isn't that fair?"

"Divil a fairer," says the saint, "that's the way to do business. Now," says he, "this is the bargain I'll make with you, King O'Toole: will you gi' me all the ground the goose flies over, the first offer, after I make her as good as new?"

"I will," says the king.

"You won't go back o' your word?" says Saint Kavin.

"Honour bright!" says King O'Toole, holding out his fist.

"Honour bright!" says Saint Kavin, back again, "it's a bargain. Come here!" says he to the poor old goose—"come here, you unfortunate ould cripple, and it's I that'll make you the sporting bird." With that, my dear, he took up the goose by the two wings —"Criss o' my cross an you," says he, markin' her to grace with the blessed sign at the same minute—and throwing her up in the air, "whew," says he, jist givin' her a blast to help her; and with that, my jewel, she took to her heels, flyin' like one o' the eagles themselves, and cutting as many capers as a swallow before a shower of rain.

Well, my dear, it was a beautiful sight to see the king standing with his mouth open, looking at his poor old goose flying as light as a lark, and better than ever she was; and when she lit at his feet, patted her on the head, and "Ma vourneen," says he, "but you are the darlint o' the world."

"And what do you say to me," says Saint Kavin, "for making her the like?"

"By jabers," says the king, "I say nothing beats the art o' man, barring the bees."

"And do you say no more nor that?" says Saint Kavin.

"And that I'm beholden to you," says the king.

"But will you gi'e me all the ground the goose flew over?" says Saint Kavin.

"I will," says King O'Toole, "and you're welcome to it," says he, "though it's the last acre I have to give."

"But you'll keep your word true," says the saint.

"As true as the sun," says the king.

"It's well for you, King O'Toole, that you said that word,"

says he; "for if you didn't say that word, the divil the bit o' your goose would ever fly agin."

When the king was as good as his word, Saint Kavin was pleased with him; and then it was that he made himself known to the king. "And," says he, "King O'Toole, you're a decent man, for I only came here to try you. You don't know me," says he, "because I'm disguised."

"Musha! then," says the king, "who are you?"

"I'm Saint Kavin," said the saint, blessing himself.

"Oh, queen of heaven!" says the king, making the sign of the cross between his eyes, and falling down on his knees before the saint; "is it the great Saint Kavin," says he, "that I've been discoursing all this time without knowing it," says he, "all as one as if he was a lump of a gossoon?—and so you're a saint?" says the king.

"I am," says Saint Kavin.

"By Jabers, I thought I was only talking to a dacent boy," says the king.

"Well, you know the difference now," says the saint. "I'm Saint Kavin," says he, "the greatest of all the saints."

And so the king had his goose as good as new to divert him as long as he lived; and the saint supported him after he came into his property, as I told you, until the day of his death—and that was soon after. For the poor goose thought he was catching a trout one Friday; but, my jewel, it was a mistake he made—and instead of a trout, it was a thieving horse-eel; and instead of the goose killing a trout for the king's supper—by dad, the eel killed the king's goose—and small blame to him; but he didn't ate her, because he darn't ate what Saint Kavin had laid his blessed hands on.

From *Celtic Fairy Tales*, edited by Joseph Jacobs.

The Duck
and the Kangaroo

EDWARD LEAR

I

Said the Duck to the Kangaroo,
"Good gracious! how you hop
Over the fields, and the water too,
As if you never would stop!

Illustrations by Edward Lear.

My life is a bore in this nasty pond;
And I long to go out in the world beyond:
I wish I could hop like you,"
Said the Duck to the Kangaroo.

II

"Please give me a ride on your back,"
   Said the Duck to the Kangaroo:
"I would sit quite still, and say nothing but 'Quack,'
   The whole of the long day through;
And we'd go the Dee, and the Jelly Bo Lee,
Over the land, and over the sea:
   Please take me a ride! oh, do!"
   Said the Duck to the Kangaroo.

III

Said the Kangaroo to the Duck,
   "This requires some little reflection.
Perhaps, on the whole, it might bring me luck:
   And there seems but one objection;
Which is, if you'll let me speak so bold,
Your feet are unpleasantly wet and cold,
   And would probably give me the roo—
   Matiz," said the Kangaroo.

IV

Said the Duck, "As I sate on the rocks,
   I have thought over that completely;
And I bought four pairs of worsted socks,
   Which fit my web-feet neatly;

And, to keep out the cold, I've bought a cloak;
And every day a cigar I'll smoke;
    All to follow my own dear true
    Love of a Kangaroo."

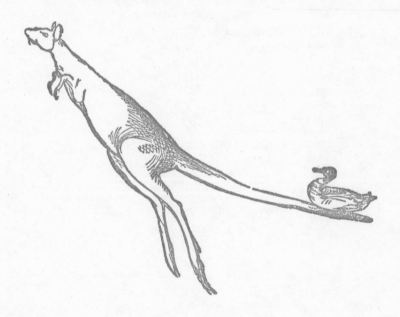

V

Said the Kangaroo, "I'm ready,
  All in the moonlight pale;
But to balance me well, dear Duck, sit steady,
  And quite at the end of my tail."

So away they went with a hop and a bound;
And they hopped the whole world three times round.
  And who so happy, oh! who,
  As the Duck and the Kangaroo?

Pecos Bill Invents Modern Cowpunching

JAMES C. BOWMAN

For some reason Americans have always taken a special delight in tall tales and broad humor. Along the frontier and especially in the West these legends—sometimes faintly based on fact but usually on nothing but soaring imagination—grew taller and more exaggerated with each telling. There were dozens of tales about Paul Bunyan, Mike Fink, Davey Crockett and a host of others. One of the most popular of these legendary heroes was Pecos Bill, a high-riding cowboy who, it was said, had been raised by a pack of coyotes.

ALL the men of the I X L were eating out of Pecos Bill's hand within less than a week after he arrived. He took to the life of a cowboy like a duck to water. He learned their best tricks, they went on to do better. Gun Smith and Chuck and the rest were very soon like children before him. Among themselves, they bragged about their noble deeds; but when Pecos was around, they couldn't help thinking that they were mere bridled cayuses.

He could stand on the ground beside a broncho, turn an air flop, and land astride the pony before it had time to tighten a muscle. He could ride bareback without a bridle. He could urge his pony at top speed over ground so rough and uneven that Gun Smith and the others were afraid even to attempt it with bit and saddle. And he was so casual and modest about everything he did that they thought Pecos the eighth wonder of the world. Almost at once he was full of ideas. And what ideas!

Up to Pecos Bill's day, when a man wanted to capture a horse or a steer, he would lay a piece of rope down on the ground, make a loop in one end of it, sit down behind a tree or a blind, and by laying a bait, try to coax the wild critter to step within the loop. He would then jerk sharply on the rope, and perhaps one time in a dozen, if he was lucky, he would succeed in making a catch. It was no uncommon thing for a man to wait around and lose an entire month's time without laying hold of a single animal.

"Well, this sort of thing has got to be changed," said Pecos Bill to himself when no one was near to hear him. "A man can't be expected to waste his entire lifetime catching a single horse or cow."

Without further delay, Pecos got hold of the longest piece of rope he could find around the ranch, and began to throw it through the air. Next he rode off alone where the others could not see what he was doing. After three days of constant practice, he found that he could lasso almost anything. He was limited only by the reach of his line.

Pecos Bill would just make a large loop in one end of his rope, swing it wildly about his head three or four times, and then, with a quick flip of his forearm and wrist, send it flying like a bullet. And as he grew more and more skilled, he added rapidly to the length of his rope.

As soon as he was entirely sure of himself, Pecos asked the boys to come out and let him show them his new invention.

"See that roan steer across there? That's Old Crookhorn, our wildest critter, ain't it?" Pecos asked quietly.

Before anyone was aware of what he was doing, Pecos had whirled his loop about his head, and sent it so fast in the direction of the four-year-old that the eye could scarcely follow it.

In an instant the old steer began to jump and bellow, and Pecos Bill to tow in the rope. Soon the astonished steer stood with lowered head before the even more surprised cowboys.

Not content with this great skill, Pecos began practicing from horseback.

In another week, he again called his cowboys out to see what he could do. They watched, with popping eyes, as he gave his rope a double turn around his saddle-bow. He then started his broncho at a hard gallop. They saw him quickly approach a rather tall, scraggly mesquite tree, whirl his loop wildly about his head and then fling it into the air. When he dragged a great hawk down from the topmost branch with the noose about its neck, the men were unable to believe their eyes.

"What sort o' wonder worker is this anyway?" they asked each other. "No human could ever throw the rope like that!"

Then Pecos Bill showed the men how it was done, and after two or three months of hard practice, each of them was able to make frequent catches at a distance of from ten to not more than twenty feet.

In the meantime, Pecos Bill had become dissatisfied with the fact that he couldn't find a longer rope. So he began to braid himself a cowhide lariat. This is how he went to work. First he looked up some old horned steers that had lived so many years within the depths of the trees that there were green algae on their backs —mossbacks, sure enough. What's more, these steers were so old their faces were gray and wrinkled.

Whenever Pecos Bill got hold of one of these old fellows, he first loosened the hide behind the ears. He then grasped the steer by the tail and with a flip of his wrist and forearm and a wild yowl, he frightened the animal so that it jumped out of its skin. The tough hides of these old mossbacks were just what Pecos needed.

Three or four years later when he had it finished, his loyal ranchers declared on all sides that the lariat was as long as the equator, and that Pecos could lasso anything this side of China.

It was thus that Pecos Bill solved one of the problems that had worried cowhands and their bosses for years.

Another thing that Pecos very soon learned was that every ranch outfit was a bitter enemy of every other outfit. When two neighboring ranchers happened to meet anywhere near the sup- posed boundary of their pasturelands, they would begin to com- plain about missing cattle. Soon one would accuse the other of rustling—a polite word for stealing—his stock. Then there would be a sudden flashing of pistols, and one or the other, and often both men would bite the dust.

"Why do they all make such fools of themselves?" Pecos Bill asked. "Why don't they invent some way of marking their horses and cattle so that they will know them wherever they happen to meet them? All this fighting and killing is sheer nonsense. The spirit of the Coyote pack is entirely lacking."

While Pecos Bill was trying to invent a plan for marking the animals, a deer fly gave him just the right suggestion when it nipped him sharply on the arm. In chasing the fly away, he just naturally happened to notice the tattooed star that was his own mark of identification. "Mother was wiser than all these cowmen put together," Pecos declared, laughing at himself for having been so slow in finding the right idea! "Why of course cattle and horses can be tattooed the same way. Then they'll be marked for life."

That very evening Pecos Bill explained his plans to Bean Hole. The cook listened, then shook his head. "But tattooin' is too infernal slow," declared Bean Hole, looking at the purple markings up and down the backs of his own arms. "It wasted more'n a whole week of my time to do these pictures. It'd be quicker to burn the mark on. I ain't been cookin' all these years for nothin'. I know that if you burn the skin deep enough, it'll leave an everlastin' scar. Look at this mark now—I've been carryin' it on my wrist for more'n twenty-seven years, and it's just as plain now as ever it was."

"You're right," shouted Pecos. "Together we've invented a new system of bookkeeping for every cowhand in the world."

That evening Pecos explained the new invention to the cowboys, who were open-mouthed at the cleverness of the plan. Rusty Peters, who was a blacksmith by trade, was set immediately to make the brands. He bent the iron so that it would read I X L when burnt upon the side of a horse or cow.

The next morning all the men were as excited as boys. They herded and roped the cattle, dragging them near the heated irons and throwing them on their side to apply the stinging brand. All day long the smoke curled. All day long the cattle bellowed.

"Keep that iron a cherry red, I'm a-tellin' you," shouted Bean

Hole, as he gave directions. "Hold it on long enough to do more'n singe the hair. Wait till it smells like the Devil's own stithy, and looks like the whole critter was burned to a cracklin'. That's not near long enough. She'll shed that mark before the snow flies. There, that's about right. Let her bawl her fill. The loss of a few mouthfuls of hot air ain't going to hurt her any."

"Keep quiet, you old bag o' wind," shouted Rusty Peters, hard at work. "I ain't a blacksmith for nothin'! I'll burn a brand across your mouth in a minute if you don't keep quiet."

By evening the entire job was completed. It was found that the I X L outfit possessed fifty-seven steers of various ages, forty-one cows, some fat and sleek, some spindly and thin, and twenty-four calves.

"This small herd ain't really enough to bother with," Pecos Bill observed in disappointment. "I thought you cowmen said you had a real ranch. Why, the woods are full of wild cattle that belong to nobody in particular. I'll just go out and drive in a few thousand of them. We'll put our trademark on them, and then they'll be ours."

"But how in tarnation will we ever keep these longhorns from runnin' straight away again?" asked Gun Smith with doubting stare. "What's the use of goin' through all this trouble disfigurin' the sides of all these cattle with our silly I X L advertisement, if we're goin' to turn 'em to the wild prairies again?"

Pecos Bill had not thought of this. The general custom among the cowmen had been to allow all the cattle to go and come whenever they liked. The ranch shack was nearly always built beside running water, and naturally, a few of the timid and lazy cows and steers would make this their home. The more ambitious stock would just as naturally wander off across the prairies and mesa and take refuge within the mesquite woods. Soon they would be as wild as deer and as difficult to catch.

This careless way of doing things meant that each ranch had a mere handful of shifting population, as far as the cattle were concerned. When the pasture and the water elsewhere were scarce, the cattle would flock to the ranch; but most of the time they would not even trouble themselves to take a French leave.

"It's dead wrong," said Pecos Bill to himself as he squatted on his haunches. "The problem to be solved is this: How are the cattle to be kept together in a herd after they are branded?"

While he was trying to work out the answer, he loped off alone to the top of a small mountain one morning before the others were awake. Far over the rolling prairies he could see many small wandering herds of cows and steers.

"Of course, if bad should come to worse, I could just round the herd up every night and throw my noose about them, and tie the cattle up till morning," he smiled. "But that ain't a good solution, for I can't bind myself that close to the ranch. I've got to reserve my energy for bigger work. All kinds of things are waiting to be invented."

At first as he sat and thought, his mind was just one grazing herd after another. He saw cattle scattered all over the prairies; he saw cattle stampeded, and he saw cattle leaving the herd to get lost in wild mesa. But after a little, things cleared up and he knew what he was going to do.

He got up, stretched the kinks out of his muscles and started at a brisk gallop for the ranch house. As soon as he arrived he called out for everybody to come.

"Here's the plan," he said excitedly. "The way to keep the herd together is for you men to ride out with the cattle every day. By waking up the drags and by holding back the leaders, the herd can be kept together and can be made to go to the best feeding grounds every day."

"You mean," said Gun Smith, with an ironical smile, "that us cowpunchers has got to be ordinary bovine critters the rest of our lives?"

"And stay with the herd all night and sleep with the hoot-owls?" asked Moon Hennessey sourly.

"Oh, yes," and the musical Mushmouth sang with a pretense of tears in his voice:

> "The centipede runs 'cross my head,
> The vinegaroon crawls in my bed,
> Tarantulas jump and scorpions play,
> The bronchs are grazin' far away,
> The rattler sounds his noisy cry,
> And the Coyotes sing their lullaby,
> While I sleep soundly beneath the sky."

"It don't appeal to me," complained Moon Hennessey.

"Oh, well, you'll be just crazy about it when you've tried it—especially if the herd stampedes in your direction," suggested Gun Smith with irony. "It's goin' to be a regular picnic, Sundays and week days together, an' there's no doubt about it."

"And if the herd gets stampeded you'll be on hand to turn the leaders and start them milling until they are bitterly disappointed in trying to run away," added Pecos Bill quietly. "Besides, sleeping out under the stars is wonderful, once you've acquired the knack. I know from long experience."

"It'll all be easier than handlin' a month-old heifer calf," laughed Gun Smith bitterly.

"Well, now that we have decided what to do, I'll go out and drive in the cattle to be branded. And while I'm away Gun Smith will be your foreman. He'll keep you out of mischief. We can't get started too soon. So, with your permission, I'll be going right away. I'll have a herd to be branded first thing in the morning."

As soon as Pecos Bill had darted out into the night, the men began to wonder whether his coming to them had been a blessing or a curse.

"Chuck, before this monstrosity of yours arrived," began Moon Hennessey, "we was leadin' a peaceful and easy life. All we was expected to do was swap lies, and eat juicy tobacco. Now, it seems, we're goin' to be set at hard labor!"

"To my way of thinkin', the change will be all to the good," answered Chuck. "And who knows—it may bring us glory and honor—and gold!"

"Well, then, since I'm the appointed foreman of this outfit until Pecos returns," Gun Smith drawled as he put his hands on his guns, "I'm goin' to give you, Chuck, the place of highest honor. While the rest of us turn in for the night, you, Chuck, will take your Old Pepper and make contact with our branded herd. If they object to your presence and attempt to trample you and your noble steed to smithereens by startin' a wild stampede, you'll simply turn the leaders and set the herd millin'. If they show signs of thirst, you will lead them beside the still water!"

"Thank you very much for the honor," answered Chuck, as he rose promptly to carry out the assigned task.

"The rest of us motherless mavericks," Gun Smith continued, "will remain here, so's to be on hand with the ropes and the brandin' irons when Old Pecos returns any minute with his promised herd of wild cattle."

"Well," added Moon Hennessey with a bored yawn, "Old Pecos will be doin' splendid if he shows up by the end of next week. There'll be no herd here tomorrow mornin', I can promise you that."

"Don't fool yourself," replied Chuck spiritedly as he turned on his heel. "You evidently ain't yet acquainted with my brother."

"Brother!" fairly hissed Moon Hennessey in a rage. "Cut out your star identification talk and go on about your business!"

Next morning the men were awakened at early dawn by the dull thud, thud, thud of innumerable hoofs, and by the monotonous bawling of the weary cattle. As the men rubbed the sleep out of their eyes and looked about, they discovered, to their astonishment, that Pecos Bill had actually returned with a herd so large that they couldn't begin to see either its beginning or end.

"What, aren't you boys up yet?" Pecos called with a smile. "I've been having a wonderful night. And I've got enough cattle here to keep all of us busy for a while, anyway."

"Enough wild critters to keep the brandin' irons sizzlin' and the smoke risin' for a month of Sundays, I'd say," conceded Gun Smith, none too happily.

But Pecos Bill had no use for conversation just then. Breakfast was gulped down, cattle struggling and bellowing; the alkali dust flying mountain high; Bean Hole rushing about like a chicken with its head off, shouting his directions amid the din and waving his kettles and pans, and Rusty Peters keeping the smoking brands busy. This was the way it went all day long. By the time the sun had set, the tired men had added three hundred and thirty-eight cattle to their herd. Three hundred and thirty-eight —hurrah for Pecos Bill!

Pecos Bill himself was so happy over the results that frequently during the following months he would go out for an evening adventure, returning promptly the following morning with hundreds more bawling wild cattle. By the end of the season the I X L ranch was one living sea of four-footed beasts.

As soon as his men had finished branding the incoming herd with the I X L trademark, Pecos Bill at once began looking around to find other worlds to conquer. He instructed the men how to live in the saddle, and how to take cat naps astride their grazing ponies. He showed them how to soothe the cattle by crooning songs to them, and how to keep the herd together without annoying even the leaders.

When the herd stampeded, as it was sure to do at times, Pecos taught the men how to turn the leaders, and thus start the entire herd milling in a circle until the cattle finally winded themselves, and stopped through sheer weariness in the very spot from which they had started in the first place.

During these days, Bean Hole was the busiest man this side of Mars. After trying for a week to feed the men by carrying food out to them from the ranch shack, he finally gave up. On four or five different occasions, as he was starting out with his kettles and pans, he actually met himself on the trail coming back with the empty dishes of the previous afternoon. If he hadn't stopped his foolishness of trying to work twenty-seven hours a day just when he did, most likely his ghost would still be wandering on the wind over the same trails.

In the despair of complete exhaustion, Bean Hole finally hitched two spans of mules to the chuck wagon, loaded it down with enough food to last a fortnight, and left the ranch shack to take care of itself. He hadn't been gone half an hour before the place looked as deserted as the ruins of Pompeii.

Very soon the entire life of the ranch was going along according to the new plan. Everything was clicking like clock work and Pecos Bill was so pleased, for the present at least, that he couldn't think of anything to invent. So he decided to go out and tell the world about what he had been doing, not for the sake of his own fame, but for the benefit of the cowmen of the entire range country.

One evening, after the cattle had settled down for the first sleep of the night, Pecos Bill announced to Gun Smith, his foreman, that it would be necessary for him to go away from the

ranch for a few days. "If anybody asks where I am," he whispered, "just tell them that I'll be back for breakfast, like as not."

Pecos then took his boots under his arm, threw his coiled rope over his shoulder, and went bounding off across the rolling prairie. When he came to a strange ranch, he would quickly put on his boots and walk in great dignity, with jangling spurs, up to the boss of the outfit. Very soon he would be telling the wide-eyed cowman his story. In this way he easily covered forty or fifty miles in an hour and a half or two hours.

Pecos Bill thus visited all the ranches of the entire Southwest within two or three months. Not forgetting a single detail, he told the men everywhere what he had done. At first they thought him the biggest liar that had ever been invented in the whole world of cowmen. But when he had limbered up his lariat, and when they had witnessed his performance, they were quite willing to believe everything he told them.

What they saw was even more wonderful than what he had said. For with perfect ease, he would lasso any animal within reach of their vision. He could lasso a grazing or galloping steer, or lay his flying noose around the neck of a bald eagle in full flight.

The flying visits led later to many heated disputes among the puzzled ranchers: "You say this Pecos Bill left Hub's Ferry at nine o'clock? But he was at Slippery Mike's by eleven, and that's a good forty miles as the crow flies, ain't it? And he was alone and on foot, wasn't he? Who is this Pecos Bill, anyway?" Every rancher seemed to have a bigger yarn to tell than his neighbor.

But they were all true—certainly! And through the efforts of Pecos Bill, ranchmen began to have a spring roundup and fall roundup. Pecos persuaded the ranchers of a given range section or river valley to drive together all the cattle of their entire district. They then sorted them into individual herds according to the particular brand of each owner. After this work was completed, each owner branded all of his calves. The strays, with no brand, and the orphan mavericks were then distributed equally and branded so that they could never again go astray. And every bit of the plan was Pecos Bill's.

In the fall the roundup was repeated so that the stray cattle could be located and given back to their rightful owners. After all the exchanges were made, the cowmen, as they took their herds back to their individual feeding grounds, found it easy to count the number of steers that were in condition for the market and the number that they would have to pasture during the coming winter.

Thus it was that each owner was given what belonged to him, according to the laws of reason, and not in accordance with the earlier outlawry of the pistol.

And so it came about very naturally, through the organization of all the scattered cowmen, that the fame of Pecos Bill rapidly spread to the four corners of the range country. From the valley of the Rio Grande, through Texas and New Mexico, Arizona and Colorado, Kansas and Nebraska, and far into the wilderness of Montana and Wyoming, cowboys, when they met, would carelessly throw one foot free from its stirrup and in a resting position shout to their nearest companion: "Say, have you heard about the rope Uncle Bill is still braidin' down on the Pecos? Why, it's already twice as long as the equator! You know, if Old Pecos Bill could only get a toe hold on the moon, he'd turn in and lasso this wanderin' planet of ours and bring it back into the Milky Way, where it belongs! Yes, and Pecos could do it easier than you or I could lasso a year-old heifer calf!"

The Princess Whom Nobody Could Silence

THERE was once upon a time a king, and he had a daughter who would always have the last word; she was so perverse and contrary in her speech that no one could silence her. So the king therefore promised that he who could outwit the Princess should have her in marriage and half the kingdom besides. There were plenty of those who wanted to try, I can assure you; for it isn't every day that a princess and half a kingdom are to be had.

The gate to the palace hardly ever stood still. The suitors came in swarms and flocks from east and west, both riding and walking. But there was no one who could silence the Princess. At last the king announced that those who tried and did not succeed should be branded on both ears with a large iron; he would not have all this running about the palace for nothing.

So there were three brothers who had also heard about the Princess, and as they were rather badly off at home, they thought they would try their luck and see if they could win the Princess and half the kingdom. They were good friends, and so they agreed to set out together.

When they had got a bit on the way Ashiepattle found a dead magpie.

"I have found something! I have found something!" cried he.

"What have you found?" asked the brothers.

"I have found a dead magpie," said he.

"Faugh! throw it away; what can you do with that?" said the other two, who always believed they were the wisest.

"Oh, I've nothing else to do. I can easily carry it," said Ashiepattle.

When they had gone on a bit farther Ashiepattle found an old willow twig, which he picked up.

"I have found something! I have found something!" he cried.

"What have you found now?" said the brothers.

"I have found a willow twig," said he.

"Pooh! what are you going to do with that? Throw it away," said the two.

"I have nothing else to do. I can easily carry it with me," said Ashiepattle.

When they had gone still farther he found a broken saucer, which he also picked up.

"Here lads, I have found something! I have found something!" said he.

"Well, what have you found now?" asked the brothers.

"A broken saucer," said he.

"Pshaw! Is it worth while dragging that along with you too? Throw it away!" said the brothers.

"Oh, I've nothing else to do. I can easily carry it with me," said Ashiepattle.

When they had gone a little bit farther he found a crooked goat-horn, and soon after he found the fellow to it.

"I have found something! I have found something, lads!" said he.

"What have you found now?" said the others.

"Two goat-horns," answered Ashiepattle.

"Ugh! throw them away! What are you going to do with them?" said they.

"Oh, I have nothing else to do. I can easily carry them with me," said Ashiepattle.

In a little while he found a wedge.

"I say, lads, I have found something! I have found something!" he cried.

"You are everlastingly finding something! What have you found now?" asked the two eldest.

"I have found a wedge," he answered.

"Oh, throw it away! What are you going to do with it?" said they.

"Oh, I have nothing else to do. I can easily carry it with me," said Ashiepattle.

As he went across the king's fields, which had been freshly manured, he stooped down and took up an old boot-sole.

"Hullo, lads! I have found something! I have found something!" said he.

"Heaven grant you may find a little sense before you get to the palace!" said the two. "What is it you have found now?"

"An old boot-sole," said he.

"Is that anything worth picking up? Throw it away! What are you going to do with it?" said the brothers.

"Oh, I have nothing else to do. I can easily carry it with me, and—who knows?—it may help me to win the Princess and half the kingdom," said Ashiepattle.

"Yes, you look a likely one, don't you?" said the other two. So they went in to the Princess, the eldest first.

"Good day!" said he.

"Good day to you!" answered she, with a shrug.

"It's terribly hot here," said he.

"It's hotter in the fire," said the Princess. The branding-iron was lying waiting in the fire.

When he saw this he was struck speechless, and so it was all over with him.

The second brother fared no better.

"Good day!" said he.

"Good day to you," said she, with a wriggle.

"It's terribly hot here!" said he.

"It's hotter in the fire," said she. With that he lost both speech and wits, and so the iron had to be brought out.

Then came Ashiepattle's turn.

"Good day!" said he.

"Good day to you!" said she, with a shrug and a wriggle.

"It is very nice and warm here!" said Ashiepattle.

"It's warmer in the fire," she answered. She was in no better humor now she saw the third suitor.

"Then there's a chance for me to roast my magpie on it," said he, bringing it out.

"I'm afraid it will sputter," said the Princess.

"No fear of that! I'll tie this willow twig round it," said the lad.

"You can't tie it tight enough," said she.

"Then I'll drive in a wedge," said the lad, and brought out the wedge.

"The fat will be running off it," said the Princess.

"Then I'll hold this under it," said the lad, and showed her the broken saucer.

"You are so crooked in your speech," said the Princess.

"No, I am not crooked," answered the lad; "but this is crooked"; and he brought out one of the goat-horns.

"Well, I've never seen the like!" cried the Princess.

"Here you see the like," said he, and brought out the other horn.

"It seems you have come here to wear out my soul!" she said.

"No, I have not come here to wear out your soul, for I have one here which is already worn out," answered the lad, and brought out the old boot-sole.

The Princess was so dumfounded at this that she was completely silenced.

"Now you are mine!" said Ashiepattle, and so he got the Princess and half the kingdom into the bargain.

From *Fairy Tales from the Far North*, edited by P. C. Asbjörnsen and Jörgen Moe.

Little Eddie Goes to Town

CAROLYN HAYWOOD

It was half-past three of a Saturday afternoon when Mrs. Wilson remembered that she needed a jar of cold cream. She looked around the house to see if one of the older boys was at home, but she only found little Eddie. Eddie was busy oiling an old typewriter that he had picked up in a junk shop for a dollar. It was his most recent treasure. About half of the keys were gone, and the rest made a noise like a string of freight cars going over a bridge. Eddie thought a little oil would help. He was busy pumping sewing machine oil into every rack in the typewriter when his mother found him.

For a few minutes she stood watching him. He looked very little. She wondered whether to send him for the cold cream. He had never been to the center of the city alone. He would have to change buses, and Mrs. Wilson wondered whether Eddie was big enough to change buses. At last she said, "Eddie, do you think you could go to the city for Mother? I need a jar of cold cream from Potter's Drug Store. Mr. Potter makes his own cold cream, and I like it much better than any other."

Eddie looked up with his eyes sparkling. "Oh Mamma!" he cried. "Sure, I can go to the city."

"You know, you have to change buses," she said. "You have to change to the H bus."

"Sure! I know," said Eddie, wiping his hands on his trousers.

"Eddie!" cried Mrs. Wilson. "How often do I have to tell you not to wipe your hands on your trousers?"

"I'm sorry," said Eddie. "I forgot."

"Well now, don't forget that you are going to get cold cream.

And remember that you change to the H bus and get off at
Twelfth Street."

"I know. I know," said Eddie. "And Potter's Drug Store is
right on the corner."

"That's right," said his mother. "I'll write a note for you, and
you can give it to Mr. Potter."

"Oh, that's the way babies go to the store," said Eddie. "I'm
no baby. I'm not going to hand Mr. Potter a piece of paper. I
can remember cold cream."

"Well, run along and get washed, and put on a clean blouse
and your other trousers," said his mother.

Eddie went off to wash. In about ten minutes he was ready.

"I'll put you on the bus," said Mrs. Wilson, handing Eddie his
bus fare. "And I'll ask the bus driver to put you off to change to
the H bus."

"Oh, Mamma," said Eddie, "let me tell him. He'll think I'm
a baby if you tell him. When I get in I'll say, 'I want to change
to the H bus.'"

"No, Eddie," said his mother, "you must say, 'Will you please
tell me where I get off to take the H bus?' Then sit close to the
driver."

"Okay," said Eddie.

"And don't lose your yellow transfer that the bus driver will
give you. That's your fare on the H bus."

"Okay," said Eddie.

"And ask Mr. Potter to show you where you get the bus to
come home. Don't forget you have to change to the E bus to
come home."

"I know," said Eddie. "I know."

"And don't forget what it is you are going for," said Mrs. Wilson. "Cold cream."

"I won't forget," said Eddie. "Rudy says if you want to re-
member something, you think of something that goes with it.
You know. If you want to remember eggs, you think of chickens.
I'll keep thinking of milk, and then I'll remember cold cream."

"You just keep thinking of cold cream," said his mother. "And
tell Mr. Potter to charge it on my bill."

"But I want to do it Rudy's way. I want to think about milk," said Eddie.

"Here comes the bus," said his mother.

The bus swung up to the curb, and before the door opened Eddie said, "You won't tell the bus driver, will you, Mamma? I want to tell him."

The door opened, and Eddie stepped into the bus. He handed his fare to the driver and said, "I'm going to the city for my mother. I have to change to the H bus. I think I know where to get off, but I guess you had better tell me." Then he added "Please."

"All right," said the driver. "Here's your transfer. Hold on to it. And sit right there."

Eddie sat down in the seat the driver pointed out. Beside Eddie sat a very fat man, so there wasn't much room for Eddie. He wriggled back on the seat, and his legs dangled over the edge.

In the seat behind Eddie sat a woman with a baby on her lap. On the seat beside her lay a large green watermelon.

The bus rolled rapidly along, and Eddie bounced a little on his seat and swayed from side to side. The straw-covered seat was very slippery, and the fat man took up the greater part of the seat.

Suddenly the bus gave a terrible lurch as it swung around the corner. All of the passengers swayed with the bus. The watermelon on the seat behind Eddie rolled off the seat. The lurch of the bus threw it forward, and it landed with a smack in the aisle of the bus. A split second later Eddie shot off his seat and "Kerplunk!" he sat right on the watermelon. The fall to the floor had already cracked the watermelon, so when Eddie sat on it, it smashed into pieces, splashing in all directions.

The bus driver drew up to the curb and stopped. "Anybody hurt?" he called out, as he turned in his seat.

Everyone in the bus was standing up. The fat man was leaning over Eddie. "Are you hurt, son? Are you hurt?" he was saying to Eddie. Eddie was lying flat on the floor now, surrounded by pieces of watermelon. He didn't look exactly scared, but he looked terribly surprised. The man held out his hands to him and Eddie took hold of them. "There's something the matter with the seat of my trousers," he said.

"Well, stand up," said the bus driver, who had left his wheel. "Let's have a look."

Eddie got up and turned his back on the driver. Then he leaned over. The whole seat of his trousers was wet.

"Does it hurt?" said the bus driver.

"Is it blood?" asked Eddie, hoping that it was.

"No," replied the bus driver. "It's watermelon. I said, does it hurt?"

"No," said Eddie. "Just awful wet."

When the lady with the baby found that Eddie was all right, she began to think about her watermelon. "What about my watermelon?" she said to the bus driver. "I paid a dollar for that watermelon."

"I'm sorry, madam," said the bus driver, "but you had no right to have the watermelon on the seat. We charge for those seats, and you didn't pay any fare for the watermelon."

"Well!" said the lady. "We'll just see about this. I'll take it up with the company."

"Very well, madam," said the driver, as he picked up the pieces of watermelon and put them in a newspaper. When he had gathered it all up, he turned to the lady. "Madam," he said, holding out the bundle, "your watermelon."

"Throw it out," said the lady.

As he opened the door of the bus, Eddie said, "Hey! What are you going to do with it?"

"I'm going to throw it down the sewer," said the bus driver.

"Oh, Mister!" Eddie cried. "Wait a minute! Can I have a piece?"

"Sure!" said the bus driver. "Help yourself!"

Eddie selected one of the larger pieces and settled back in his seat, while everyone, even the lady with the baby, laughed.

The fat man on the seat beside him bounced up and down when he laughed. "Here," he said, placing his newspaper on Eddie's lap, "have a napkin."

Eddie hadn't half finished his piece of watermelon when the bus driver called out, "Walnut Street. Change to the H bus. This is it, son."

Eddie scrambled off his seat, knocking the newspaper from his lap. The bus stopped, and Eddie stepped out.

"So long!" the bus driver called to him.

"So long!" Eddie called back. Then, as the door was closing, he held up the piece of watermelon and shouted, "Thanks!"

He finished the watermelon while he waited for the H bus. As it came into sight, he threw the watermelon rind down a near-by sewer. He stepped into the bus, and hoped that no one would notice his trousers. They still felt wet, and they were beginning to feel sticky.

"Fares!" said the bus driver. And then Eddie thought of his transfer ticket for the first time. He looked in both of his hands but it wasn't there. He put his hand in his trouser pocket, and pulled out a handful of odds and ends. A bunch of rusty keys, some bottle tops, a few marbles, a couple of large screws, some nuts and bolts, a small flashlight, a piece of white chalk, some broken crayons, a ball of string, and a quarter. But there was no transfer ticket.

"Sit down," said the bus driver. "I can't wait all day."

Eddie sat down and plunged his hand into his other pocket.

He pulled out a handful of cornflakes. He had put them there after breakfast to nibble on. Then he had forgotten them. Now in the excitement of looking for the transfer ticket, the cornflakes fell in a shower to the floor.

At the next stop the bus driver looked around. "How are you coming?" he said to Eddie.

"I've got it some place," said Eddie.

"Try the pocket of your blouse," the driver suggested.

Eddie poked his fingers into his blouse pocket. A wide grin spread over his face, and he pulled out the yellow transfer ticket. "I knew I had it," he said, as he handed it to the driver. Then he added, "Oh, I forgot. We didn't go past Twelfth Street, did we?"

"Two more stops," said the driver.

Eddie ate his few remaining cornflakes, and at the second stop he jumped out the moment the doors opened.

He walked into Potter's Drug Store and up to the counter. Mr. Potter came out from behind a glass window through which Eddie could see shelves filled with bottles. Every time he came into Potter's he wished that he could go behind that window and play with all of those bottles.

"Hello!" said Mr. Potter. "You're Mrs. Wilson's little boy, aren't you?"

"Yes, sir," replied Eddie. "I'm Eddie."

"Well, what can I do for you, Eddie?" Mr. Potter asked.

"Mamma sent me for some . . . some . . . some . . ."

"Yes?" said Mr. Potter. "Some what?"

"Uh, some . . ." What was it his mother had sent him for? Eddie couldn't remember.

"Did she write it down for you?" asked Mr. Potter.

"No," said Eddie. "But I remember what it was."

"You do?" said Mr. Potter.

"Yes. It was, ah . . . It was, ah . . . Milk!"

"Milk!" exclaimed Mr. Potter. "Eddie, I don't think your mother sent you here for milk."

"Well, it wasn't just milk, but it was some kind of milk," said Eddie.

"Oh, I know!" said Mr. Potter. "Milk of magnesia." And with this, Mr. Potter placed a package on the counter.

"I don't think it was milk of magnesia," said Eddie.

"Maybe it was shoe milk," said Mr. Potter. "There's a shoe milk to clean white shoes. Do you think it was shoe milk?" Mr. Potter lifted a package off a shelf and placed it beside the milk of magnesia.

"Shoe milk. Shoe milk," repeated Eddie. "It didn't sound like that."

Mr. Potter's face lighted up. "I know," he said, "it was probably malted milk. Was it malted milk, Eddie?"

"Malted milk," said Eddie. "Malted milk. Well, now, maybe it was." Mr. Potter brought out the bottle of malted milk.

"No," said Eddie, wrinkling up his brow. "I don't think it was malted milk."

Mr. Potter placed his palms on the counter and leaned towards Eddie.

"Eddie," he said, "do you think it was buttermilk soap? Try to think hard. Was it buttermilk soap?"

"Buttermilk soap," muttered Eddie. "Buttermilk soap."

Mr. Potter placed a cake of buttermilk soap beside the other packages.

"Maybe it was," said Eddie, "but I'm not quite sure."

"You're sure it wasn't milkweed lotion?" said Mr. Potter.

"What's that for?" Eddie asked.

"It's for your hands. Keeps them soft," replied Mr. Potter.

"Milkweed, milkweed," Eddie mumbled to himself. "Milkweed."

"Well, one of these must be right," said Mr. Potter. "Tell you what we'll do. I'll put all of these things in a bag and you take them home to your mother. She can bring back the ones she doesn't want."

"Okay!" said Eddie, joyfully. "That's a good idea, Mr. Potter."

Mr. Potter placed all of the packages in a large paper bag. "I'll charge this on your mother's bill," he said. "You tell her she can return what she doesn't want."

Eddie took the bag in his arm. Then he said, "My mother said, 'Will you please show me where to get on the bus to go home?'"

"Why, of course," replied Mr. Potter, coming out from behind the counter. "Come along."

Mr. Potter walked outside with Eddie. "You get the H bus right over on that corner. Now wait until the light changes."

Eddie watched the traffic signal. When it turned green, Mr. Potter said, "Now, go ahead. And remember to change to the E bus at Walnut Street."

Eddie ran across the street with his large package. As he reached the pavement he could see the H bus coming. Just as it swung up to the curb, Eddie thought of milk again. Milk. The door opened and he put one foot on the step. Then he jumped back. He looked at the traffic signal. It was green. He dashed across the street and into the drug store. He ran up to the counter and put down his bundle. Then he shouted, "Cold cream! It was cold cream!"

Mr. Potter came out from behind his window. "So! It was cold cream! Are you sure?"

Eddie nodded his head very vigorously. "Yes, Mr. Potter. I know it was cold cream. Do you want to know how I know?"

"Yes," said Mr. Potter. "How do you know it's cold cream?"

"'Cause I kept remembering milk," said Eddie.

The Night the Ghost Got In

JAMES THURBER

THE ghost that got into our house on the night of November 17, 1915, raised such a hullabaloo of misunderstandings that I am sorry I didn't just let it keep on walking, and go to bed. Its advent caused my mother to throw a shoe through a window of the house next door and ended up with my grandfather shooting a patrolman. I am sorry, therefore, as I have said, that I ever paid any attention to the footsteps.

They began about a quarter past one o'clock in the morning, a rhythmic, quick-cadenced walking around the dining-room table. My mother was asleep in one room upstairs, my brother Herman in another; grandfather was in the attic, in the old walnut bed which, as you will remember, once fell on my father. I had just stepped out of the bathtub and was busily rubbing myself with a towel when I heard the steps. They were the steps of a man walking rapidly around the dining-room table downstairs. The light from the bathroom shone down the back steps, which dropped directly into the dining-room; I could see the faint shine of plates on the plate-rail; I couldn't see the table. The steps kept going round and round the table; at regular intervals a board creaked, when it was trod upon. I supposed at first that it was my father or my brother Roy, who had gone to Indianapolis but were expected home at any time. I suspected next that it was a burglar. It did not enter my mind until later that it was a ghost.

After the walking had gone on for perhaps three minutes, I tiptoed to Herman's room. "Psst!" I hissed, in the dark, shaking him. "Awp," he said, in the low, hopeless tone of a despondent beagle—he always half suspected that something would "get him" in the night. I told him who I was. "There's something downstairs!" I said. He got up and followed me to the head of the back staircase. We listened together. There was no sound. The steps had ceased. Herman looked at me in some alarm: I had only the bath towel around my waist. He wanted to go back to bed, but I gripped his arm. "There's something down there!" I said. Instantly the steps began again, circled the dining-room table like a man running, and started up the stairs toward us, heavily, two at a time. The light still shone palely down the stairs; we saw nothing coming; we only heard the steps. Herman rushed to his room and slammed the door. I slammed shut the door at the stairs top and held my knee against it. After a long minute, I slowly opened it again. There was nothing there. There was no sound. None of us ever heard the ghost again.

The slamming of the doors had aroused mother: she peered out of her room. "What on earth are you boys doing?" she demanded. Herman ventured out of his room. "Nothing," he said, gruffly, but he was, in color, a light green. "What was all that running around downstairs?" said mother. So she had heard the steps, too! We just looked at her. "Burglars!" she shouted intuitively. I tried to quiet her by starting lightly downstairs.

"Come on, Herman," I said.

"I'll stay with mother," he said. "She's all excited."

I stepped back onto the landing.

"Don't either of you go a step," said mother. "We'll call the police." Since the phone was downstairs, I didn't see how we were going to call the police—nor did I want the police—but mother made one of her quick, incomparable decisions. She flung up a window of her bedroom which faced the bedroom windows of the house of a neighbor, picked up a shoe, and whammed it through a pane of glass across the narrow space that separated the two houses. Glass tinkled into the bedroom occupied by a retired engraver named Bodwell and his wife. Bodwell had been for some years in rather a bad way and was subject to mild "attacks." Most everybody we knew or lived near had *some* kind of attacks.

It was now about two o'clock of a moonless night; clouds hung black and low. Bodwell was at the window in a minute, shouting, frothing a little, shaking his fist. "We'll sell the house and go back to Peoria," we could hear Mrs. Bodwell saying. It was some time before mother "got through" to Bodwell. "Burglars!" she shouted. "Burglars in the house!" Herman and I hadn't dared to tell her that it was not burglars but ghosts, for she was even more afraid of ghosts than of burglars. Bodwell at first thought that she meant there were burglars in his house, but finally he quieted down and called the police for us over an extension phone by his bed. After he had disappeared from the window, mother suddenly made as if to throw another shoe, not because there was further need of it but, as she later explained, because the thrill of heaving a shoe through a window glass had enormously taken her fancy. I prevented her.

The police were on hand in a commendably short time: a Ford sedan full of them, two on motorcycles, and a patrol wagon with about eight in it and a few reporters. They began banging at our front door. Flashlights shot streaks of gleam up and down the walls, across the yard, down the walk between our house and Bodwell's. "Open up!" cried a hoarse voice. "We're men from Headquarters!" I wanted to go down and let them in, since there they were, but mother wouldn't hear of it. "You haven't a stitch on," she pointed out. "You'd catch your death." I wound the towel around me again. Finally the cops put their shoulders to our big heavy front door with its thick beveled glass and broke it in: I could hear a rending of wood and a splash of glass on the floor of the hall. Their lights played all over the living-room and criss-crossed nervously in the dining-room, stabbed into hallways, shot up the front stairs and finally up the back. They caught me standing in my towel at the top. A heavy policeman bounded up the steps. "Who are you?" he demanded. "I live here," I said. "Well, whattsa matta, ya hot?" he asked. It was, as a matter of fact, cold; I went to my room and pulled on some trousers. On my way out, a cop stuck a gun into my ribs. "Whatta you doin' here?" he demanded. "I live here," I said.

The officer in charge reported to mother. "No sign of nobody, lady," he said. "Musta got away—whatt'd he look like?" "There were two or three of them," mother said, "whooping and carrying on and slamming doors." "Funny," said the cop. "All ya windows and doors was locked on the inside tight as a tick."

Downstairs, we could hear the tromping of the other police. Police were all over the place; doors were yanked open, drawers were yanked open, windows were shot up and pulled down, furniture fell with dull thumps. A half-dozen policemen emerged out of the darkness of the front hallway upstairs. They began to ransack the floor: pulled beds away from walls, tore clothes off hooks in the closets, pulled suitcases and boxes off shelves. One of them found an old zither that Roy had won in a pool tournament. "Looky here, Joe," he said, strumming it with a big paw. The cop named Joe took it and turned it over. "What is it?" he asked me. "It's an old zither our guinea pig used to sleep on," I said. It was true that a pet guinea pig we once had would never sleep anywhere except on the zither, but I should never have said so. Joe and the other cop looked at me a long time. They put the zither back on a shelf.

"No sign o' nuthin'," said the cop who had first spoken to mother. "This guy," he explained to the others, jerking a thumb at me, "was nekked. The lady seems historical." They all nodded, but said nothing; just looked at me. In the small silence we all heard a creaking in the attic. Grandfather was turning over in bed. "What's 'at?" snapped Joe. Five or six cops sprang for the attic door before I could intervene or explain. I realized that it would be bad if they burst in on grandfather unannounced, or even announced. He was going through a phase in which he believed that General Meade's men, under steady hammering by Stonewall Jackson, were beginning to retreat and even desert.

When I got to the attic, things were pretty confused. Grandfather had evidently jumped to the conclusion that the police were deserters from Meade's army, trying to hide away in his attic. He bounded out of bed wearing a long flannel nightgown over long woolen underwear, a nightcap, and a leather jacket around his chest. The cops must have realized at once that the indignant white-haired old man belonged in the house, but they had no chance to say so. "Back, ye cowardly dogs!" roared grandfather. "Back t' the lines, ye lily-livered cattle!" With that, he fetched the officer who found the zither a flat-handed smack alongside his head that sent him sprawling. The others beat a re-

treat, but not fast enough; grandfather grabbed Zither's gun from its holster and let fly. The report seemed to crack the rafters; smoke filled the attic. A cop cursed and shot his hand to his shoulder. Somehow, we all finally got downstairs again and locked the door against the old gentleman. He fired once or twice more in the darkness and then went back to bed. "That was grandfather," I explained to Joe, out of breath. "He thinks you're deserters." "I'll say he does," said Joe.

The cops were reluctant to leave without getting their hands on somebody besides grandfather; the night had been distinctly a defeat for them. Furthermore, they obviously didn't like the "layout"; something looked—and I can see their viewpoint—phony. They began to poke into things again. A reporter, a thin-faced, wispy man, came up to me. I had put on one of mother's blouses, not being able to find anything else. The reporter looked at me with mingled suspicion and interest. "Just what the hell is the real lowdown here, Bud?" he asked. I decided to be frank with him. "We had ghosts," I said. He gazed at me a long time as if I were a slot machine into which he had, without results, dropped a nickel. Then he walked away. The cops followed him, the one grandfather shot holding his now-bandaged arm, cursing and blaspheming. "I'm gonna get my gun back from that old bird," said the zither-cop. "Yeh," said Joe. "You—and who else?" I told them I would bring it to the station house the next day.

"What was the matter with that one policeman?" mother asked, after they had gone. "Grandfather shot him," I said. "What for?" she demanded. I told her he was a deserter. "Of all things!" said mother. "He was such a nice-looking young man."

Grandfather was fresh as a daisy and full of jokes at breakfast next morning. We thought at first he had forgotten all about what had happened, but he hadn't. Over his third cup of coffee, he glared at Herman and me. "What was the idee of all them cops tarryhootin' round the house last night?" he demanded. He had us there.

FROM
The Middle Moffat

ELEANOR ESTES

Jane has never really felt that her place in the Moffat family was as good as her sister's or brothers'. Because her mother always introduced Sylvie as "my oldest child," Joey as "my oldest son," and Rufus as "the youngest in the family," Janey came out simply as, "This is Jane." But when she got the idea of calling herself "the middle Moffat," that seemed to give her name a proper ending. All four Moffats are to appear in the school play, The Three Bears, and appropriately enough, the middle Moffat is cast as the middle bear—but some unexpected surprises follow.

The Middle Bear

WHEN a play was given at the Town Hall, Sylvie was usually the only one of the four Moffats who was in it. However, once in a while the others were in a play. For instance, Rufus had been the smallest of the seven dwarfs. And once Janey had been a butterfly. She had not been an altogether successful butterfly, though, for she had tripped on the sole of her stocking, turning a somersault all across the stage. And whereas Joey was rarely in a play, he was often in charge of switching the lights on and off.

Jane liked the plays at the Town Hall. In fact she liked them better than the moving pictures. In the moving pictures Jane always found it difficult to tell the good man from the bad man. Especially if they both wore black mustaches. Of course the pianist usually played ominous music just before the bad man came on the scene, and that helped. Even so, Jane preferred the plays at the Town Hall. There she had no trouble at all telling the good from the bad.

Now there was to be a play at the Town Hall, "The Three Bears," and all four of the Moffats were going to be in it. Miss Chichester, the dancing school teacher, was putting it on. But the money for the tickets was not going into her pocket or into the Moffats' pocket, even though they were all in the play. The money was to help pay for the new parish house. The old one had burned down last May and now a new one was being built. "The Three Bears" was to help raise the money to finish it. A benefit performance, it was called.

In this benefit performance, Sylvie was to play the part of Goldilocks. Joey was to be the big bear, Rufus the little bear, and Janey the middle bear. Jane had not asked to be the middle bear. It just naturally came out that way. The middle Moffat was going to be the middle bear.

As a rule Joey did not enjoy the idea of acting in a play any more than he liked going to dancing school. However, he felt this play would be different. He felt it would be like having a disguise on, to be inside of a bear costume. And Jane felt the same way. She thought the people in the audience would not recognize her as the butterfly who turned a somersault across the stage, because she would be comfortably hidden inside her brown bear costume. As for Rufus, he hoped that Sylvie, the Goldilocks of this game, would not sit down too hard on that nice little chair of his and really break it to bits. It was such a good chair, and he wished he had it at home.

Mama was making all the costumes, even the bear heads. A big one for Joey, a little one for Rufus, and a middle-sized one for Jane. Of course she wasn't making them out of bear fur; she was using brown outing flannel.

Now Jane was trying on her middle bear costume. She stepped into the body of the costume and then Mama put the head on her.

"Make the holes for the eyes big enough," Jane begged. "So I'll see where I'm going and won't turn somersaults."

"Well," said Mama, "if I cut the eyes any larger you will look like a deep sea diver instead of a bear."

"Oh, well . . ." said Jane hastily. "A bear's got to look like a bear. Never mind making them any bigger, then."

Besides being in the play, each of the Moffats also had ten tickets to sell. And since Rufus really was too little to go from house to house and street to street selling tickets, the other three Moffats had even more to dispose of. Forty tickets!

At first Jane wondered if a girl should sell tickets to a play she was going to be in. Was that being conceited? Well, since the money was for the new parish house and not for the Moffats, she finally decided it was all right to sell the tickets. Besides, she thought, who would recognize her as the girl who sold tickets once she was inside her bear costume?

Sylvie sold most of her tickets like lightning to the ladies in the choir. But Joey's and Janey's tickets became grimier and grimier, they had such trouble disposing of them. Nancy Stokes said she would help even though she went to a different parish house. She and Joey and Jane went quietly and politely up on people's verandas and rang the bell.

"Buy a ticket for the benefit of the new parish house?" was all they meant to say. But very often no one at all answered the bell.

"They can't all be away," said Nancy. "Do you think they hide behind the curtains when they see us coming?"

"Oh, no," said Jane. "You see it'd be different if the money was for us. But it isn't. It's a benefit. Why should they hide?"

One lady said she was very sorry but she was making mincemeat. "See?" she said, holding up her hands. They were all covered with mincemeat. So she could not buy a ticket. Not possibly, and she closed the door in their faces.

"She could wash her hands," said Nancy angrily. The children called this lady "mincemeat," ever after. Of course she never knew it.

Yes, the tickets were very hard to sell. But little by little the pile did dwindle. If only everybody were like Mrs. Stokes, they would go very fast. She bought four tickets! Jane was embarrassed.

"Tell your mother she doesn't have to buy all those tickets just 'cause all of us are in the play," she instructed Nancy.

But all the Stokes insisted they really wanted to go. And even if none of the Moffats were in it, they would still want to go, for the play would help to build a new parish house. What nice people! thought Jane. Here they were, a family who went to the white church, buying tickets to help build a parish house for Janey's church. She hoped she would be a good middle bear, so they would be proud they knew her.

At last it was the night of the play. The four Moffats knew their lines perfectly. This was not surprising, considering they all lived in the same house and could practice their lines any time they wanted to. And, besides this, they had had two rehearsals, one in regular clothes and one in their bear costumes.

When Jane reached the Town Hall, she was surprised to find there were many features on the program besides "The Three Bears." The Gillespie twins were going to give a piano duet. "By the Brook," it was called. A boy was going to play the violin. Someone else was going to toe dance. And Miss Beale was going to sing a song. A big program. And the Moffats, all of them except Mama, were going to watch this whole performance from behind the scenes. They could not sit in the audience with the regular people with their bear costumes on, for that would give the whole show away.

Jane fastened her eye to a hole in the curtain. Mama had not yet come. Of course Mama would have to sit out front there with the regular people, even though she had made the costumes. The only people who had arrived so far were Clara Pringle and Brud. They were sitting in the front row and Jane wondered how they had gotten in because the front door that all the regular people were supposed to use wasn't even open yet.

When Jane wasn't peering through a hole in the curtain, Joey or Rufus was. Each one hoped he would be the first to see Mama when she came in. Or now and then they tried to squeeze through the opening at the side of the asbestos curtain. But the gnarled little janitor shook his head at them. So they stayed inside.

Sylvie was busy putting make-up on herself and on the dancers' faces. Jane watched them enviously. The only trouble with wearing a bear costume, she thought, was that she couldn't have her face painted. Well, she quickly consoled herself, she certainly would not have stage fright inside her bear head. Whereas she might if there were just paint on her face. "Somebody has been sitting in my chair," she rehearsed her lines. She stepped into her bear costume. But before putting on her head, she helped Rufus into his bear uniform. He didn't call it a costume. A uniform. A bear uniform. Jane set his head on his shoulders, found his two eyes for him so he could see out, and the little bear was ready.

Joey had no difficulty stepping into his costume and even in finding his own two eyes. Now the big bear and the little bear were ready. Jane looked around for her head, to put it on. Where was it?

"Where's my head?" she asked. "My bear head."

Nobody paid any attention to her. Miss Chichester was running back and forth and all around, giving an order here and an order there. Once as she rushed by, causing a great breeze, Jane yelled to make herself heard, "How can we act 'The Three Bears' unless I find my middle bear head?"

"Not just now. I'm too busy," was all Miss Chichester said.

Everybody was too busy to help Jane find her head. Sylvie was helping the toe dancer dress. Joey was busy running around doing this and doing that for Miss Chichester. And the little old janitor was busy tightening ropes and making sure the lights were working. Rufus could not be torn from a hole in the curtain. He was looking for Mama.

Jane sighed. Everybody's busy, she thought. She rummaged around in a big box of costumes. Maybe her bear head had been stuck in it. She found a dragon head and tried it on. How would that be? She looked in the mirror. The effect was interesting. But, no, she could not wear this, for a bear cannot be a dragon.

Goodness, thought Jane. The curtain will go up, and the middle bear won't be a whole bear. This was worse than tripping over her stocking the time she was a butterfly. Maybe Joey and Rufus somehow or another had two heads on. They didn't, though, just their own. Phew, it was warm inside these bear costumes. Jane stood beside Rufus and looked through another small hole in the curtain. Oh! The big door was open! People were beginning to arrive. And what kind of a bear would she be without a head? Maybe she wouldn't be allowed to be a bear at all. But there certainly could not be three bears without a middle one.

"Don't worry," said Rufus, not moving an inch from his spot. "Lend you mine for half the play . . ."

"Thanks," said Jane. "But we all have to have our heads on all through the whole thing."

The Stokes were coming in! Jane felt worried. The only person who might be able to fix a new bear head for her in a hurry was Mama. Oh, if she had only made a couple of spare heads. But Mama wasn't coming yet. Jane resolved to go and meet her. She put on her tam and her chinchilla coat over her bear costume. Then she ran down the three narrow steps into the Hall. She crouched low in her coat in order not to give away the fact that she was clad in a bear costume. Nobody on this side of the curtain was supposed to know what people on her side of the curtain had on until the curtain rolled up. Surprise. That's what was important in a play.

Mr. Buckle was coming in now, walking towards the front row. Jane stooped low, with her knees bent beneath her. In front her coat nearly reached the ground. From the way she looked from the front, few would guess that she was the middle bear. Of course her feet showed. They were encased in the brown costume. But she might be a brownie or even a squirrel.

"Hello, Mr. Buckle," said Jane. "I'm in a hurry . . ."

"Where are you going, middle Moffat?" he asked. "Aren't you the prima donna?"

"No. Just the middle bear."

"Well, that's fine. The middle Moffat is the middle bear."

"Yes. Or I was until I lost my head."

"Oh, my," said Mr. Buckle. "This then is not your head?" he asked, pointing to her tam.

"Yes, but not my bear head. I don't mean bare head. Bear head! B-e-a-r. That kind of head."

"Mystifying. Very mystifying," said Mr. Buckle, settling himself slowly in a seat in the front row.

"You'll see later," said Jane, running down the aisle.

She ran all the way home. But the house was dark. Mama had already left. And she must have gone around the other way or

Jane would have passed her. Jane raced back to the Town Hall.
There! Now! The lights were dim. The entertainment had begun.
Jane tried to open the side door. Chief Mulligan was guarding
this entrance. He did not want to let her in at first. He thought
she was just a person. But when she showed him her costume, he
opened the door just wide enough for her. The bear costume was
as good as a password.

The toe dancer was doing the split. Jane tiptoed up the three
steps and went backstage, wondering what would happen now.
The show always goes on. There was some comfort in that
thought. Somehow, someone would fix her head. Or possibly
while she was gone her middle bear head had been found. She
hoped she would not have to act with her head bare.

Miss Chichester snatched her.

"Oh, there you are, Jane! Hop into your costume, dear."

"I'm in it," said Jane. "But I can't find my middle bear head."

"Heavens!" said Miss Chichester, grasping her own head.
"What else will go wrong?"

Jane looked at her in surprise. What else *had* gone wrong? Had
others lost worse than their heads?

"Where's the janitor?" Miss Chichester asked. "Maybe he let
his grandchildren borrow it."

Jane knew he hadn't, but she couldn't tell Miss Chichester for
she had already flown off. And then Janey had an idea.

"I know what," she said to Joey. "Pin me together." And she
pulled the neck part of her costume up over her head. Joey pinned
it with two safety pins, and he cut two holes for her eyes. This
costume was not comfortable now. Pulling it up and pinning it
this way lifted Jane's arms so she had trouble making them hang
down the way she thought a bear's should. However, at any rate,
she now had a bear head of sorts.

"Do I look like a bear?" she asked Rufus.

"You look like a brown ghost," Rufus replied.

"Don't you worry," said Sylvie, coming up. "You look like a
very nice little animal."

"But I'm supposed to be a bear, not a nice little animal," said
Jane.

"Well," said Sylvie, "people will know you are supposed to be

a bear because Rufus and Joey both have their bear heads on."

So Jane resigned herself to not being a perfect bear. She tried to comfort herself with the thought that she would still be in disguise. She hoped her acting would be so good it would counterbalance her bad head. "Somebody has been eating my porridge," she practiced.

Miss Chichester appeared. "The janitor said 'No,' " she said. She thoughtfully surveyed Jane a moment. "Hm-m-m, a makeshift," she observed. "Well, it's better than nothing," she agreed with Jane. But she decided to switch the order of the program around in order to give everybody one last chance to find the middle bear's real head. She sent Miss Beale out onto the stage. Everybody hoped that while Miss Beale was singing "In an Old-fashioned Garden," the head would appear. But it didn't.

"Keep a little in the background," said Miss Chichester to Jane. "Perhaps people will not notice."

"If I can only see where the background is," thought Jane. For she found it even harder to keep her eyes close to the holes cut in her costume than it had been to the real ones in her regular bear head.

Now the heavy curtain rolled up. It didn't stick halfway up as it sometimes did, and Sylvie, Goldilocks, in a blue pinafore and socks, ran out onto the stage midst loud applause. The play had begun! Sylvie had a great deal of acting to do all by herself before the three bears came home. But she wasn't scared. She was used to being on the stage alone.

Jane's heart pounded as she and Joey and Rufus waited for their cue to come home. If only she didn't trip and turn a somersault, for she really could not see very well. Somehow she managed to see out of only one eye at a time. These eye holes must have been cut crooked. One hole kept getting hooked on her nose.

"Now!" Miss Chichester whispered. "Cue! Out with you three bears."

Joe, Jane, and Rufus, the three bears, lumbered out onto the stage. They were never supposed to just walk, always lumber and lope.

The applause was tremendous. It startled the three bears. The

Town Hall was packed. Somebody must have sold a lot of tickets. "There's Mama," said Rufus. He said it out loud.

He wasn't supposed to say anything out loud except about his porridge, his chair, and his bed. But anyway he said, "There's Mama." Jane could not see Mama. Lumbering out onto the stage had dislocated her costume so that now she could not see at all. Fortunately the footlights shone through the brown flannel of her costume so she could keep away from the edge of the stage and not fall off.

The Moffats all knew their lines so well they did not forget them once. The only trouble was they did not have much chance to say them because the applause was so great every time they opened their mouths. At last, however, they reached the act about the three beds. An extra platform had been set up on the stage to look like the upstairs of a three bears' house. The three bears lumbered slowly up the steps.

Suddenly shouts arose all over the Hall:

"Her head! Her head! The middle bear's head!"

"Sh-sh-sh," said others. "See what's going to happen."

As Jane could not see very well she had no idea what these shouts referred to. She had the same head on now that she had had on all during this play so far. Why then all these shouts? Or had she really stayed in the background the way Miss Chichester had asked her to, and the audience had only just discovered about the make-shift?

"Oh," whispered Joey to Jane. "I see it. It's your real bear head and it's on the top of my bed post."

"O-o-o-h!" said Jane. "Get it down."

"How can I?" said Joe. "With all these people watching me?"

"Try and get it when you punch your bed," urged Jane.

Joey was examining his big bear's bed now. "Hm-m-m," he said fiercely. "Somebody has been lying on my bed. . . ." But he couldn't reach the middle bear's head. He did try. But he couldn't quite reach it, and there was more laughter from the audience.

Jane pulled her costume about until she could see through the eyehole. Ah, there was her head! On the post of the big bear's bed. No wonder people were laughing. What a place for the middle bear's head. Here she was, without it. And there it was, without her. Jane resolved to get it. Somehow or other she would rescue her head before this play was completely over. Now was her chance. It was her turn to talk about her bed. Instead, Jane said:

"Somebody has been trying on my head, and there it is!"

Jane hopped up on Joey's bed. She grabbed her middle bear head.

"Yes," she repeated. "Somebody has been trying on my head," but as she added, "and here it is!" the safety pins that held her make-shift head together popped open. The audience burst into roars of laughter as Janey's own real head emerged. Only for a second though. For she clapped her middle bear head right on as fast as she could, and hopped off the bed. Goodness, she thought, I showed my real face and I didn't have any paint on it.

Unfortunately Jane still could not see, for she had stuck her bear head on backwards. But the audience loved it. They clapped and they stamped. Bravo! Bravo! Bravo, middle bear! Big boys at the back of the hall put their fingers in their mouths and whistled. And it was a long, long time before Jane could say:

"Somebody has been sleeping in my bed," and the play could go on. At last Rufus discovered Goldilocks in his little bed, and she leaped out of the window. That was the end of the play, and the curtain rolled down.

When the bowing began, Miss Chichester tried to send Jane in backwards, thinking the back of her was the front of her. Fortunately, Rufus held Jane by one paw, and Joey held the other. So she didn't get lost. And the three bears lumbered dizzily on and off many times, sometimes with Sylvie, and sometimes alone. And somebody yelled for "The mysterious middle bear!" It must have been the oldest inhabitant.

Miss Chichester turned Jane's head around for this bow and at last Jane really did look like a perfect middle bear. Furthermore, she could see out. There was Mama, laughing so hard the tears were rolling down her cheeks. And there was Nancy Stokes with all the Stokes, and Olga was there. And there was Mr. Buckle beaming up at the stage. Jane bowed and lumbered off the stage. She felt good now. Acting was fun, she thought, espe-

cially if you could be disguised in a bear uniform. And this time she had not turned a somersault across the stage as she had the time she was a butterfly. True, she had lost her head. But she had found it. And the show had gone on, the way people always say they do.

Moreover, the Moffats had nice warm bear pajamas to sleep in for the rest of the winter. Of course they didn't go to bed with the bear heads on. But the rest of the costumes were nice and warm.

Clever Manka

The Story of a Girl Who Knew What to Say

PARKER FILLMORE

THERE was once a rich farmer who was as grasping and un-scrupulous as he was rich. He was always driving a hard bargain and always getting the better of his poor neighbors. One of these neighbors was a humble shepherd who in return for service was to receive from the farmer a heifer. When the time of payment came the farmer refused to give the shepherd the heifer and the shepherd was forced to lay the matter before the burgomaster.

The burgomaster, who was a young man and as yet not very experienced, listened to both sides and when he had deliberated he said:

"Instead of deciding this case, I will put a riddle to you both and the man who makes the best answer shall have the heifer. Are you agreed?"

The farmer and the shepherd accepted this proposal and the burgomaster said:

"Well then, here is my riddle: What is the swiftest thing in the world? What is the sweetest thing? What is the richest? Think out your answers and bring them to me at this same hour to-morrow."

The farmer went home in a temper.

"What kind of a burgomaster is this young fellow!" he growled. "If he had let me keep the heifer I'd have sent him a bushel of pears. But now I'm in a fair way of losing the heifer for I can't think of any answer to his foolish riddle."

"What is the matter, husband?" his wife asked.

"It's that new burgomaster. The old one would have given me the heifer without any argument, but this young man thinks to decide the case by asking us riddles."

When he told his wife what the riddle was, she cheered him greatly by telling him that she knew the answers at once.

"Why, husband," said she, "our gray mare must be the swiftest thing in the world. You know yourself nothing ever passes us on the road. As for the sweetest, did you ever taste honey any sweeter than ours? And I'm sure there's nothing richer than our chest of golden ducats that we've been laying by these forty years."

The farmer was delighted.

"You're right, wife, you're right! That heifer remains ours!"

The shepherd when he got home was downcast and sad. He had a daughter, a clever girl named Manka, who met him at the door of his cottage and asked:

"What is it, father? What did the burgomaster say?"

The shepherd sighed.

"I'm afraid I've lost the heifer. The burgomaster set us a riddle and I know I shall never guess it."

"Perhaps I can help you," Manka said. "What is it?"

So the shepherd gave her the riddle and the next day as he was setting out for the burgomaster's, Manka told him what answers to make.

When he reached the burgomaster's house, the farmer was already there rubbing his hands and beaming with self-importance.

The burgomaster again propounded the riddle and then asked the farmer his answers.

The farmer cleared his throat and with a pompous air began:

"The swiftest thing in the world? Why, my dear sir, that's my gray mare, of course, for no other horse ever passes us on the road. The sweetest? Honey from my beehives, to be sure. The richest? What can be richer than my chest of golden ducats!"

And the farmer squared his shoulders and smiled triumphantly.

"H'm," said the young burgomaster, dryly. Then he asked:

"What answers does the shepherd make?"

The shepherd bowed politely and said:

"The swiftest thing in the world is thought for thought can run any distance in the twinkling of an eye. The sweetest thing of all is sleep for when a man is tired and sad what can be sweeter? The richest thing is the earth for out of the earth comes all the riches of the world."

"Good!" the burgomaster cried. "Good! The heifer goes to the shepherd!"

Later the burgomaster said to the shepherd:

"Tell me, now, who gave you those answers? I'm sure they never came out of your own head."

At first the shepherd tried not to tell, but when the burgomaster pressed him he confessed that they came from his daughter, Manka. The burgomaster, who thought that he would like to make another test of Manka's cleverness, sent for ten eggs. He gave them to the shepherd and said:

"Take these eggs to Manka and tell her to have them hatched out by tomorrow and to bring me the chicks."

When the shepherd reached home and gave Manka the burgomaster's message, Manka laughed and said: "Take a handful of millet and go right back to the burgomaster. Say to him: 'My daughter sends you this millet. She says that if you plant, grow it, and have it harvested by tomorrow, she'll bring you the ten chicks and you can feed them the ripe grain.'"

When the burgomaster heard this, he laughed heartily.

"That's a clever girl of yours," he told the shepherd. "If she's as comely as she is clever, I think I'd like to marry her. Tell her to come to see me, but she must come neither by day nor by night, neither riding nor walking, neither dressed nor undressed."

When Manka received this message she waited until the next dawn when night was gone and day not yet arrived. Then she wrapped herself in a fishnet and, throwing one leg over a goat's back and keeping one foot on the ground, she went to the burgomaster's house.

Now I ask you: did she go dressed? No, she wasn't dressed. A fishnet isn't clothing. Did she go undressed? Of course not, for wasn't she covered with a fishnet? Did she walk to the burgomaster's? No, she didn't walk for she went with one leg thrown over a goat. Then did she ride? Of course she didn't ride for wasn't she walking on one foot?

When she reached the burgomaster's house she called out:

"Here I am, Mr. Burgomaster, and I've come neither by day nor by night, neither riding nor walking, neither dressed nor undressed."

The young burgomaster was so delighted with Manka's cleverness and so pleased with her comely looks that he proposed to her at once and in a short time married her.

"But understand, my dear Manka," he said, "you are not to use that cleverness of yours at my expense. I won't have you interfering in any of my cases. In fact if ever you give advice to any one who comes to me for judgment, I'll turn you out of my house at once and send you home to your father."

All went well for a time. Manka busied herself in her housekeeping and was careful not to interfere in any of the burgomaster's cases.

Then one day two farmers came to the burgomaster to have a dispute settled. One of the farmers owned a mare which had foaled in the marketplace. The colt had run under the wagon of the other farmer and thereupon the owner of the wagon claimed the colt as his property.

The burgomaster, who was thinking of something else while the case was being presented, said carelessly:

"The man who found the colt under his wagon is, of course, the owner of the colt."

As the owner of the mare was leaving the burgomaster's house, he met Manka and stopped to tell her about the case. Manka was ashamed of her husband for making so foolish a decision and she said to the farmer:

"Come back this afternoon with a fishing net and stretch it across the dusty road. When the burgomaster sees you he will come out and ask you what you are doing. Say to him that you're catching fish. When he asks you how you can expect to catch fish in a dusty road, tell him it's just as easy for you to catch fish in a dusty road as it is for a wagon to foal. Then he'll see the injustice of his decision and have the colt returned to you. But remember one thing: you mustn't let him find out that it was I who told you to do this."

That afternoon when the burgomaster chanced to look out the window he saw a man stretching a fishnet across the dusty road. He went out to him and asked: "What are you doing?"

"Fishing."

"Fishing in a dusty road? Are you daft?"

"Well," the man said, "it's just as easy for me to catch fish in a dusty road as it is for a wagon to foal."

Then the burgomaster recognized the man as the owner of the mare and he had to confess that what he said was true.

"Of course the colt belongs to your mare and must be returned to you. But tell me," he said, "who put you up to this? You didn't think of it yourself."

The farmer tried not to tell but the burgomaster questioned him until he found out that Manka was at the bottom of it. This made him very angry. He went into the house and called his wife.

"Manka," he said, "do you forget what I told you would happen if you went interfering in any of my cases? Home you go this very day. I don't care to hear any excuses. The matter is settled. You may take with you the one thing you like best in my house for I won't have people saying that I treated you shabbily."

Manka made no outcry.

"Very well, my dear husband, I shall do as you say: I shall go to my father's cottage and take with me the one thing I like best in your house. But don't make me go until after supper. We have been very happy together and I should like to eat one last meal with you. Let us have no more words but be kind to each other as we've always been and then part as friends."

The burgomaster agreed to this and Manka prepared a fine supper of all the dishes of which her husband was particularly fond. The burgomaster opened his choicest wine and pledged Manka's health. Then he set to, and the supper was so good that he ate and ate and ate. And the more he ate, the more he drank until at last he grew drowsy and fell sound asleep in his chair. Then without awakening him Manka had him carried out to the wagon that was waiting to take her home to her father.

The next morning when the burgomaster opened his eyes, he found himself lying in the shepherd's cottage.

"What does this mean?" he roared out.

"Nothing, dear husband, nothing!" Manka said. "You know you told me I might take with me the one thing I liked best in your house, so of course I took you! That's all."

For a moment the burgomaster rubbed his eyes in amazement. Then he laughed loud and heartily to think how Manka had outwitted him.

"Manka," he said, "you're too clever for me. Come on, my dear, let's go home."

So they climbed back into the wagon and drove home.

The burgomaster never again scolded his wife but thereafter whenever a very difficult case came up he always said:

"I think we had better consult my wife. You know she's a very clever woman."

FROM
Freddy the Detective

WALTER R. BROOKS

---

*Freddy is a very clever pig and the most ambitious animal
on Mr. Bean's farm. He decides to become a detective but
his first attempt to solve a case ends in his being fooled by
the rats, who then tease him about it unmercifully. A steady
diet of readings in Sherlock Holmes gives him new confidence, and he is sure that he will now get some good ideas
about how to be a detective.*

Freddy Solves Some Mysteries

Bᴜᴛ Freddy really had no ideas at all. There was no good using
force; he had tried that, and all he had got out of it was a broken
tooth that sent his family into fits of laughter whenever he
smiled. Anyway, detectives seldom used force; they used guile.
He went back to his library and got comfortable and tried to
think up some guile to use on the rats. And as usual when he lay
perfectly still and concentrated for a short time, he fell asleep.

He was awakened by a timid but persistent tapping at the
door. "Come in," he said sleepily, and then as a white nose and
two white ears appeared round the edge of the door, he jumped
up. "Ah, Mrs. Winnick," he said as the rest of an elderly rabbit
followed the ears into the room; "long time since I have seen
you. What can I do for you today?"

Mrs. Winnick was a widow who lived down by the edge of the
woods. In her day she had been as pretty a young rabbit as you
could wish to see, but since the loss of her husband the cares of

providing for a large family had taken every bit of her time and energy. She took no part in the gay social life of the other animals in the neighborhood, and they seldom saw her, though they were good to her, and one or other of them was always taking a fresh head of lettuce or a couple of carrots down to her, for they suspected that she and the children did not always get enough food.

"Oh, Mr. Freddy," she burst out, "it's about Egbert. He's disappeared, and whatever I shall do I don't know. He was always such a good boy, too—kind and helpful, and willing to look after the baby. With the other children it's play, play, play all day long, but Egbert—" And she began to cry. . . .

"Come, come," said Freddy briskly. "Just tell me all about it, and we'll see what can be done. I'm sure it's not as bad as you think. Now, do you want me to help you find Egbert?" And as she nodded tearful assent, "Well," he continued, "let's get at the facts. Let's see—Egbert. He's your eighth oldest, isn't he? Or ninth?"

"Twelfth," she replied, "and always such a good—"

"Yes," said Freddy quickly. "And when did you last see him?"

After asking a good many questions Freddy got Mrs. Winnick's story. The night before Egbert had taken several of the children up through the woods to Jones's Creek to get some watercress. At nine o'clock the children had come home without him. They had not found any good watercress, and Egbert had said that he would go farther down the creek to a place he knew where there was sure to be some, but that they must go home, as it was their bedtime, and their mother would worry. Mrs. Winnick had put the children to bed and had presently gone to bed herself. But this morning Egbert's bed was empty. He had not come home, and nothing had been seen or heard of him since.

Freddy consoled the weeping widow as best he could. "I'll get to work on it right away," he said, "and meanwhile don't worry. I'll soon have Egbert back for you. By the way, who sent you to me?"

"It was the children," said the rabbit. "They'd heard about your setting up to be a detective, and they wanted me to come and see you. Not that I have any faith in it—excuse me, sir. But you haven't been at it very long, have you?"

"No," Freddy admitted, "but there always has to be a first time, doesn't there? Even Sherlock Holmes made a start once, didn't he? Don't you worry, ma'am. I've made a deep study of the subject, and there isn't an animal in the country that knows more about detecting than I do. Why, I've read a whole book about it."

Mrs. Winnick seemed satisfied with this and went off home, stopping after every three or four hops to cry a little and blow her nose. Freddy wasted no time, but set out at once for the creek. He found the watercress bed which Egbert had visited with his little brothers and sisters, then went slowly on downstream, keeping a sharp lookout for any signs of the missing rabbit. Once he saw where some wintergreen leaves had been nibbled, and once, in a sandy place, he saw the plain imprint of a rabbit's foot, so he knew he was on the right track. And then where the stream widened out, just before it took a bend round to the right to join the river, he found another big bed of cress, and in the swampy shore a large number of rabbit's footprints.

Freddy had been happy when he started out. Mrs. Winnick's visit had cheered him up a lot. Here was a new problem. He would solve it and prove to his friends that he was a real detective after all. But now this problem was just as bad as the other one. What was he going to do? These were Egbert's footprints all right, but what good did they do him? There ought to be some clue that he could follow up. There always was in the Sherlock Holmes stories. "You can't solve a case without clues," he muttered unhappily. "These might be clues to Sherlock Holmes, but to me they're just a lot of footprints." And he sat down on the bank to think.

He was thinking so hard that for some time he did not see a small rabbit who hopped down out of the woods to the cress bed, picked a few stalks, then hopped back up among the trees. The rabbit had made several trips before Freddy suddenly caught sight of him.

The rabbit hadn't seen Freddy either, and when the pig started up suddenly, he dodged quickly behind a bush.

"So *you're* the one who made all those footprints in the mud here, are you?" said Freddy.

"Yes, sir," came a small anxious voice from behind the bush. "Isn't it all right, sir?"

"Sure it's all right," said the pig. "Come out; I won't hurt you. I'm looking for a rabbit about your size. Haven't seen one around, have you?"

The rabbit hopped timidly out. "No, sir," he said. "Who was he, sir?"

"Ah," said Freddy mysteriously, "*I'm* the one to be asking the questions. I'm a detective. Just you answer up briskly, young fellow. Haven't seen any other rabbits around, eh?"

"No, sir—"

"No other footprints in the mud when you came here?"

"I don't think so, sir. You see, I—"

"How long have you been here?"

"Since last night, sir. You see, I came to get some watercress, and as I was—"

Freddy stopped him. "That's enough," he said severely. "Please just answer the questions I ask you, without adding anything of your own. Just answer yes or no. You heard no unusual noises?"

"Yes, sir—I mean no, sir," said the rabbit, who was getting confused.

"What do you mean—'yes, sir, no, sir'?" said Freddy. "Please give me a straight answer. Did you or did you not hear any unusual noises?"

"No, sir—I mean—" The rabbit gulped. "—no, sir."

"Good," said the pig. "That's the stuff; a straight answer to a straight question. And—ha, h'm—let me see—" He hadn't found out anything, and yet he couldn't think of any more questions to ask. "Well, ah—what are you doing here anyway?"

But the rabbit didn't answer. "Come, come," said Freddy sharply. "Answer me! What are you—"

But the rabbit interrupted him by bursting into tears. "You told me to answer yes or no," he sobbed, "and you can't answer that question yes or no. I c-came here to get watercress, an' I was just going home an' I found a little bird with a hurt wing, an' I thought I ought to stay with it, an' I know my mother'll worry, b-but I don't like to leave the bird all alone, an' now you come

an' ask me a lot of questions I don't know the answers to, an'—"
Here he broke down entirely and cried so hard that he got the
hiccups.

Freddy was a kind-hearted animal, but he had been so absorbed in asking questions in a thoroughly detective-like manner
that he hadn't really noticed that he was frightening the rabbit
so badly that the poor little creature couldn't give him any information even if he had it to give. In this Freddy was more like a
real detective than he realized. Some detectives will ask a simple
question like "What is your name?" in so frightening a voice that
the person he asks can't even remember whether he has a name
or not.

"There, there," said Freddy, patting the rabbit on the back,
"I'm sorry I scared you. It's all right. Where is this bird?"

"Up in a hollow behind that tree," hiccuped the little animal.

"All right," said Freddy. "I'll look after him for you. You run
along home. I've got to find this other rabbit I was telling you
about, but first I'll see that the bird is taken care of. Run along
and tell your mother not to worry any more."

The rabbit wasted no time, but trotted off, still crying, and
hiccuping occasionally, and Freddy went in search of the bird. He
found it presently—a fledgling wood thrush, too young to talk
yet. Beside it was a small heap of watercress which the rabbit had
evidently been trying to feed it.

"Tut, tut," said Freddy. "Feeding an infant like that watercress! He'll be sick. And he's hidden here so that his mother
couldn't possibly find him. That rabbit has a kind heart, but he
certainly isn't very bright." He picked up the little thrush carefully in his mouth and carried it, fluttering feebly, out into an
open space, then went back into the bushes and sat down. In five
minutes there was a rush of wings, and the mother thrush
alighted beside the hungry fledgling and began consoling him
with little chirps. Freddy slipped away without waiting to be
thanked.

"Now," he said to himself, "for Egbert. Though how in the
world I'm to find him I don't know. But I've *got* to or I'll never
dare to show my face in the farmyard again. I wish I'd never tried
to be a detective, that's what I wish!"

On a chance he decided to go a little farther down the creek, at least as far as the hermit's house, a deserted cabin which stood on the other side of the stream. Perhaps some of the waterside animals might have seen the missing rabbit.

But he had not gone far before something drove all thought of Egbert from his mind. There were sounds coming from the hermit's house. Shouts and rough laughter and occasional pistol shots. What a chance for a detective! Freddy crept forward; then, finding that the bushes on the opposite bank were too high to permit him to see what was going on, he plunged into the water, swam quietly across, and worked his way up toward the house. And this is what he saw:

Hanging from the limb of a tall tree in front of the house was a swing made of two ropes and a board for a seat. A big man with a cap pulled down over his eyes, and his coat collar turned up, was swinging in long, dizzy swoops. He had a revolver in his hand, and at the top of his swing, when he was level with the top of the house, he would shoot the revolver and try to hit the chimney. A smaller man was sitting in a rocking chair on the porch. He wore a black mask over his face, and no cap, and was knitting busily away at a woolen muffler.

Pretty soon the big man stopped swinging. "Come now, Looey," he shouted. "It's your turn now."

The small man shook his head. "No, Red, I must get this muffler done. We'll both want to wrap up warm tomorrow night; we'll be out late."

"Oh, come on," said Red. "Take a couple of shots anyway. Bet you can't beat me. I got two out of seven."

The other got up rather unwillingly. "Well, all right. But you have got to promise to be more careful. I worry about you all the time. You remember that last bank we robbed; it was a rainy night, and you didn't wear your rubbers, and you caught a bad cold."

"Yes, yes, Looey," Red replied. "I'll be careful. Come on, now. Into the swing."

"You'll have to push me, Red," said Looey, taking a large revolver from the pocket of his coat. He seated himself in the swing, and the big man started him swinging. Higher and higher he went, until at each push Red was running right under him. Then when he was high enough, he aimed the revolver, and bang! a brick flew from the chimney.

"Hooray for Looey!" shouted Red. "A bull's-eye! Shoot again!"

Freddy, peering out from his hiding-place, was so excited he could hardly breathe. Here was real work for a detective, and no mistake. For these men were certainly robbers. And if he could capture them, his name as a detective was made.

But just then, as Looey was whizzing for the tenth time up into the treetops, one of the ropes broke; he let go his hold and went up in a great curve like a rocket, then came hurtling down through the foliage and into the very bush behind which Freddy was hiding.

He wasn't hurt, for the bush had broken his fall, and he picked himself up immediately, and his eye fell on the amazed pig. Freddy did not wait to see what would happen. With a squeal of fright he bolted.

"A pig! Quick, Red, a nice fat pig!" shouted Looey, and started after him, the other robber close behind. There was much shouting and a great banging of revolvers, and two or three bullets whizzed past Freddy's head, but he was a good runner and in a very few minutes had left them far behind.

He ran on for a while, then sat down to rest under a beech tree —and realized suddenly that he didn't know where he was. The woods on this side of the creek extended for many miles. If he could find the creek, he would be all right—but he did not know where the creek was. And the day was cloudy; he could not tell his direction from the position of the sun. "Well, I suppose the best thing to do is to keep on going," he said to himself. "May meet a squirrel or a jay who can tell me where I am." And he started on.

But though he walked and walked, he met no one, and there was no sign of the creek. He had just about decided that he would have to stay out all night when he noticed some footprints. "H'm, someone been along here not many minutes ago," he said. "Looks like a pig, too. Wonder what another pig is doing in these woods. I guess I'll follow them and see if I can catch up."

So he went on, following the footprints, until he came to a place where the other pig had sat down to rest before going on. There was the plain print of a curly tail in the leaf mold under a beech tree. Freddy sat down too, and then suddenly something about the place seemed familiar to him. This beech tree, those bushes over there—"Why, this is where I sat down to rest myself a long time ago! Those are my own footprints I've been following!"

This realization made him feel very foolish, as well it might, for it *is* rather silly for a detective to try to shadow himself. Still, he realized that all he had to do was to follow those footprints *backward* instead of forward, and he would come out by the hermit's house. Which he did, and presently he heard the sound of voices.

But this time he did not stop to see what the robbers were doing. He gave the house a wide berth, jumped into the creek, swam across, and in a few minutes more was back on familiar ground.

"I'll just stop in and see if anything has been heard of Egbert," he said to himself. So he turned down toward the Widow Winnick's home. Half a dozen small rabbits were playing about on the edge of the woods as he came up, and one of them called down the rabbit-hole: "Mother! Mr. Freddy's here!"

Almost at once Mrs. Winnick's head popped up through the opening. But it was a changed Mrs. Winnick that beamed happily at him.

"Oh, Mr. Freddy!" she cried. "How can I ever thank you? My Egbert! You found him for me!"

"But," stammered the bewildered Freddy, "I didn't—" And then he stopped. For one of the little rabbits who were standing around him in a respectful and admiring circle hiccuped, and said politely: "Excuse me." And Freddy saw it all. Of course! That rabbit had been Egbert all the time!

He recovered himself just in time. "Oh, don't thank me, Mrs. Winnick. Don't thank me," he said rather grandly. "It was nothing, I assure you—nothing at all. Indeed, I am very grateful to you for having sent me down in that direction, for I have made some very important discoveries. However, I am glad Egbert got back safely. All the other children are well, I hope. Good, good;

I am very glad to hear it. Good evening." And he went on home-ward.

"Well," he said to himself, "I guess as a detective I'm not so bad after all. Restored a lost child to his mother and discovered a band of robbers, all in one day! Huh, Sherlock Holmes never did more than that, I bet."

Freddy disguises himself in men's clothing and sets out to solve another mystery.

It was nearly dark in the woods, though above him the treetops were bright green and gold in the light of the setting sun. Since he could not swim the creek in his men's clothes, to get to the hermit's house he had to cut through the woods to the bridge and then walk back on the other side. He walked on his hind legs, be-cause he felt that he needed all the practice he could get if he was to make anybody think he was a man. But the trousers bothered his legs, and he stumbled over roots and tripped over vines and fell into holes until, long before he reached the creek, he was so bruised and hot and out of breath that he sat down on a log to rest. "My goodness," he said to himself, "I'm glad I'm not a man! How they ever manage to do anything or get anywhere in all these clumsy hot clothes I can't imagine! Lords of creation, they call themselves! Humph, I'd rather be a pig any time."

Pretty soon he got up and went on again, and at last he reached the bridge. On the farther side of the bridge a narrow, grassy road ran off to the left toward the hermit's house. Freddy followed it. He began to feel rather nervous, but he was a brave pig and he had no thought of turning back.

By this time it was dark. The windows in the hermit's house were lighted up, but they were so dirty that Freddy couldn't see what was going on inside. He could hear music, however—some-one was playing the harmonium, and a man's voice was singing. The song was "Sweet and Low," but both singer and accompa-nist were going as fast as they could, and they were never to-gether for more than one note. The singer would be ahead, then the player would put on a burst of speed and pass him, only to get behind again when he stopped to take breath.

Freddy thought this was the funniest singing he had ever heard, and he went up to the front door and peeked through the keyhole just as the song came to an end. The big man, who was sitting at the harmonium, was wiping sweat from his forehead. "You won that time, Looey," he was saying, "but it's the chords in that second part that slow me up."

"I'll race you on 'Boola Boola,'" said Looey.

"No you won't either," said Red. "You always win on that because you leave out about six 'Boolas,' and I can't keep track when I'm playing. Let's take something where all the words aren't alike. Let's do 'Annie Laurie.' One, two, three—go!"

The noise was terrible. If you don't believe it, try singing "Annie Laurie" as fast as you can. Freddy couldn't stand it any longer, and he rapped on the door.

The musicians were going so fast that they couldn't stop for about four bars. Then there was a moment's silence, followed by the clump of heavy shoes, and the door was flung open. Freddy touched his cap and bowed politely.

"My gosh, what's this?" said Red. "Come in, young feller. What can I do for you?"

Freddy stepped inside. The room was lit by three kerosene lamps, but the lamp chimneys were so dirty that they gave very little light, and he felt reasonably sure that if he kept his cap on, they wouldn't know he was a pig. Nevertheless he was scared when they both came close to him and squatted down with their hands on their knees and stared at him.

At first they didn't say anything. They stared at him for a minute, then stood up and stared at each other, then squatted down and stared at him again.

"Well, I'll be jiggered!" said Red.

"So'll I!" said Looey. "He's a—what do you call those little men—a wharf, isn't it?"

"A dwarf," said Red. "You ought to know that, Looey."

"Well, wharf or dwarf, what does it matter what we call him? The point is, what does he call himself? What's your name, guy?"

Freddy pointed to his mouth and shook his head.

"He's dumb," said Looey. "What good's a dumb dwarf? Let's throw him out and go on with the music."

Freddy had in his pocket the chart that he had prepared, but although from long practice in handling books and papers he had got so that he could use his forefeet almost as if they were hands, he was afraid that if he took it out and gave it to them they would see that he had hoofs instead of hands, and would realize that he was a pig.

Fortunately at this moment Red said: "Wait! I've got an idea!"

"I hope it's better than the one you had last Thursday," said Looey.

"This is a good one," said Red. "Listen, this dwarf is little, and he's dumb. That means he can get in places where we can't get in, and that he can't tell anybody about it afterwards. How about that back window in the Centerboro National Bank?"

"Gosh!" exclaimed Looey. "That *is* an idea!" he turned to Freddy. "Say, dwarf, would you like to make a lot of money?"

Freddy nodded enthusiastically.

"Fine! You come with us and do just what we tell you to, and we'll give you fifty cents. Come on, Red, get your things on." And almost before he knew what had happened, Freddy was walking back up the dark road with one of the robbers on each side of him.

He hadn't had a chance to show them his chart, and he hadn't the least idea what sort of adventure he was in for now. "Something pretty shady, I bet," he said to himself. "But no use worrying. I'm in with them now, and if I can't catch them after this, I'm a pretty poor detective."

At the bridge they stopped, Red dove into the bushes, and pretty soon there was the sputter of an engine and he drove out into the road in a badly battered open car. Red hoisted Freddy in, and they started off in the direction of Centerboro. Nothing was said on the way. Both the robbers had on raincoats, black masks, and rubbers, and carried pistols in their hands. Looey had hard work driving with the pistol in his hand, and once when he had to shift gears, it went off. It was pointed at the windshield when it went off, and Freddy was surprised not to see the glass fly to pieces, but Looey only laughed.

"We don't carry loaded pistols when we're at work," he explained; "it's too easy to have an accident."

As they drove down Main Street, Freddy saw that there were lights in all the stores, just as the sheriff had told him there would be. They slowed up when they came to the bank, and he saw a watchman sitting on the front steps with a gun across his knees. But he paid no attention to them as they turned into the alley next to the bank.

Looey stopped the car in the alley, and they all got out. Red took a stepladder out of the back seat and put it against the bank wall under a small window. "There you are," he said. "They don't bother to lock this window because it's too small for anybody to get through. But you can get through, and when you're inside, we'll throw this sack in after you, and all you have to do is stuff all the money into the sack, throw it out, and then come out yourself. See?"

Freddy saw all right. He saw that he was going to be a robber in spite of himself, and there was nothing else to do. But he had reckoned without the stepladder. Climbing the back stairs at the farm with Mr. Bean's trousers on had been bad enough, but this was hopeless. He scrambled up three steps, then caught his left foot in his right trouser leg, stumbled, squealed, and Freddy and the ladder and Looey came down with a crash on the cobblestones of the alley.

At once the night was full of noise. Windows went up, police whistles blew, men ran out into the streets and began shouting and firing off their guns. Looey scrambled to his feet, tossed Freddy into the car, and climbed in beside him as Red started up the engine. With a roar they dashed out of the alley and up Main Street at full speed. Half a dozen cars swung out into the street behind them as they dodged and twisted to avoid the men who tried to stop them. Red drove magnificently; he almost seemed to dodge the bullets that were fired at them, for none of them hit the car. In less than a minute they were thundering back up the road on which they had come into town, with the pursuit streaming out behind them. In a few minutes more they came to the bridge and crossed it; then Red put on the brakes so quickly that they were all nearly flung through the windshield, swung the car round, snapped off the lights, and drove into the bushes where the car had been hidden before.

One by one the pursuing cars flashed past their hiding-place. When the last one had gone by, the two robbers climbed slowly out of the car.

"You can go on back where you came from, dwarf," said Looey in a disgusted voice.

"You ought to be ashamed of yourself," said Red. "Now we haven't got any stepladder, all on account of you. I was going to put up fresh curtains in the living room tomorrow, but how I'm to do it without a stepladder I don't know."

"Go on," said Looey, "beat it. We don't want anything more to do with you. You haven't got any more sense than a pig."

Freddy grinned to himself in the dark; then he took the paper out of his pocket and handed it to Red.

"What's this?" said the robber. He lit a match to look, then called in an excited voice to his companion: "Look, Looey, he's got a map of that farmer's place—the one that lives across the creek—and it shows where his money is hidden."

They bent over the paper, lighting match after match to examine it. "Map of Mr. Bean's barn, showing location of hidden treasure," it said at the top, and under this Freddy had drawn a chart of the barn, but from one of the box stalls he had drawn a long arrow, at the end of which was written: "Under the floor of this stall is hidden a box containing ten thousand dollars in gold."

The robbers were greatly excited. "This is what he came to give us," said Looey. "Maybe he ain't such a bad dwarf after all." He turned to Freddy. "I'm sorry I said that about your being a pig. Are you sure the money is there?"

Freddy nodded emphatically.

"It's worth trying," said Red. "But, just the same, I ain't taking any chances. We'll take this fellow to the house and tie him up while we go over and see if the money's there. If it is, all right; we'll give him his share. But if it ain't—" He glared at the detective. "Well, he'll regret it, that's all."

This didn't suit Freddy at all, but there was nothing else to be done. They took him back to the hermit's house and tied him in a chair and then set out—on foot, this time, as there would be too many people looking for their automobile on the road.

Freddy was almost in despair. He had made no arrangements

for the capture of the robbers. If they went to the barn, they would find nothing in the box stall but a dozen or more animal prisoners. If they came back empty-handed a second time this evening, what would happen to him? To think about it made his clothes feel even more tight and uncomfortable than they already were.

But he didn't think about it long, for the robbers had not been gone more than a minute when there was a movement in a dark corner of the room, and a tiny voice said: "That you, Freddy?"

"Cousin Augustus!" exclaimed Freddy. "Gosh, I'm glad to hear your voice! Gnaw these ropes through, will you, like a good fellow? I've got to get to the farm before those fellows get there or I'll miss an important capture."

Cousin Augustus's teeth were sharp; in a very few minutes Freddy was free and had thrown off his disguise. "Ha," he exclaimed, "this feels like something! Now I'm equal to anything! But I wonder if I can get there before they do. Tell me, Gus, is there any bird round here that you could wake up and get to take a message to Jock?"

"Sure," said the mouse, "there's a wren lives under the eaves of the porch. I'll just slip up and take a peek in his nest and see if he'll go."

Cousin Augustus wasted no time. In two minutes he was back, accompanied by a very sleepy and rather cross wren, who, however, when he realized that it was Freddy, the renowned detective, who wanted his help, was only too anxious to oblige.

"Fly over and wake up Jock or Robert," said Freddy, "and tell them to clear all the prisoners out of the second box stall right away. Tell 'em they mustn't waste a second. There are two robbers coming over there, and I want them to get into that stall without any difficulty. Tell Jock to get all the other animals up and have them hide in the barn and keep quiet until the men get in the stall. I'll be there before there's anything else to be done."

The wren repeated the message to be sure he had it straight, and flew off, and then Freddy dashed down to the creek, dove in and swam across, and galloped off through the woods toward the farm. It was much easier going on four feet than it had been on two, and it wasn't long before he reached the pasture. From there on he went more carefully, and by the time he reached the barn he was creeping along like a shadow.

Faint sounds came from the barn, and now and then a light flickered and was gone again. The robbers were there, then! Freddy slipped inside and into Hank's stall. "Hello, Hank," he whispered. "Everything going all right?"

"Far as I know," said Hank. "Though what it all means is beyond me. Just a few minutes ago Jock and Robert and Mrs. Wiggins came in here and made all the prisoners go into one stall, and then they hid—they're over there in the corner—and then two men sneaked in, and it sounds as if they were tearing up the floor. What's it all about anyway?"

But there was no time to explain. Freddy tiptoed across the floor to the door of the stall. Sure enough, there were Red and Looey, working by the light of an electric torch, heaving at a plank in the floor. With great caution Freddy pushed the heavy door slowly shut and dropped the peg into the hasp.

The robbers heard nothing, and Freddy made no noise, for he had a reason for letting them go on with their work. He went over to the corner where his friends were hiding.

"I guess you can come out now," he said. "We've got 'em safe and fast. This is a great night's work! But what I've been through since I left here you wouldn't believe!"

He started to tell them the tale of his adventures, but suddenly there was a great rattling at the door of the stall. The robbers had found out that they were locked in.

Jock laughed. "Let 'em just try to get out!" he said. "That door will hold an elephant. Anyway I sent down for Peter, in case anything should go wrong. He can handle 'em all right."

Freddy started to go on with his story, when they heard a car drive into the yard, and a loud voice shouted: "Hey, farmer! Wake up!"

"I know that voice," said Freddy. "It's the city detective. Well, let's see how many robbers he's caught tonight!"

The animals went to the barn door. A light had sprung up in an upper window, and pretty soon Mr. Bean's head, in its red nightcap with a white tassel, was poked out into the night.

"Stop raisin' all that rumpus, or I'll come down and take my horsewhip to ye!"

"I want to know if you've seen an open car go by here in the past hour," shouted the detective.

"I got something better to do at night than to sit up and watch for open cars," said Mr. Bean. "Now go 'long about your business. I won't have my animals woke up an' disturbed this way."

"I'm huntin' for two robbers in an open car!" shouted Mr. Boner.

"Well, I ain't two robbers in an open car," replied the farmer. "I'm a self-respectin' citizen in a nightshirt, an' what's more, I got a shotgun in my hand, and if you ain't gone in two minutes—"

Just then another car drove into the yard, and the sheriff got out. Mr. Bean's manner changed as soon as he recognized the newcomer. "Oh, how d'e do, sheriff?" he said. "Who is this feller? Friend of yours?"

The sheriff explained. They were combing the countryside for the two robbers who had been frightened away while trying to rob the Centerboro bank, and they wondered if Mr. Bean had seen or heard anything of them.

"I been in bed for three hours," said the farmer. "But there's Freddy comin' across from the barn. Looks like he might have somethin' to show you. Now I'm goin' back to bed. Look around all you like, but for goodness' sake be quiet about it. I want them animals to get their sleep." And he shut down the window.

Meantime Freddy had come up to the sheriff. He raised a foreleg and waved it toward the barn.

"What is it, Freddy?" asked the sheriff. "You know somethin', I bet."

"Oh, that pig again!" exclaimed the disgusted detective. "Come along, sheriff, there ain't anything here."

"Not so fast," replied the sheriff. "I'm goin' to see." And he followed Freddy to the barn and up to the door of the stall, which was still being shaken by the imprisoned robbers.

"H'm," said the sheriff, lugging out his big pistol. "Looks like you'd caught something this time. Stand aside, animals." And he pulled out the peg.

The door gave way suddenly, and out tumbled Looey and Red.

"Stick up your hands!" said Mr. Boner, stepping forward. And as the discomfited robbers backed up against the wall with their hands in the air, he turned to the sheriff. "There's your prisoners, sheriff," he said dramatically. "I knew they were here all the time. That's why I stopped in here in the first place."

"Yeah?" said Looey. "Is that so! Well, let me tell you something. It wasn't you that caught us, city detective. You couldn't catch a lame snail."

"No back talk from you!" exclaimed Mr. Boner angrily. "If it wasn't me that caught you, who was it?"

"It was a little feller in a checked cap, if you want to know," said Looey. "And if all you detectives was as smart as him, you'd have caught us long ago."

"Here's your 'little feller,'" said the sheriff, pushing Freddy forward.

"There you go with your pig again," snorted the disgusted Boner. "I drove into this barnyard to look for 'em, didn't I? And they're here, ain't they? Well, then, who caught 'em? And who's going to believe that a pig could have done it?"

"The pig done it," said the sheriff doggedly, "and the pig ought to get the credit, *and* the reward!"

Looey and Red were staring at Freddy in amazement. "A pig!" exclaimed Red. "My gosh, Looey, a *pig!*"

"Pig, all right," replied Looey wearily. "Gee, we're a hot pair of robbers. Caught by a pig!" And then as Mr. Boner started in again to argue that it was he that should get the reward, Looey added: "Well, take us away and lock us up. Anywhere where we won't have to listen to this guy talk any more."

Mr. Bean, in his long white nightshirt and carrying a lantern, had appeared a few moments earlier in the barn door. "Trying to take the credit from my animals, is he?" he muttered. "We'll soon fix that." And he put his head outside and called softly: "Peter! Get rid of this fellow for us, will you?"

"And I want to tell *you* something too, Mr. Sheriff," Mr. Boner was saying. "You ain't done anything on this case, any more than your friend the pig has, and I'm going to give my own story of the capture to the newspapers, and don't you try to stop me. They're going to say that Mr. Montague Boner, the famous detective, was successful in putting an end to the depredations in upstate banking circles last night. With his brilliant capture of the two—"

Here he stopped, and abruptly, for something rough and furry had rubbed up against him. He turned to look. Peter, the bear, was standing on his hind legs beside him, his mouth wide open, his arms spread out, looking twice his size in the flickering lantern-light.

Mr. Boner opened his mouth almost as wide as Peter's, and out of it came a long yell. Then he dashed for the door. He yelled as he reached the yard, and he continued to yell as he turned out of the gate and dashed off up the road, with Peter loping along easily a few feet behind him. The animals crowded to the door; they could see nothing, but they could hear those diminishing yells dying away in the direction of Centerboro, until at last through the calm night they came back as a thin thread of sound, like the whine of a mosquito. And presently that was gone too, and there was silence.

"Thank you, Mr. Bean, and animals all," said the sheriff. "I'll be getting along now. I'll be up in the morning, Freddy, to have you show me where all that stolen money is. I'll bring the reward with me. Come along, you two. Couple o'nice cells all made up for you, with clean towels and flowers in the vases and everything. Night, all."

Mr. Bean said good night; then he turned to the animals. "Now don't sit up talking half the night," he said gruffly. "Lots of time to go over it all tomorrow. I'm proud of you, Freddy." He patted the pig clumsily on the shoulder. "Good night." And he stumped off toward the house.

The Walloping Window-blind

CHARLES EDWARD CARRYL

A capital ship for an ocean trip
  Was *The Walloping Window-blind;*
No gale that blew dismayed her crew
  Or troubled the captain's mind.
The man at the wheel was taught to feel
  Contempt for the wildest blow,
And it often appeared, when the weather had cleared,
  That he'd been in his bunk below.

The boatswain's mate was very sedate,
  Yet fond of amusement, too;
And he played hopscotch with the starboard watch
  While the captain tickled the crew.
And the gunner we had was apparently mad,
  For he sat on the after-rail,
And fired salutes with the captain's boots,
  In the teeth of the booming gale.

The captain sat in a commodore's hat,
  And dined, in a royal way,
On toasted pigs and pickles and figs
  And gummery bread, each day.
But the cook was Dutch, and behaved as such;
  For the food that he gave the crew
Was a number of tons of hot-cross buns,
  Chopped up with sugar and glue.

And we all felt ill as mariners will,
   On a diet that's cheap and rude;
And we shivered and shook as we dipped the cook
   In a tub of his gluesome food.
Then nautical pride we laid aside,
   And we cast the vessel ashore
On the Gulliby Isles, where the Poohpooh smiles,
   And the Anagazanders roar.

Composed of sand was that favored land,
   And trimmed with cinnamon straws;
And pink and blue was the pleasing hue
   Of the Tickletoeteaser's claws.
And we sat on the edge of a sandy ledge
   And shot at the whistling bee;
And the Binnacle-bats wore water-proof hats
   As they danced in the sounding sea.

On rubagub bark, from dawn to dark,
  We fed, till we all had grown
Uncommonly shrunk,—when a Chinese junk
  Came by from the torriby zone.
She was stubby and square, but we didn't much care,
  And we cheerily put to sea;
And we left the crew of the junk to chew
  The bark of the rubagub tree.

Oranges and Lemons

ELEANOR FARJEON

THERE was once a Prince who grew oranges and lemons in a white palace on the Italian hills. All over the hills there were palaces of other princes who also grew oranges and lemons, blue-and-white palaces and red-and-yellow palaces, but the Prince in the white palace grew the biggest fruit because he lived highest up the hill, and his trees caught the most sun. The Blue-and-White Prince and the Red-and-Yellow Prince came to visit him, followed by their pages carrying their best orange- and lemon-trees in green tubs, and when they reached the courtyard of the White Prince they put their trees down beside his and looked from one to the other. Then they shook their heads sadly and said,

"Yes! Yours are the biggest!"

And they went down the hill again, with their pages carrying the tubs behind them.

But on the very top of the hill there was a black castle with a tall tower, and in it lived a Princess whom nobody had ever seen. Every evening at sunset she came and stood on the top of her tower and looked at the sun going down and the moon coming up; and one evening the Prince got his telescope, and instead of looking through it at the sun and the moon, he looked at the Princess. She was all in black, and she wore a black mask on her face, so that even the White Prince could say no more than other people that he had seen her.

He went into his olive-orchard and called Beppe, his man, who sat whistling in a tree like a bird.

"Beppe," said the White Prince, "you must go to the castle

on the hill, and ask the Black Princess to come down and look at my oranges and lemons."

"It shall be done," said Beppe, and up the hill he went, whistling like a bird.

Before long he came back again.

"What does she say?" asked the White Prince.

"She says," said Beppe, "that she has no need to look at your oranges and lemons, because she has bigger and finer ones of her own."

"I don't believe it!" said the White Prince. "Go back and ask her if I may come and see her oranges and lemons, and if they are really bigger than mine I will give her my palace and all that is in it."

"It shall be done," said Beppe, and up the hill he went, whistling like a bird.

Before long he came back again.

"What does she say?" asked the White Prince.

"She says," said Beppe, "that she will not let any one look at her oranges and lemons who can't find his way in for himself; but she will put her trees upon the castle wall, and you can look at them through your telescope if you like. If you don't like, you needn't."

The White Prince got red then, because he knew she had seen him staring at her through the telescope while she was looking at the sky. To hide his confusion he said,

"How did you find *Your* way into the castle? The way you got in, I can get in."

"I didn't," said Beppe. "I called through the keyhole, and she called back."

So *that* was no help.

"Did you look through the keyhole?" he asked next.

"I did," said Beppe.

"And what does she look like?"

"She wore her black mask," said Beppe.

So *that* was no help.

That evening, when the Black Princess came as usual to the top of her tower to watch the sun going down and the moon coming up, she carried in her arms two little green tubs, which she set on the wall where the White Prince could see them. But when he looked through his telescope he saw nothing in the tubs but two little trees with glossy green leaves, and on one was a lime and on the other a tangerine.

Then he got very annoyed with her for making game of him, and he called Beppe to him and said,

"Go to the Black Princess and say that her fruit is almost too small to be seen."

"It shall be done," said Beppe, and up the hill he went, whistling like a bird, and back he came again in no time.

"What does she say?" asked the White Prince.

"She says," said Beppe, "that you must have looked at her fruit through the wrong end of the telescope. And she says that if you were a little nearer, the fruit would look a little bigger."

This made the Prince so cross that he didn't sleep all night. In the morning he went up the hill to the Black Castle himself, and when he got there he banged on the door.

"Who is there?" called a sweet voice from the other side.

"The Prince of Oranges and Lemons!" said he.

"Oh, I know you now!" said the voice. "But I think you are only the Prince of Limes and Tangerines. What do you want?"

"I want to come in!"

"Find the way in!" said she. And no more would she say.

Downhill he went empty-handed, and uphill he came with his key. But his key was too big and her keyhole too small.

Downhill he went with his key, and uphill he came with his ladder. But her wall was too high, and his ladder was too short.

Downhill he went with his ladder, and uphill he came with his cannon. But her gate was too strong and his shot was too weak.

Then he sat down in despair by the wall, and said, "There is no way in!"

"There are a hundred ways in!" laughed a tiny voice by his ear.

He looked round to see who had spoken, but there was nobody there; only the insects humming in the sun, and the green lizards basking on the walls. As he turned his head his shadow fell on the nearest one, and it scuttled into a crack like a fairy.

He looked at the crack, and at the hundred other cracks in the wall, each of which was a way in for a lizard.

"Oh! if only I were no bigger than a lizard!" cried the Prince.

"That's easy enough!" laughed the tiny voice by his ear. "Go and get your telescope."

Downhill he went with his cannon, and uphill he came with his telescope.

"What next?" asked the Prince.

"Stand by a crack in the wall," said the tiny voice, "and point the telescope at yourself."

"Which end of the telescope?" asked the Prince.

"The end that makes you look little, of course!"

So the Prince pointed the wrong end of the telescope at a crack in the wall, and stood himself between the telescope and the crack. As quick as a wink he grew as small as a lizard, and slipped through the crack like a fairy. Then he ran with all his tiny might up the Black Tower, and came out on the turret just as the moon was coming up and the sun going down. There, like a giantess, stood the Black Princess, watching them through her mask.

The Prince tugged at her skirt crying, "Here I am! here I am! I have found the way in!"

The Princess looked down and down until she saw him and said, "So you have, my Prince of Lizards! It only remains for you to tell me what you think of my oranges and lemons." And she pointed to the wall, where stood the two biggest trees in the two most monstrous tubs that the Prince had ever seen, and on one hung an orange as big as the sun, and on the other a lemon as big as the moon.

The Prince looked at them for a long while, shook his head sadly, and said, "Yes! yours are the biggest."

"In that case," said she, "you must give me your palace and all that is in it."

"A promise is a promise," said the Prince. "But first take off your mask."

She did so, and when the black mask was removed the Prince saw that her face was as beautiful as the sun by day and the moon

by night. She let the mask lie where it fell, and picking up the Prince with one hand and her trees with the other, came out of the Castle for the very first time. When she saw the telescope lying on the ground, she picked that up, too, and went downhill to the Prince's Palace.

She set down the trees and the Prince and the telescope in the middle of the floor and looked all round her, and said, "It is a beautiful palace, and I am glad it is mine."

"It is yours with all that is in it," said the Prince. "If you take it you must take me, too. A promise is a promise."

"But you are almost too small to be seen!" cried she.

"You are looking through the wrong end of the telescope," said the Prince. "If you come a little nearer I will look a little bigger."

So she came a little nearer, and as she did so he placed himself in front of the right end of the telescope. As quick as a wink he grew as big as a man. By the time the Princess reached him, she had stopped looking like a giantess, and was just as small as a woman. And on the floor he saw two trees that were tiny enough to be carried in one hand, and on one was a lime and on the other a tangerine.

"Are those the trees you showed me up in your castle?" asked the Prince.

"To be sure they are," said she, "and very fine trees, too. Nobody in Italy has bigger fruit than I have."

The Prince gave her a kiss and said, "Very well! let us come out and look at *my* orange- and lemon-trees, and bring yours with you."

They went out on the terrace where his beautiful fruit-trees stood in their tubs, and the fruit shone gold and yellow in the sunset and the moonrise. The Prince made the Princess put down her little tubs beside his big ones, and said, "Beppe shall judge, once and for all."

Then he called to his man, who was sitting in an olive-tree watching the sky from the orchard below.

"Beppe! which are the biggest, hers or mine?"

But Beppe, instead of looking at the fruit on the trees, looked like a stupid at the sun and moon in the sky, and said, "Hers are," and went on whistling like a bird.

There was nothing more to be done but for the Prince and Princess to get married. And so they did.

FROM
Alice in Wonderland

LEWIS CARROLL

Alice in Wonderland *was written nearly a hundred years ago by a professor of mathematics at an English college. He wrote them first just to amuse the three young daughters (the middle one was named Alice) of the dean of the college. But when they were published they became so popular that millions of people—both grownups and children—have read and loved them. This selection is from the second part of the book, called* Through the Looking-Glass, *when Alice meets Humpty Dumpty, the egg-shaped gentleman who talks in riddles.*

Humpty Dumpty

HOWEVER, the egg only got larger and larger, and more and more human: when she had come within a few yards of it, she saw that it had eyes and a nose and mouth; and, when she had come close to it, she saw clearly that it was HUMPTY DUMPTY himself. "It can't be anybody else!" she said to herself. "I'm as certain of it, as if his name were written all over his face!"

It might have been written a hundred times, easily, on that enormous face. Humpty Dumpty was sitting, with his legs crossed like a Turk, on the top of a high wall—such a narrow one that Alice quite wondered how he could keep his balance—and, as his eyes were steadily fixed in the opposite direction, and he didn't take the least notice of her, she thought he must be a stuffed figure, after all.

"And how exactly like an egg he is!" she said aloud, standing with her hands ready to catch him, for she was every moment expecting him to fall.

"It's *very* provoking," Humpty Dumpty said after a long silence, looking away from Alice as he spoke, "to be called an egg—*very!*"

"I said you *looked* like an egg, Sir," Alice gently explained. "And some eggs are very pretty, you know," she added, hoping to turn her remark into a sort of compliment.

"Some people," said Humpty Dumpty, looking away from her as usual, "have no more sense than a baby!"

Alice didn't know what to say to this: it wasn't at all like conversation, she thought, as he never said anything to *her*; in fact, his last remark was evidently addressed to a tree—so she stood and softly repeated to herself:

> *"Humpty Dumpty sat on a wall:*
> *Humpty Dumpty had a great fall.*
> *All the King's horses and all the King's men*
> *Couldn't put Humpty Dumpty in his place again."*

"That last line is much too long for the poetry," she added, almost out loud, forgetting that Humpty Dumpty would hear her.

"Don't stand chattering to yourself like that," Humpty Dumpty said, looking at her for the first time, "but tell me your name and your business."

"My *name* is Alice, but—"

"It's a stupid name enough!" Humpty Dumpty interrupted impatiently. "What does it mean?"

"*Must* a name mean something?" Alice asked doubtfully.

"Of course it must," Humpty Dumpty said with a short laugh: "*my* name means the shape I am—and a good handsome shape it is, too. With a name like yours, you might be any shape, almost."

"Why do you sit out here all alone?" said Alice, not wishing to begin an argument.

"Why, because there's nobody with me!" cried Humpty Dumpty. "Did you think I didn't know the answer to *that*? Ask another."

"Don't you think you'd be safer down on the ground?" Alice went on, not with any idea of making another riddle, but simply in her good-natured anxiety for the queer creature. "That wall is so *very* narrow!"

"What tremendously easy riddles you ask!" Humpty Dumpty growled out. "Of course I don't think so! Why, if ever I *did* fall off—which there's no chance of—but *if* I did—" Here he pursed up his lips, and looked so solemn and grand that Alice could hardly help laughing. "*If* I *did* fall," he went on, "*the King has promised me*—ah, you may turn pale, if you like! You didn't think I was going to say that, did you? *The King has promised me—with his very own mouth—*to—to—"

"To send all his horses and all his men," Alice interrupted, rather unwisely.

"Now I declare that's too bad!" Humpty Dumpty cried, breaking into a sudden passion. "You've been listening at doors—and behind trees—and down chimneys—or you couldn't have known it!"

"I haven't indeed!" Alice said very gently. "It's in a book."

"Ah, well! They may write such things in a *book*," Humpty Dumpty said in a calmer tone. "That's what you call a History of England, that is. Now, take a good look at me! I'm one that has spoken to a King, *I* am: mayhap you'll never see such another: and, to show you I'm not proud, you may shake hands with me!" And he grinned almost from ear to ear, as he leant forwards (and as nearly as possible fell off the wall in doing so) and offered Alice his hand. She watched him a little anxiously as she took it. "If he smiled much more the ends of his mouth might meet behind," she thought: "and then I don't know *what* would happen to his head! I'm afraid it would come off!"

"Yes, all his horses and all his men," Humpty Dumpty went on. "They'd pick me up again in a minute, *they* would! However, this conversation is going on a little too fast: let's go back to the last remark but one."

"I'm afraid I can't quite remember it," Alice said, very politely.

"In that case we start afresh," said Humpty Dumpty, "and it's my turn to choose a subject—" ("He talks about it just as

Illustration after John Tenniel.

if it was a game!" thought Alice.) "So here's a question for you. How old did you say you were?"

Alice made a short calculation, and said, "Seven years and six months."

"Wrong!" Humpty Dumpty exclaimed triumphantly. "You never said a word like it!"

"I thought you meant 'How old *are* you?'" Alice explained.

"If I'd meant that, I'd have said it," said Humpty Dumpty.

Alice didn't want to begin another argument, so she said nothing.

"Seven years and six months!" Humpty Dumpty repeated thoughtfully. "An uncomfortable sort of age. Now if you'd asked *my* advice, I'd have said, 'Leave off at seven'—but it's too late now."

"I never ask advice about growing," Alice said indignantly.

"Too proud?" the other inquired.

Alice felt even more indignant at this suggestion. "I mean," she said, "that one can't help growing older."

"*One* can't, perhaps," said Humpty Dumpty; "but *two* can. With proper assistance, you might have left off at seven."

"What a beautiful belt you've got on!" Alice suddenly remarked. (They had had quite enough of the subject of age, she thought: and, if they really were to take turns in choosing subjects, it was *her* turn now.) "At least," she corrected herself on second thoughts, "a beautiful cravat, I should have said—no, a belt, I mean—I beg your pardon!" she added in dismay, for Humpty Dumpty looked thoroughly offended, and she began to wish she hadn't chosen that subject. "If only I knew," she thought to herself, "which was neck and which was waist!"

Evidently Humpty Dumpty was very angry, though he said nothing for a minute or two. When he *did* speak again, it was in a deep growl.

"It is a—*most—provoking*—thing," he said at last, "when a person doesn't know a cravat from a belt!"

"I know it's very ignorant of me," Alice said, in so humble a tone that Humpty Dumpty relented.

"It's a cravat, child, and a beautiful one, as you say. It's a present from the White King and Queen. There now!"

"Is it really?" said Alice, quite pleased to find that she *had* chosen a good subject, after all.

"They gave it me," Humpty Dumpty continued thoughtfully, as he crossed one knee over the other and clasped his hands round it, "they gave it me—for an un-birthday present."

"I beg your pardon?" Alice said with a puzzled air.

"I'm not offended," said Humpty Dumpty.

"I mean, what *is* an un-birthday present?"

"A present given when it isn't your birthday, of course."

Alice considered a little. "I like birthday presents best," she said at last.

"You don't know what you're talking about!" cried Humpty Dumpty. "How many days are there in a year?"

"Three hundred and sixty-five," said Alice.

"And how many birthdays have you?"

"One."

"And if you take one from three hundred and sixty-five, what remains?"

"Three hundred and sixty-four, of course."

Humpty Dumpty looked doubtful. "I'd rather see that done on paper," he said.

Alice couldn't help smiling as she took out her memorandum-book, and worked the sum for him:

$$\begin{array}{r} 365 \\ \underline{1} \\ \underline{364} \end{array}$$

Humpty Dumpty took the book, and looked at it carefully. "That seems to be done right—" he began.

"You're holding it upside down!" Alice interrupted.

"To be sure I was!" Humpty Dumpty said gayly, as she turned it round for him. "I thought it looked a little queer. As I was saying, that *seems* to be done right—though I haven't time to look it over thoroughly just now—and that shows that there are three hundred and sixty-four days when you might get un-birthday presents—"

"Certainly," said Alice.

"And only *one* for birthday presents, you know. There's glory for you!"

"I don't know what you mean by 'glory,'" Alice said.

Humpty Dumpty smiled contemptuously. "Of course you don't—till I tell you. I meant 'there's a nice knock-down argument for you!'"

"But 'glory' doesn't mean 'a nice knock-down argument,'" Alice objected.

"When *I* use a word," Humpty Dumpty said, in rather a scornful tone, "it means just what I choose it to mean—neither more nor less."

"The question is," said Alice, "whether you *can* make words mean so many different things."

"The question is," said Humpty Dumpty, "which is to be master—that's all."

Alice was too much puzzled to say anything; so after a minute Humpty Dumpty began again. "They've a temper, some of them —particularly verbs: they're the proudest—adjectives you can do anything with, but not verbs—however, *I* can manage the whole lot of them! Impenetrability! That's what *I* say!"

"Would you tell me, please," said Alice, "what that means?"

"Now you talk like a reasonable child," said Humpty Dumpty, looking very much pleased. "I meant by 'impenetrability' that we've had enough of that subject, and it would be just as well if you'd mention what you mean to do next, as I suppose you don't mean to stop here all the rest of your life."

"That's a great deal to make one word mean," Alice said in a thoughtful tone.

"When I make a word do a lot of work like that," said Humpty Dumpty, "I always pay it extra."

"Oh!" said Alice. She was too much puzzled to make any other remark.

"Ah, you should see 'em come round me of a Saturday night," Humpty Dumpty went on, wagging his head gravely from side to side, "for to get their wages, you know."

(Alice didn't venture to ask what he paid them with; and so you see I can't tell *you*.)

"You seem very clever at explaining words, Sir," said Alice. "Would you kindly tell me the meaning of the poem called 'Jabber-wocky'?"

"Let's hear it," said Humpty Dumpty. "I can explain all the poems that ever were invented—and a good many that haven't been invented just yet."

This sounded very hopeful, so Alice repeated the first verse:—

> "*'Twas brillig, and the slithy toves*
> *Did gyre and gimble in the wabe:*
> *All mimsy were the borogoves,*
> *And the mome raths outgrabe.*"

"That's enough to begin with," Humpty Dumpty interrupted: "there are plenty of hard words there. '*Brillig*' means four o'clock in the afternoon—the time when you begin *broiling* things for dinner."

"That'll do very well," said Alice: "and '*slithy*'?"

"Well, '*slithy*' means 'lithe and slimy.' 'Lithe' is the same as 'active.' You see it's like a portmanteau—there are two meanings packed up into one word."

"I see it now," Alice remarked thoughtfully: "and what are 'toves'?"

"Well, 'toves' are something like badgers—they're something like lizards—and they're something like corkscrews."

"They must be very curious-looking creatures."

"They are that," said Humpty Dumpty: "also they make their nests under sun-dials—also they live on cheese."

"And what's to 'gyre' and to 'gimble'?"

"To 'gyre' is to go round and round like a gyroscope. To 'gimble' is to make holes like a gimblet."

"And 'the wabe' is the grass-plot round a sun-dial, I suppose?" said Alice, surprised at her own ingenuity.

"Of course it is. It's called 'wabe,' you know, because it goes a long way before it, and a long way behind it—"

"And a long way beyond it on each side," Alice added.

"Exactly so. Well then, 'mimsy' is 'flimsy and miserable' (there's another portmanteau for you). And a 'borogove' is a thin shabby-looking bird with its feathers sticking out all round—something like a live mop."

"And then 'mome raths'?" said Alice. "I'm afraid I'm giving you a great deal of trouble."

"Well, a 'rath' is a sort of green pig: but 'mome' I'm not certain about. I think it's short for 'from home'—meaning that they'd lost their way, you know."

"And what does 'outgrabe' mean?"

"Well, 'outgribing' is something between bellowing and whistling, with a kind of sneeze in the middle: however, you'll hear it done, maybe—down in the wood yonder—and, when you've once heard it, you'll be quite content. Who's been repeating all that hard stuff to you?"

"I read it in a book," said Alice. "But I had some poetry repeated to me much easier than that, by—Tweedledee, I think it was."

"As to poetry, you know," said Humpty Dumpty, stretching out one of his great hands, "I can repeat poetry as well as other folk, if it comes to that—"

"Oh, it needn't come to that!" Alice hastily said, hoping to keep him from beginning.

"The piece I'm going to repeat," he went on without noticing her remark, "was written entirely for your amusement."

Alice felt that in that case she really *ought* to listen to it; so she sat down, and said "Thank you" rather sadly.

> *"In winter, when the fields are white,*
> *I sing this song for your delight—*

only I don't sing it," he added, as an explanation.

"I see you don't," said Alice.

"If you can *see* whether I'm singing or not, you've sharper eyes than most," Humpty Dumpty remarked severely. Alice was silent.

> *"In spring, when woods are getting green,*
> *I'll try and tell you what I mean."*

"Thank you very much," said Alice.

> *"In summer, when the days are long,*
> *Perhaps you'll understand the song:*
>
> *"In autumn, when the leaves are brown,*
> *Take pen and ink, and write it down."*

"I will, if I can remember it so long," said Alice.

"You needn't go on making remarks like that," Humpty Dumpty said: "They're not sensible, and they put me out."

> *"I sent a message to the fish:*
> *I told them 'This is what I wish.'*
>
> *"The little fishes of the sea,*
> *They sent an answer back to me.*
>
> *"The little fishes' answer was,*
> *'We cannot do it, Sir, because——'"*

"I'm afraid I don't quite understand," said Alice.

"It gets easier further on," Humpty Dumpty replied.

> "I sent to them again to say
> 'It will be better to obey.'

> "The fishes answered, with a grin,
> 'Why, what a temper you are in!'

> "I told them once, I told them twice:
> They would not listen to advice.

> "I took a kettle large and new,
> Fit for the deed I had to do.

> "My heart went hop, my heart went thump:
> I filled the kettle at the pump.

> "Then some one came to me and said,
> 'The little fishes are in bed.'

> "I said to him, I said it plain,
> 'Then you must wake them up again.'

> "I said it very loud and clear:
> I went and shouted in his ear."

Humpty Dumpty raised his voice almost to a scream as he repeated this verse, and Alice thought, with a shudder, "I wouldn't have been the messenger for *anything!*"

> "But he was very stiff and proud:
> He said, 'You needn't shout so loud!'

> "And he was very proud and stiff:
> He said, 'I'd go and wake them, if——'

> "I took a corkscrew from the shelf:
> I went to wake them up myself.

> "And when I found the door was locked,
> I pulled and pushed and kicked and knocked.

> "And when I found the door was shut,
> I tried to turn the handle, but——"

There was a long pause.

"Is that all?" Alice timidly asked.

"That's all," said Humpty Dumpty. "Good-bye."

This was rather sudden, Alice thought: but, after such a *very* strong hint that she ought to be going, she felt it would hardly be civil to stay. So she got up, and held out her hand. "Good-bye, till we meet again!" she said as cheerfully as she could.

"I shouldn't know you again if we *did* meet," Humpty Dumpty replied in a discontented tone, giving her one of his fingers to shake; "you're so exactly like other people."

"The face is what one goes by, generally," Alice remarked in a thoughtful tone.

"That's just what I complain of," said Humpty Dumpty. "Your face is the same as everybody has—the two eyes, so—" (marking their places in the air with his thumb) "nose in the middle, mouth under. It's always the same. Now if you had the two eyes on the same side of the nose, for instance—or the mouth at the top—that would be *some* help."

"It wouldn't look nice," Alice objected. But Humpty Dumpty only shut his eyes, and said, "Wait till you've tried."

Alice waited a minute to see if he would speak again, but, as he never opened his eyes or took any further notice of her, she said "Good-bye!" once more, and, getting no answer to this, she quietly walked away: but she couldn't help saying to herself, as she went, "Of all the unsatisfactory—" (she repeated this aloud, as it was a great comfort to have such a long word to say) "of all the unsatisfactory people I *ever* met—" She never finished the sentence, for at this moment a heavy crash shook the forest from end to end.

Alice's Evidence

LEWIS CARROLL

"They told me you had been to her,
    And mentioned me to him:
She gave me a good character,
    But said I could not swim.

He sent them word I had not gone
    (We know it to be true):
If she should push the matter on,
    What would become of you?

I gave her one, they gave him two,
    You gave us three or more;
They all returned from him to you,
    Though they were mine before.

If I or she should chance to be
    Involved in this affair,
He trusts to you to set them free,
    Exactly as we were.

My notion was that you had been
    (Before she had this fit)
An obstacle that came between
    Him, and ourselves, and it.

Don't let him know she liked them best,
    For this must ever be
A secret, kept from all the rest,
    Between yourself and me."

From Alice's Adventures in Wonderland.

Conal and Donal and Taig

SEUMAS MacMANUS

O<small>NCE</small> there were three brothers named Conal, Donal and Taig, and they fell out regarding which of them owned a field of land. One of them had as good a claim to it as the other, and the claims of all of them were so equal that none of the judges, whomsoever they went before, could decide in favor of one more than the other.

At length they went to one judge who was very wise indeed and had a great name, and every one of them stated his case to him.

He sat on the bench, and heard Conal's case and Donal's case and Taig's case all through, with very great patience. When the three of them had finished, he said he would take a day and a night to think it all over, and on the day after, when they were all called into court again, the Judge said that he had weighed the evidence on all sides, with all the deliberation it was possible to give it, and he decided that one of them hadn't the shadow of a shade of a claim more than the others, so that he found himself facing the greatest puzzle he had ever faced in his life.

"But," says he, "no puzzle puzzles me long. I'll very soon decide which of you will get the field. You seem to me to be three pretty lazy-looking fellows, and I'll give the field to whichever of the three of you is the laziest."

"Well, at that rate," says Conal, "it's me gets the field, for I'm the laziest man of the lot."

"How lazy are you?" says the Judge.

"Well," said Conal, "if I was lying in the middle of the road, and there was a regiment of troopers coming galloping down it, I'd sooner let them ride over me than take the bother of getting up and going to the one side."

"Well, well," says the Judge, says he, "you are a lazy man surely, and I doubt if Donal or Taig can be as lazy as that."

"Oh, faith," says Donal, "I'm just every bit as lazy."

"Are you?" says the Judge. "How lazy are you?"

"Well," said Donal, "if I was sitting right close to a big fire, and you piled on it all the turf in a townland and all the wood in a barony, sooner than have to move I'd sit there till the boiling marrow would run out of my bones."

"Well," says the Judge, "you're a pretty lazy man, Donal, and I doubt if Taig is as lazy as either of you."

"Indeed, then," says Taig, "I'm every bit as lazy."

"How can that be?" says the Judge.

"Well," says Taig, "if I was lying on the broad of my back in the middle of the floor and looking up at the rafters, and if soot drops were falling as thick as hailstones from the rafters into my open eyes, I would let them drop there for the length of the lee-long day sooner than take the bother of closing the eyes."

"Well," says the Judge, "that's very wonderful entirely, and," says he, "I'm in as great a quandary as before, for I see you are the three laziest men that ever were known since the world began, and which of you is the laziest it certainly beats me to say. But I'll tell you what I'll do," says the Judge, "I'll give the field to the oldest man of you."

"Then," says Conal, "it's me gets the field."

"How is that?" says the Judge; "how old are you?"

"Well, I'm that old," says Conal, "that when I was twenty-one years of age I got a shipload of awls and never lost nor broke one of them, and I wore out the last of them yesterday mending my shoes."

"Well, well," says the Judge, says he, "you're surely an old man, and I doubt very much that Donal and Taig can catch up to you."

"Can't I?" says Donal; "take care of that."

"Why," said the Judge, "how old are you?"

"When I was twenty-one years of age," says Donal, "I got a shipload of needles, and yesterday I wore out the last of them mending my clothes."

"Well, well, well," says the Judge, says he, "you're two very, very old men, to be sure, and I'm afraid poor Taig is out of his chance anyhow."

"Take care of that," says Taig.

"Why," said the Judge, "how old are you, Taig?"

Says Taig, "When I was twenty-one years of age I got a shipload of razors, and yesterday I had the last of them worn to a stump shaving myself."

"Well," says the Judge, says he, "I've often heard tell of old men," he says, "but anything as old as what you three are never was known since Methusalem's cat died. The like of your ages," he says, "I never heard tell of, and which of you is the oldest, that surely beats me to decide, and I'm in a quandary again. But I'll tell you what I'll do," says the Judge, says he, "I'll give the field to whichever of you minds [remembers] the longest."

"Well, if that's it," says Conal, "it's me gets the field, for I mind the time when if a man tramped on a cat he usen't to give it a kick to console it."

"Well, well, well," says the Judge, "that must be a long mind entirely; and I'm afraid, Conal, you have the field."

"Not so quick," says Donal, says he, "for I mind the time when a woman wouldn't speak an ill word of her best friend."

"Well, well, well," says the Judge, "your memory, Donal, must certainly be a very wonderful one, if you can mind that time. Taig," says the Judge, says he, "I'm afraid your memory can't compare with Conal's and Donal's."

"Can't it," says Taig, says he. "Take care of that, for I mind the time when you wouldn't find nine liars in a crowd of ten men."

"Oh, Oh, Oh!" says the Judge, says he, "that memory of yours, Taig, must be a wonderful one." Says he: "Such memories as you three men have were never known before, and which of you has the greatest memory it beats me to say. But I'll tell you what I'll do now," says he; "I'll give the field to whichever of you has the keenest sight."

"Then," says Conal, says he, "it's me gets the field; because," says he, "if there was a fly perched on the top of yon mountain, ten miles away, I could tell you every time he blinked."

"You have wonderful sight, Conal," says the Judge, says he, "and I'm afraid you've got the field."

"Take care," says Donal, says he, "but I've got as good. For I could tell you whether it was a mote in his eye that made him blink or not."

"Ah, ha, ha!" says the Judge, says he, "this is wonderful sight surely. Taig," says he, "I pity you, for you have no chance for the field now."

"Have I not?" says Taig. "I could tell you from here whether that fly was in good health or not by counting his heart beats."

"Well, well, well," says the Judge, says he, "I'm in as great a quandary as ever. You are three of the most wonderful men that ever I met, and no mistake. But I'll tell you what I'll do," says he; "I'll give the field to the supplest man of you."

"Thank you," says Conal. "Then the field is mine."

"Why so?" says the Judge.

"Because," says Conal, says he, "if you filled that field with hares, and put a dog in the middle of them, and then tied one of my legs up my back, I would not let one of the hares get out."

"Then, Conal," says the Judge, says he, "I think the field is yours."

"By the leave of your judgeship, not yet," says Donal.

"Why, Donal," says the Judge, says he, "surely you are not as supple as that?"

"Am I not?" says Donal. "Do you see that old castle over there without door, or window, or roof in it, and the wind blowing in and out through it like an iron gate?"

"I do," says the Judge. "What about that?"

"Well," says Donal, says he, "if on the stormiest day of the year you had that castle filled with feathers, I would not let a feather be lost, or go ten yards from the castle until I had caught and put it in again."

"Well, surely," says the Judge, says he, "you are a supple man,

Donal, and no mistake. Taig," says he, "there's no chance for you now."

"Don't be too sure," says Taig, says he.

"Why," says the Judge, "you couldn't surely do anything to equal these things, Taig?"

Says Taig, says he: "I can shoe the swiftest race-horse in the land when he is galloping at his topmost speed, by driving a nail every time he lifts his foot."

"Well, well, well," says the Judge, says he, "surely you are the three most wonderful men that ever I did meet. The likes of you never was known before, and I suppose the likes of you will never be on the earth again. There is only one other trial," says he, "and if this doesn't decide, I'll have to give it up. I'll give the field," says he, "to the cleverest man amongst you."

"Then," says Conal, says he, "you may as well give it to me at once."

"Why? Are you that clever, Conal?" says the Judge, says he.

"I am that clever," says Conal, "I am that clever, that I would make a skin-fit suit of clothes for a man without any more measurement than to tell me the color of his hair."

"Then, boys," says the Judge, says he, "I think the case is decided."

"Not so quick, my friend," says Donal, "not so quick."

"Why, Donal," says the Judge, says he, "you are surely not cleverer than that?"

"Am I not?" says Donal.

"Why," says the Judge, says he, "what can you do, Donal?"

"Why," says Donal, says he, "I would make a skin-fit suit for a man and give me no more measurement than let me hear him cough."

"Well, well, well," says the Judge, says he, "the cleverness of you two boys beats all I ever heard of. Taig," says he, "poor Taig, whatever chance either of these two may have for the field, I'm very, very sorry for you, for you have no chance."

"Don't be so very sure of that," says Taig, says he.

"Why," says the Judge, says he, "surely, Taig, you can't be as clever as either of them. How clever are you, Taig?"

"Well," says Taig, says he, "if I was a judge, and too stupid to

decide a case that came up before me, I'd be that clever that I'd look wise and give some decision."

"Taig," says the Judge, says he, "I've gone into this case and deliberated upon it, and by all the laws of right and justice, I find and decide that you get the field."

FROM
Honk: the Moose

PHIL STONG

The two boys, Waino and Ivar, have been out hunting all day with an air gun. But they haven't managed to shoot anything, not even a tiny rabbit. When they return to the livery stable run by Ivar's father, they find some totally unexpected big game—a moose.

What Do You Do with a Moose?

Waino was in the corner between Papa's desk and the wall. Ivar knew, really, that the air gun wouldn't kill a moose. He picked up a pitchfork and went bravely to the door.

The doorknob twisted again. "You get away from there," Ivar shouted. "Go on back in the woods where you belong."

There was a pause. "What's the matter in there? Why's the door locked?"

"Papa!" Ivar said, and threw back the bolt.

Ivar's father was not fat but he was about as big as two men. His face was all pink and white and his eyes were as good-humored as Ivar's. He smiled at the two boys, now.

"What's the matter?" he asked again. "You look like you yust seen a ghost." Because he had spoken only Finnish and Swedish as a boy, it was still hard for him to say "J." He said "Y" instead. Ivar, who was an American boy, said "J" but he never noticed that his father said "Y." He always heard him speak that way.

"A moose," Ivar said.

"A moose," Waino added.

"What!" Then Ivar's father laughed, and the floor shook a

little. "You yust seen a moose, what? Well, he wouldn't chase you here."

"Out in the stable," Ivar told him.

Ivar's father laughed a good deal, and everything shook. "A moose in the stable. I think you've got a bat in the belfry, Ivar. I guess a horse got loose. You go up and see if your mother has any errands—I'll take care of the moose."

"It's a moose, Papa—honestly!"

"You should see things straight, Ivar," his father said. "A Suomi should see things straight. It is a horse, and because you were afraid you say it is a moose. Come on, we'll see this moose, now. A Suomi should not be afraid, either—"

He opened the door and stepped out into the aisle. "We will see."

An instant afterward he scooped the two boys up in his strong hands and almost threw them back into the office. He followed them and locked the door. "It's a moose," he said.

Ivar's father thought for a moment and then the same stubborn bravery that had made Ivar go out against the moose made his father rise and go to the door. "You lock the door after me and stay here. We'll see about this. If I call, you go out the window and run for the policeman."

He opened the door and went out, but Ivar disobeyed. He was not going to let his father talk to a moose unless he was there to help. He walked out quietly behind his father, so, of course, Waino went too.

The moose had eaten so much hay that he was growing sleepy. He still nibbled at the hay, which he could just reach as it hung over from the loft, but he didn't want it very much. Only, since the hay was there, he might as well eat it while he had the chance.

"Wonderful!" said Ivar's father. "How could anything eat so much? You please shoo now," he added to the moose.

Honk rolled one eye toward him and went on eating. This made Ivar's father angry. "Hay costs twenty dollars a ton. You have already eaten a ton. How do you pay?" In fact, the moose had stuffed himself with hay, after the long, hungry days in the woods, until he looked like a balloon that had been blown up only at the front end. The other end was still skinny.

"It's honestly—"

"Yes, I know," Ivar's father interrupted him. "It's a moose. How he got there, I don't know."

"The winter is bad—maybe he was cold."

Ivar's father smiled at Waino, at the same time keeping an eye on the moose. "Not cold—mooses don't care if it is cold. But I guess he was hungry. He must have come here in the afternoon when nobody was looking."

"What are you going to do with him, Mr. Ketonen?" Waino asked eagerly. For a young boy he always showed a very practical mind.

"What am I going to do with him?" Ivar's father said, a little bit crossly. "What does one do with a moose? I am going to do what one always does with mooses."

"What's that?" Ivar asked curiously.

"I am going to shoo him out of my barn. What will the horses think?"

"What *will* they, Papa?"

"They will think I don't keep a good livery stable. Mooses!"

At this moment Honk's legs collapsed. He felt very good, but tired. He rolled one eye at the people and then he sank on his side and rolled himself once or twice. After that, with a contented sigh, he went to sleep.

This made Ivar's father angry again. "You get out of here. You can't sleep here." He prodded the moose in the side. Honk did not even open his eyes.

Ivar began to feel a little sorry for the moose. He could see how sleepy the animal was and he thought of mornings when he had had to get up to go to school in spite of the fact that he was having a splendid time sleeping.

"I wish I was mean enough to stick him with a pitchfork," Ivar's father said unhappily. "Listen, you!" he said fiercely to the moose. "If you don't go away I'll get the policeman; and do you know what he'll do to you? He'll shoot you."

The moose did not open his eyes even then. He said "HAAAWNK" very softly and sleepily.

"All right," said Mr. Ketonen firmly. "Ivar, you go for the policeman."

"Aw, Papa—!"

"Aw, Mr. Ketonen—!" said Waino.

"Can I run a livery barn with a moose in it? He'll eat me out of house and home. He'll get in the way. Besides, mooses are dangerous."

"That one isn't, Papa. Look at him."

"How do we know what he'll be like when he wakes up? You go get the policeman, Ivar."

"All right."

Ivar and Waino left the stable. Night had fallen—it was almost suppertime—and the bright corner lights of the little mining town twinkled and glittered on the snowy streets. They found Mr. Ryan, the policeman, in the mayor's office, over the fire station. His belt with its two enormous revolvers was hung from a nail on the wall. He was reading the evening paper.

He merely glanced over his paper at Ivar and Waino.

"Well," he said severely, "I knew when I saw you start out with that gun you'd get into trouble. What've you done? Killed a moose hunting out of season—or maybe several mooses?"

The boys knew that this was a joke, but they were too breathless to laugh.

"Papa wants you to come put a moose out of his stable."

Mr. Ryan liked to joke. He stared at them for a moment and then he frowned.

"Playing jokes on an officer of the law, uh? I'll just take you back to the jail and let you pick your rooms right now. And remember," he said slowly, "what we have here for supper is bread and water—and that's what we have for breakfast and for dinner."

"No, Mr. Ryan, please, it isn't a joke. Papa wants you to come put a moose out of his livery stable."

"No, Mr. Ryan, please, it isn't a joke—" Waino said.

Mr. Ryan grinned and reached for his belt. For a minute he'd thought the boys were trying to make him believe a real moose was in the stable and then he remembered that "moose" was Minnesota slang for a big man.

It was pretty late for tramps up on the Iron Range and, anyway, Ivar Ketonen (young Ivar was named for his father) was about as big a "moose" himself as anyone would want to see. He wasn't the kind that would ask for help or need it, usually.

At the same time, if Ketonen needed help he might need it pretty badly. Mr. Ryan started at a swift walk that made the boys trot. Mr. Ryan was a small Irishman but he was very strong and braver than he was strong.

"What's this moose doing?" he asked Ivar.

"He's asleep, Mr. Ryan."

Mr. Ryan laughed. "We'll give him a better place to sleep up here in the jail. Did he make any trouble?"

"No, he just ate a lot of—"

"Oh, broke into the house, uh? Well, that's bad." Mr. Ryan grew serious. "He oughtn't to have done that. We'd have fed him and let him go tomorrow. Now, I guess, we'll have to keep him. That's bad—breaking into places."

"Yes, sir," Ivar said anxiously.

"He steal anything?"

"No, sir. Just a lot of—"

"Nothing but food, poor fellow. Well, we'll see what we can do for him. He must have been mighty hungry. Didn't know enough to come around to me. I'd have fed him and given him a bed. He might be all right after all." Mr. Ryan hated to arrest people—he hated to see them get into trouble. But he wasn't afraid to arrest *anybody* if he thought he deserved to be in trouble.

Waino said timidly, "He's a kind of a sad moose, Mr. Ryan."

Mr. Ryan sighed. "Poor fellow. Hungry and just saw a door open. It's been a hard winter. We'll see what we can do."

They had come to the door of the livery stable. Mr. Ryan believed the boys when they said the "moose" was sad, but he didn't know how much they knew about tramps. He hooked his thumb over the edge of his belt close to one of the revolvers and opened the door quickly.

"Ivar?" Mr. Ryan called to Ivar's father.

"Frank?"

"Everything all right?"

"Everything is not all right. What are you going to do about this moose? What's he doing here?"

Mr. Ryan walked quickly and boldly down the aisle. The boys heard him gasp. "It's a moose!"

"I said it was a moose," Ivar told him. He added, rather anxiously, "What are you going to do with him, Mr. Ryan?"

Waino said, "What are you going to do with him, Mr. Ryan?"

Mr. Ryan did not know what to do. He was too soft-hearted to shoot a sleeping moose, so he phoned the mayor.

City Council

Mr. Nels Olavsson, the Mayor of Birora, had been having a good supper. There was soup with all kinds of vegetables and lots of soup meat to eat with horseradish; there was a whitefish from Lake Superior, and cream sauce; there were potatoes boiled with the jackets on and spinach with oil and vinegar dressing and some of his wife's canned tomatoes; and there would have been mince pie—but the telephone rang.

While he was gone Mama brought the hot mince pie to their three daughters—twelve, nine and five—and put a piece at Mr. Olavsson's place.

When he came back they all looked up together and they saw that he was putting on his mackinaw and his fur hat. The three little girls with their yellow hair quit eating pie and looked at their father, but it was Mama who asked, "What happened, Papa?"

"Nothing," he said, "but Mister Ryan has gone crazy and I must go down and see what I can do."

"*Mister Ryan?* Eat your pie, Papa. Mister Ryan wouldn't go crazy."

"He has gone crazy," Mayor Olavsson said firmly, pulling on his furry mittens. "He asked me to come down to Ivar Ketonen's because there was a moose in the stable."

"Can I come and see the moose?" Gunda asked. She was nine.

"I want to see the moose," said Christine, the youngest. "You never took me to see a moose, Papa."

"A moose in a livery stable!" said Olga, who was twelve.

"There aren't any mooses in livery stables. They're in the woods. Can I come and see him too, Papa?"

"No—because the moose is in Mr. Ryan's head. It isn't a real moose. There wouldn't be a moose in a stable."

"Your pie is getting cold," Mama warned.

"I don't know when I'll be back," Mr. Olavsson said and hurried out.

Mrs. Olavsson put the pie back in the stove to keep warm. Mr. Olavsson walked down the street as fast as a fat man could. The snow puffed out like little fountains in front of his boots.

"Hello, Ivar," he called cautiously at the door of the livery stable.

"Hello, Nels." Then he heard Mr. Ryan call in the same tone of voice he always used, "Hello, Nels. Come on in."

The Mayor went in very slowly and he left the door off the latch so that he could get out again quickly. "Now, Frank," he said, "let's let the moose go and you come with me to the doctor—"

"Let the moose go!" Mr. Ryan said. "I'm not holding the moose. I wish he would go. I'd give anything if he'd go. You come let him go."

He was so mad that Mr. Olavsson was pretty sure he wasn't crazy. He went on down the aisle of the livery stable. "What's this moose you're talking about—did you say moose or mouse?"

"*Mouse*," Mr. Ryan said grimly as the Mayor drew nearer.

Mr. Olavsson saw Honk. "My goodness! That's not a mouse —that's a *moose!*"

"Oh, you don't mean it!" Mr. Ryan said.

"But—what's he doing here?"

Mr. Ryan looked all over Honk. "Maybe he's learning to play the piano—or maybe he's knitting—or maybe he's reading a good book—but it looks to me like he was just sleeping."

Ivar felt that he had known this moose a long time now and he laughed. Waino laughed. The Mayor frowned at them.

"I mean—how did he get here?"

Ivar's papa shook but he did not open his mouth to laugh. "I didn't have any moose so I had him sent by mail."

Mr. Olavsson did not even smile at this. "Just wandered in?"

"Yust wandered in," Ivar's father said.

"What are you going to do with him?"

Ivar's father shrugged his shoulders. "It's not *my* moose. This is the town moose. If it isn't, why is it in the town? If it is, why do you send it in to eat almost more than a ton of hay?"

Ivar and Waino were sitting on the moose and Mr. Ryan and Ivar's father were standing toward one end of him.

"He looks kind of skinny and he looks kind of he doesn't feel good," Mr. Olavsson said. "Poor old Moose—it's been a hard winter."

"He was hungry," Ivar said.

"I can see," the Mayor said. "Why didn't you shoot him?"

"You can't shoot a moose when he's asleep," Mr. Ryan objected.

"No, don't shoot him," Ivar and Waino said together and they bounced up and down on the moose so much that it said "HAWWNK."

Mr. Ryan and Mr. Olavsson went into the office at once, but Ivar's father stayed and said: "Boys, your mothers might want you to run some errands. You better go on home while we figure this out."

"But they can't shoot poor old Honk," Ivar said, and though this was the moose's name, it was the first time anyone had mentioned it.

"No, they can't shoot poor old Honk," Waino said.

"We'll do what we think is best," Mr. Olavsson said crossly, from the office door.

"You aren't going to have him shot?" Mr. Ryan asked.

"No—we'll dispose of him."

When Ivar and Waino heard this they bounced up and down on Honk as hard as they could. They hoped he would wake up and go away before he was "disposed of." But Honk only said "H-H-H-AWWWWNNNK!" very slowly, without opening his eyes.

Ivar's father took a firm stand. "Me—I can't afford to feed a moose and I don't want him here. But I'd sooner see him here than disposed of. If this town won't take care of its mooses, I guess I'll have to."

Mr. Olavsson looked at Mr. Ryan, but anyone could see that Mr. Ryan was on Ivar Ketonen's side.

"I can't do this all by myself," the Mayor said. "I'll call the city council."

"You don't have to do that," Ivar's father said. "I shall at my own cost build a pen for him at once, until he tries to go away, and then I shall let him."

"No, Ivar," said the Mayor, unhappily, "you don't have to do that. I'll call the council and ask them what to do."

"One thing you will not do and that is to shoot that poor moose."

Five minutes later the same thing was happening in three different houses in Birora.

"Mr. Olavsson is clear crazy this time," said Mr. Lunn, snapping on his ear-muffs.

At the same time—"but think of it! The Mayor going out of his mind!" Mr. Town Clerk Hulburd was saying to his family.

At the same time Mr. Councilman Hoaglund was shaking his head sadly. "He shouldn't have worked so hard on the tax list. Think of it! Mr. Olavsson kept saying and saying that there *was* a moose in the stable."

An hour later they were all sitting around a table in Ivar's father's office looking very puzzled.

"You can't shoot him—a sad moose like that," Mr. Olavsson was saying for the hundredth time.

"No—the poor fellow, he's starving!" Mr. Lunn said.

"You mean he *was* starving," Ivar's father corrected, thinking of his hay.

"I'll tell you," Mayor Olavsson said finally. "The town will pay for the hay and Frank can stay here tonight with his revolver. If the moose makes any fuss, then he must shoot him. But if he just goes away, everything will be all right."

They agreed on that. Sometime in the night Honk went quietly away.

Limericks

EDWARD LEAR

There was a Young Lady of Hull,
Who was chased by a virulent Bull;
But she seized on a spade, and called out, "Who's afraid?"
Which distracted that virulent Bull.

Illustrations by Edward Lear.

There was an Old Man in a tree,
Who was horribly bored by a Bee;
When they said, "Does it buzz?" he replied,
    "Yes, it does!
It's a regular brute of a Bee."

There was an old man on the Border,
Who lived in the utmost disorder;
He danced with the cat, and made tea in his hat,
Which vexed all the folks on the Border.

There was an Old Lady whose folly
Induced her to sit in a holly;
Whereon, by a thorn her dress being torn,
She quickly became melancholy.

Jack and the Robbers

RICHARD C. CHASE

Tʜɪs here's another tale about Jack when he was still a small-like boy. He was about twelve, I reckon, and his daddy started tryin' to make him help with the work around the place. But Jack he didn't like workin' much. He would piddle around a little and then he'd go on back to the house, till one day his daddy whipped him. He just tanned Jack good. Jack didn't cry none, but he didn't like it a bit. So early the next mornin' he slipped off without tellin' his mother and struck out down the public road. Thought he'd go and try his fortune somewhere off from home.

He got down the road a few miles and there was an old ox standin' in a field by a rail fence, a-bellowin' like it was troubled over somethin'—

> "Um-m-muh!
> Um-m-m—muh-h-h!"

"Hello!" says Jack. "What's the matter?"

"I'll just tell you," says the old ox. "I'm gettin' too old to plow and I heard the men talkin' about how they'd have to kill me to-morrow and get shet of me."

"Come on down here to the gap," says Jack, "and you can slip off with me."

So the old ox followed the fence to where the gap was at and Jack let the bars down and the old ox got out in front of Jack, and they went on down the public road.

Jack and the ox traveled on, and pretty soon they came where

there was an old donkey standin' with his head hangin' down over the gate, a-goin'—

"Wahn-n-n-eh!
Wahn-n-n-eh!
Wahn-n-n-eh!"

"Hello," says Jack. "What's troublin' you?"

"Law me!" says the old donkey. "The boys took me out to haul in wood this mornin' and I'm gettin' so old and weak I couldn't do no good. I heard 'em say they were goin' to kill me tomorrow, get shet of me."

"Come on and go with us," says Jack.

So he let the old donkey out and they pulled on down the public road. The old donkey told Jack to get up on his back and ride.

They went on a piece, came to an old hound dog settin' in a man's yard. He would bark awhile and then howl awhile—

"A-woo! woo! woo!
A-oo-oo-oo!"

—sounded awful lonesome.

"Hello," says Jack. "What you a-howlin' so for?"

"Oh, law me!" says the old dog. "The boys took me coon-huntin' last night, cut a tree where the coon had got up in it. I got hold on the coon all right, but my teeth are all gone and hit got loose from me. They said they were goin' to kill me today, get shet of me."

"Come on, go with us," says Jack.

So the old dog scrouged under the gate.

The old donkey says to him, "Get up on my back and ride, if you want to."

Jack holp the old dog up behind him, and they went on down the public road.

Came to an old tomcat climbin' along the fence. Hit was

a-squallin' and meowin', stop ever' now and then, sit down on
the top rail—

"Meow-ow!
Meow-ow-ow!"

—sounded right pitiful.

"Hello!" says Jack. "What's the matter you squallin' so?"

"Oh, law!" says the old cat. "I caught a rat out in the barn
this mornin', but my teeth are gettin' so old and bad I let him
go. I heard 'em talkin' about killin' me to get shet of me, 'cause
I ain't no good to catch rats no more."

"Come on and go with us," says Jack.

So the old cat jumped down off the fence.

The old donkey says, "Hop up there on my back and you can
ride."

The old cat jumped up, got behind the dog, and they went on
down the public road.

Came to where they saw an old rooster settin' on a fence post,
crowin' like it was midnight, makin' the awfulest lonesome
racket—

"Ur rook-a-roo!
Ur-r-r rook-a-roo-oo-oo!"

"Hello!" says Jack. "What's troublin' you?"

"Law me!" says the old rooster. "Company's comin' today
and I heard 'em say they were goin' to kill me, put me in a pie!"

"Come on with us," says Jack.

Old rooster flew on down, got behind the cat, says, "All right,
boys. Let's go!"

So they went right on down the highway. That was about all
could get on the old donkey's back. The old rooster was right on
top its tail and a-havin' a sort of hard time stayin' on. They
traveled on, traveled on, till hit got plumb dark.

"Well," says Jack, "we got to get off the road and find us a place
to stay tonight."

Directly they came to a little path leadin' off in the woods, decided to take that, see could they find a stayin' place in there. Went on a right smart piece further, and 'way along up late in the night they came to a little house, didn't have no clearin' around it. Jack hollered hello at the fence, but there didn't nobody answer.

"Come on," says the old donkey. "Let's go investigate that place."

Well, there wasn't nobody ever came to the door and there wasn't nobody around back of the house, so directly they went on in. Found a right smart lot of good somethin' to eat in there.

Jack says, "Now, who in the world do you reckon could be a-livin' out here in such a wilderness of a place as this?"

"Well," says the old donkey, "hit's my o-pinion that a gang of highway robbers lives out here."

So Jack says, "Then hit looks like to me we might as well take up and stay here. If they've done stole all these vittles, we got as much right to 'em as they have."

"Yes," says the old dog, "that's exactly what I think, too. But if we stay, I believe we better get fixed for a fight. I expect they'll be comin' back in here about midnight."

"That's just what I was goin' to say," says the old cat. "I bet it's pretty close to midnight right now."

"Hit lacks about a hour," says the old rooster.

"Come on, then," says Jack. "Let's all of us get set to fight 'em.

The ox said he'd stay out in the yard. The old donkey said he'd take up his stand on the porch just outside the door. The dog said he'd get in behind the door and fight from there. The old tomcat got down in the fireplace, and the old rooster flew up on the comb of the roof, says, "If you boys need any help now, just call on me, call on me-e-e!"

They all waited awhile. Heard somebody comin' directly; hit was seven highway robbers. They came on till they got pretty close to the house, then they told one of 'em to go on in and start up a fire so's they could have a light to see to get in and so they could divide out the money they'd stole that day.

One man went on in the house, the other six waited outside the gate.

That man went to the fireplace, got down on his knees to blow up the fire. The cat had his head right down on the hearth-rock and that man thought its eyes was coals of fire. Time he blowed in that old cat's eyes, it reached out its claws right quick and scratched him down both cheeks. The robber hollered and headed for the door. The dog ran out and bit him in the leg. He shook it off and ran on the porch and the old donkey raised up and kicked him on out in the yard. The ox caught him up on its horns and ran to the fence and threw him out in the brush. About that time the old rooster settin' up there on top of the house started in to crowin' right big.

The other robbers, time they heard all that racket, they put out from there just as fast as they could run. The one they'd sent in the house finally got up and started runnin' like a streak, caught up with 'em in no time. They said to him, says, "What in the world was that in there?"

"Oh, I'm killed! I'm killed!" says the man. "I won't live over fifteen minutes!"

The other said, "Well, 'fore ye die, tell us what it was caused all that racket back yonder."

"Law me! The house is plumb full of men, and they've even got one on the roof. I went to blow up the fire and a man in the fireplace raked me all over the face with an awl. Started to run and a man behind the door took me in the leg with a butcher knife. Time I got out the door, a man out there hit me with a knot-maul, knocked me clean off the porch. A man standin' in the yard caught me on a pitchfork and threw me over the fence. And then that man up on the roof hollered out,

> *'Chunk him on up here!*
> *Chunk him on up here.'*

Ain't no use in us goin' back there with all of them men in the house. Let's leave here quick 'fore they come after us."

So them highway robbers ran for their life, and kept on runnin' till they were plumb out the country.

Jack and the ox and the old donkey and the dog and the cat and the rooster, they took possession of that house, and just had 'em a big time.

But the last time I was down that way, Jack had gone on back home to his folks. He was out in the yard a-cuttin' his mother a big pile of stovewood.

The Last of the Dragons

E. NESBIT

OF COURSE you know that dragons were once as common as motorbuses are now, and almost as dangerous. But as every well-brought-up prince was expected to kill a dragon and rescue a princess, the dragons grew fewer and fewer, till it was often quite hard for a princess to find a dragon to be rescued from. And at last there were no more dragons in France and no more dragons in Germany, or Spain, or Italy, or Russia. There were some left in China, and are still, but they are cold and bronzy, and there never were any, of course, in America. But the last real live dragon left was in England, and of course that was a very long time ago, before what you call English History began. This dragon lived in Cornwall in the big caves amidst the rocks, and was a very fine big dragon, quite seventy feet long from the tip of its fearful snout to the end of its terrible tail. It breathed fire and smoke, and rattled when it walked, because its scales were made of iron. Its wings were like half-umbrellas—or like bat's wings, only several thousand times bigger. Everyone was very frightened of it, and well they might be.

Now the King of Cornwall had one daughter, and when she was sixteen, of course, she would have to go and face the dragon. Such tales are always told in royal nurseries at twilight, so the Princess knew what she had to expect. The dragon would not eat her, of course—because the prince would come and rescue her. But the Princess could not help thinking it would be much pleasanter to have nothing to do with the dragon at all—not even to be rescued from him.

"All the princes I know are such very silly little boys," she told her father. "Why must I be rescued by a prince?"

"It's always done, my dear," said the King, taking his crown off and putting it on the grass, for they were alone in the garden, and even kings must unbend sometimes.

"Father, darling," said the Princess presently, when she had made a daisy chain and put it on the King's head, where the crown ought to have been. "Father, darling, couldn't we tie up one of the silly little princes for the dragon to look at—and then I could go and kill the dragon and rescue the Prince? I fence much better than any of the princes we know."

"What an unladylike idea!" said the King, and put his crown on again, for he saw the Prime Minister coming with a basket of new-laid Bills for him to sign. "Dismiss the thought, my child. I rescued your mother from a dragon, and you don't want to set yourself up above her, I should hope?"

"But this is the *last* dragon. It is different from all other dragons."

"How?" asked the King.

"Because it *is* the last," said the Princess, and went off to her fencing lesson, with which she took great pains. She took great pains with all her lessons—for she could not give up the idea of fighting the dragon. She took such pains that she became the strongest and boldest and most skillful and most sensible princess in Europe. She had always been the prettiest and nicest.

And the days and years went on, till at last the day came which was the day before the Princess was to be rescued from the dragon. The prince who was to do this deed of valor was a pale prince, with large eyes and a head full of mathematics and philosophy, but he had unfortunately neglected his fencing lessons. He was to stay the night at the palace, and there was a banquet.

After supper the Princess sent her pet parrot to the Prince with a note. It said:

"Please, Prince, come on to the terrace. I want to talk to you without anybody else hearing.—The Princess."

So, of course, he went—and he saw her gown of silver a long way off shining among the shadows of the trees like water in starlight. And when he came quite close to her he said:

"Princess, at your service," and bent his cloth-of-gold-covered knee and put his hand on his cloth-of-gold-covered heart.

"Do you think," said the Princess earnestly, "that you will be able to kill the dragon?"

"I will kill the dragon," said the Prince firmly, "or perish in the attempt."

"It's no use your perishing," said the Princess.

"It's the least I can do," said the Prince.

"What I'm afraid of is that it'll be the most you can do," said the Princess.

"It's the only thing I can do," said he, "unless I kill the dragon."

"Why you should do anything for me is what I can't see," said she.

"But I want to," he said. "You must know that I love you better than anything in the world."

When he said that he looked so kind that the Princess began to like him a little.

"Look here," she said, "no one else will go out tomorrow. You know they tie me to a rock, and leave me—and then everybody scurries home and puts up the shutters and keeps them shut till you ride through the town in triumph shouting that you've killed the dragon, and I ride on the horse behind you weeping for joy."

"I've heard that that is how it is done," said he.

"Well, do you love me well enough to come very quickly and set me free—and we'll fight the dragon together?"

"It wouldn't be safe for you."

"Much safer for both of us for me to be free, with a sword in my hand, than tied up and helpless. *Do* agree."

He could refuse her nothing. So he agreed. And next day everything happened as she had said.

When he had cut the cords that tied her to the rocks they stood on the lonely mountainside looking at each other.

"It seems to me," said the Prince, "that this ceremony could have been arranged without the dragon."

"Yes," said the Princess, "but since it has been arranged with the dragon—"

"It seems such a pity to kill the dragon—the last in the world," said the Prince.

"Well, then, don't let's," said the Princess. "Let's tame it not to eat princesses but to eat out of their hands. They say everything can be tamed by kindness."

"Tamed by kindness means giving them things to eat," said the Prince. "Have you got anything to eat?"

She hadn't, but the Prince owned that he had a few biscuits. "Breakfast was so very early," said he, "and I thought you might have felt faint after the fight."

"How clever," said the Princess, and they took a biscuit in each hand. And they looked here and they looked there, but never a dragon could they see.

"But here's its trail," said the Prince, and pointed to where the rock was scarred and scratched so as to make a track leading to the mouth of a dark cave. It was like cart ruts in a Sussex road, mixed with the marks of sea gulls' feet on the sea sand. "Look, that's where it's dragged its brass tail and planted its steel claws."

"Don't let's think how hard its tail and its claws are," said the Princess, "or I shall begin to be frightened—and I know you can't tame anything, even by kindness, if you're frightened of it. Come on. Now or never."

She caught the Prince's hand in hers, and they ran along the path towards the dark mouth of the cave. But they did not run into it. It really was so very *dark*.

So they stood outside, and the Prince shouted: "What ho! Dragon there! What ho within!" And from the cave they heard an answering voice and great clattering and creaking. It sounded as though a rather large cotton mill were stretching itself and waking up out of its sleep.

The Prince and the Princess trembled, but they stood firm.

"Dragon—I say, Dragon!" said the Princess. "Do come out and talk to us. We've brought you a present."

"Oh, yes—I know your presents," growled the dragon in a huge rumbling voice. "One of those precious princesses, I suppose? And I've got to come out and fight for her. Well, I tell you straight, I'm not going to do it. A fair fight I wouldn't say no to —a fair fight and no favor—but one of these put-up fights where you've got to lose—No. So I tell you. If I wanted a princess I'd come and take her, in my own time—but I don't. What do you suppose I'd do with her, if I'd got her?"

"Eat her, wouldn't you?" said the Princess in a voice that trembled a little.

"Eat a fiddlestick end," said the dragon very rudely. "I wouldn't touch the horrid thing."

The Princess's voice grew firmer.

"Do you like biscuits?" she asked.

"No," growled the dragon.

"Not the nice little expensive ones with sugar on the top?"

"No," growled the dragon.

"Then what *do* you like?" asked the Prince.

"You go away and don't bother me," growled the dragon, and they could hear it turn over, and the clang and clatter of its turning echoed in the cave like the sound of the steam hammers in the arsenal at Woolwich.

The Prince and Princess looked at each other. What *were* they to do? Of course it was no use going home and telling the King that the dragon didn't want princesses—because His Majesty was very old-fashioned and would never have believed that a new-fashioned dragon could ever be at all different from an old-fashioned dragon. They could not go into the cave and kill the dragon. Indeed, unless it attacked the Princess it did not seem fair to kill it at all.

"It must like something," whispered the Princess, and she called out in a voice as sweet as honey and sugar cane:

"Dragon! Dragon, dear!"

"WHAT?" shouted the dragon coming towards them through the darkness of the cave. The Princess shivered, and said in a very small voice:

"Dragon—Dragon, dear!"

And then the dragon came out. The Prince drew his sword and the Princess drew hers—the beautiful silver-handled one that the Prince had brought in his motor-car. But they did not attack; they moved slowly back as the dragon came out, all the vast scaly length of it, and lay along the rock—its great wings half

spread and its golden sheen gleaming and sparkling in the sun. At last they could retreat no farther—the dark rock behind them stopped their way—and with their backs to the rock they stood swords in hand and waited.

The dragon drew nearer and nearer—and now they could see that it was not breathing fire and smoke as they had expected—it came crawling slowly towards them wriggling a little as a puppy does when it wants to play and isn't quite sure whether you're not cross with it.

And then they saw that great tears were coursing down its brazen cheeks.

"Whatever's the matter?" said the Prince.

"Nobody," sobbed the dragon, "ever called me 'dear' before!"

"Don't cry, dragon dear," said the Princess. "We'll call you 'dear' as often as you like. We want to tame you."

"I *am* tame," said the dragon. "That's just it. That's what nobody but you has ever found out. I'm so tame that I'd eat out of your hands."

"Eat what, dragon dear?" said the Princess. "Not biscuits?"

The dragon slowly shook its heavy head.

"Not biscuits?" said the Princess tenderly. "What, then, dragon dear?"

"Your kindness quite undragons me," it said. "No one has ever asked any of us what we like to eat—always offering us princesses, and then rescuing them—and never once, 'What'll you take to drink the King's health in?' Cruel hard I call it," and it wept again.

"But what would you like to drink our health in?" said the Prince. "We're going to be married today, aren't we, Princess?"

She said that she supposed so.

"What'll I take to drink your health in?" asked the dragon. "Ah, you're something like a gentleman, you are, sir. I don't mind if I do, sir. I'll be proud to drink your and your good lady's health in a tiddy drop of"—its voice faltered—"to think of you asking me so friendly like," it said. "Yes, sir, just a tiddy drop of puppuppuppuppupetrol—that—that's what does a dragon good, sir—"

"I've lots in the car," said the Prince, and was off down the mountain like a flash. He was a good judge of character, and he knew that with this dragon the Princess would be safe.

"If I might make so bold," said the dragon, "while the gentleman's away—p'raps just to pass the time you'd be so kind as to call me 'dear' again, and if you'd shake claws with a poor old dragon that's never been anybody's enemy but its own—well, the last of the dragons'll be the proudest dragon there's ever been since the first of them."

It held out an enormous paw, and the great steel hooks that were its claws closed over the Princess's hand as softly as the claws of the Himalayan bear will close over the bit of bun you hand it through the bars at the zoo.

And so the Prince and Princess went back to the palace in triumph, the dragon following them like a pet dog. And all through the wedding festivities no one drank more earnestly to the happiness of the bride and bridegroom than the Princess's pet dragon, whom she had at once named Fido.

And when the happy pair were settled in their own kingdom, Fido came to them and begged to be allowed to make itself useful.

"There must be some little thing I can do," it said, rattling its wings and stretching its claws. "My wings and claws and so on ought to be turned to some account—to say nothing of my grateful heart."

So the Prince had a special saddle or howdah made for it—very long it was—like the tops of many tramcars fitted together. One hundred and fifty seats were fitted to this, and the dragon, whose greatest pleasure was now to give pleasure to others, delighted in taking parties of children to the seaside. It flew through the air quite easily with its hundred and fifty little passengers, and would lie on the sand patiently waiting till they were ready to return. The children were very fond of it and used to call it Dear, a word which never failed to bring tears of affection and gratitude to its eyes. So it lived, useful and respected, till quite the other day— when someone happened to say, in its hearing, that dragons were out of date, now so much new machinery had come. This so distressed it that it asked the King to change it into something less old-fashioned, and the kindly monarch at once changed it into a mechanical contrivance. The dragon, indeed, became the first airplane.

A Centipede
Was Happy Quite

AUTHOR UNKNOWN

A centipede was happy quite,
  Until a frog in fun
Said, "Pray, which leg comes after which?"
This raised her mind to such a pitch,
She lay distracted in the ditch
  Considering how to run.

FROM

The Adventures of Tom Sawyer

MARK TWAIN

Tom wanted to make a good impression on Becky Thatcher and so he set out to win the prize at Sunday School. Of course Tom, being Tom, didn't go about it the usual way— he had a new method that was quicker and easier than learning his catechism. But this time Tom's method backfired.

How Tom Won the Bible Prize

THE sun rose upon a tranquil world, and beamed down upon the peaceful village like a benediction. Breakfast over, Aunt Polly had family worship; it began with a prayer built from the ground up of solid courses of Scriptural quotations, welded together with a thin mortar of originality; and from the summit of this she delivered a grim chapter of the Mosaic Law, as from Sinai.

Then Tom girded up his loins, so to speak, and went to work to "get his verses." Sid had learned his lesson days before. Tom bent all his energies to the memorizing of five verses, and he chose part of the Sermon on the Mount, because he could find no verses that were shorter. At the end of half an hour Tom had a vague general idea of his lesson, but no more, for his mind was traversing the whole field of human thought, and his hands were busy with distracting recreations. Mary took his book to hear him recite, and he tried to find his way through the fog:

"Blessed are the—a—a—"

"Poor—"

"Yes—poor; blessed are the poor—a—a—"

"In spirit—"

"In spirit; blessed are the poor in spirit, for they—they—"

"*Theirs*—"

"For *theirs*. Blessed are the poor in spirit, for *theirs* is the kingdom of heaven. Blessed are they that mourn, for they—they—"

"Sh—"

"For they—a—"

"S, H, A—"

"For they S, H—Oh I don't know what it is!"

"*Shall!*"

"Oh, *shall!* for they shall—for they shall—a—a—shall mourn—a—a—blessed are they that shall—they that—a—they that shall mourn, for they shall—a—shall *what?* Why don't you tell me, Mary? what do you want to be so mean for?"

"Oh, Tom, you poor thick-headed thing, I'm not teasing you. I wouldn't do that. You must go and learn it again. Don't you be discouraged, Tom, you'll manage it—and if you do, I'll give you something ever so nice. There, now, that's a good boy."

"All right! what is it, Mary, tell me what it is."

"Never you mind, Tom. You know if I say it's nice, it *is* nice."

"You bet you that's so, Mary. All right, I'll tackle it again."

And he did "tackle it again"—and under the double pressure of curiosity and prospective gain, he did it with such spirit that he accomplished a shining success. Mary gave him a brand-new "Barlow" knife worth twelve and a half cents; and the convulsion of delight that swept his system shook him to his foundations. True, the knife would not cut anything, but it was a "sure enough" Barlow, and there was inconceivable grandeur in that—though where the western boys ever got the idea that such a weapon could possibly be counterfeited to its injury, is an imposing mystery and will always remain so, perhaps. Tom contrived to scarify the cupboard with it, and was arranging to begin on the bureau, when he was called off to dress for Sunday-school.

Mary gave him a tin basin of water and a piece of soap, and he went outside the door and set the basin on a little bench there; then he dipped the soap in the water and laid it down; turned up his sleeves; poured out the water on the ground, gently, and then entered the kitchen and began to wipe his face diligently on the towel behind the door.

But Mary removed the towel and said:

"Now ain't you ashamed, Tom. You mustn't be so bad. Water won't hurt you."

Tom was a trifle disconcerted. The basin was refilled, and this time he stood over it a little while, gathering resolution; took in a big breath and began. When he entered the kitchen presently, with both eyes shut and groping for the towel with his hands, an honorable testimony of suds and water was dripping from his face. But when he emerged from the towel, he was not yet satisfactory, for the clean territory stopped short at his chin and his jaws, like a mask; below and beyond this line there was a dark expanse of unirrigated soil that spread downward in front and backward around his neck. Mary took him in hand, and when she was done with him he was a man and a brother, without distinction of color, and his saturated hair was neatly brushed, and its short curls wrought into a dainty and symmetrical general effect. [He privately smoothed out the curls, with labor and difficulty, and plastered his hair close down to his head; for he held curls to be effeminate, and his own filled his life with bitterness.] Then Mary got out a suit of his clothing that had been used only on Sundays during two years—they were simply called his "other clothes"—and so by that we know the size of his wardrobe. The girl "put him to rights" after he had dressed himself; she buttoned his neat roundabout up to his chin, turned his vast shirt collar down over his shoulders, brushed him off and crowned him with his speckled straw hat. He now looked exceedingly improved and uncomfortable. He was fully as uncomfortable as he looked; for there was a restraint about whole clothes and cleanliness that galled him. He hoped that Mary would forget his shoes, but the hope was blighted; she coated them thoroughly with tallow, as was the custom, and brought them out. He lost his temper and said he was always being made to do everything he didn't want to do.

But Mary said, persuasively:

"Please, Tom—that's a good boy."

So he got into the shoes snarling. Mary was soon ready, and

the three children set out for Sunday-school—a place that Tom hated with his whole heart; but Sid and Mary were fond of it.

Sabbath-school hours were from nine to half-past ten; and then church service. Two of the children always remained for the sermon voluntarily, and the other always remained too—for stronger reasons. The church's high-backed, uncushioned pews would seat about three hundred persons; the edifice was but a small, plain affair, with a sort of pine board tree-box on top of it for a steeple. At the door Tom dropped back a step and accosted a Sunday-dressed comrade:

"Say, Billy, got a yaller ticket?"

"Yes."

"What'll you take for her?"

"What'll you give?"

"Piece of lickrish and a fish-hook."

"Less see 'em."

Tom exhibited. They were satisfactory, and the property changed hands. Then Tom traded a couple of white alleys for three red tickets, and some small trifle or other for a couple of blue ones. He waylaid other boys as they came, and went on buying tickets of various colors ten or fifteen minutes longer. He entered the church, now, with a swarm of clean and noisy boys and girls, proceeded to his seat and started a quarrel with the first boy that came handy. The teacher, a grave, elderly man, interfered; then turned his back a moment, and Tom pulled a boy's hair in the next bench, and was absorbed in his book when the boy turned around; stuck a pin in another boy presently, in order to hear him say "Ouch!" and got a new reprimand from his teacher. Tom's whole class were of a pattern—restless, noisy, and troublesome. When they came to recite their lessons, not one of them knew his verses perfectly, but had to be prompted all along. However, they worried through, and each got his reward—in small blue tickets, each with a passage of Scripture on it; each blue ticket was pay for two verses of the recitation. Ten blue tickets equaled a red one, and could be exchanged for it; ten red tickets equaled a yellow one: for ten yellow tickets the superintendent gave a very plainly bound Bible (worth 40 cents in those easy times), to the pupil. How many of my readers would have the in-

dustry and application to memorize two thousand verses, even for a Doré Bible? And yet Mary had acquired two Bibles in this way—it was the patient work of two years—and a boy of German parentage had won four or five. He once recited three thousand verses without stopping; but the strain upon his mental faculties was too great, and he was little better than an idiot from that day forth—a grievous misfortune for the school, for on great occasions, before company, the superintendent (as Tom expressed it) had always made this boy come out and "spread himself." Only the older pupils managed to keep their tickets and stick to their tedious work long enough to get a Bible, and so the delivery of one of these prizes was a rare and noteworthy circumstance; the successful pupil was so great and conspicuous for that day, that on the spot every scholar's heart was fired with a fresh ambition that often lasted a couple of weeks. It is possible that Tom's mental stomach had never really hungered for one of those prizes, but unquestionably his entire being had for many a day longed for the glory and the eclat that came with it.

In due course the superintendent stood up in front of the pulpit, with a closed hymn book in his hand and his forefinger inserted between its leaves, and commanded attention. When the Sunday-school superintendent makes his customary little speech, a hymn book in the hand is as necessary as is the inevitable sheet of music in the hand of a singer who stands forward on the platform and sings a solo at a concert—though why, is a mystery: for neither the hymn book nor the sheet of music is ever referred to by the sufferer. This superintendent was a slim creature of thirty-five, with a sandy goatee and short sandy hair; he wore a stiff standing-collar whose upper edge almost reached his ears and whose sharp points curved forward abreast the corners of his mouth—a fence that compelled a straight lookout ahead, and a turning of the whole body when a side view was required; his chin was propped on a spreading cravat which was as broad and as long as a bank note, and had fringed ends; his boot toes were turned sharply up, in the fashion of the day, like sleigh-runners —an effect patiently and laboriously produced by the young men by sitting with their toes pressed against a wall for hours together. Mr. Walters was very earnest of mien, and very sincere and honest at heart; and he held sacred things and places in such reverence, and so separated them from worldly matters, that unconsciously to himself his Sunday-school voice had acquired a peculiar intonation which was wholly absent on weekdays. He began after this fashion:

"Now children, I want you all to sit up just as straight and pretty as you can and give me all your attention for a minute or two. There—that is it. That is the way good little boys and girls should do. I see one little girl who is looking out of the window—I am afraid she thinks I am out there somewhere—perhaps up in one of the trees making a speech to the little birds. [Applausive titter.] I want to tell you how good it makes me feel to see so many bright, clean little faces assembled in a place like this, learning to do right and be good." And so forth and so on. It is not necessary to set down the rest of the oration. It was of a pattern which does not vary, and so it is familiar to us all.

The latter third of the speech was marred by the resumption of fights and other recreations among certain of the bad boys and by fidgetings and whisperings that extended far and wide, washing even to the bases of isolated and incorruptible rocks like Sid and Mary. But now every sound ceased suddenly, with the subsidence of Mr. Walters' voice, and the conclusion of the speech was received with a burst of silent gratitude.

A good part of the whispering had been occasioned by an event which was more or less rare—the entrance of visitors; Lawyer Thatcher, accompanied by a very feeble and aged man; a fine, portly, middle-aged gentleman with iron-gray hair; and a dignified lady who was doubtless the latter's wife. The lady was leading a child. Tom had been restless and full of chafings and repinings; conscience-smitten, too—he could not meet Amy Lawrence's eye, he could not brook her loving gaze. But when he saw this small new-comer his soul was all ablaze with bliss in a moment. The next moment he was "showing off" with all his might—cuffing boys, pulling hair, making faces—in a word, using every art that seemed likely to fascinate a girl and win her applause. His exaltation had but one alloy—the memory of his humiliation in this angel's garden—and that record in sand was fast washing out, under the waves of happiness that were sweeping over it now.

The visitors were given the highest seat of honor, and as soon as Mr. Walters' speech was finished, he introduced them to the school. The middle-aged man turned out to be a prodigious personage—no less a one than the county judge—altogether the most august creation these children had ever looked upon—and they wondered what kind of material he was made of—and they half wanted to hear him roar, and were half afraid he might, too. He was from Constantinople, twelve miles away—so he had traveled, and seen the world—these very eyes had looked upon the county court-house—which was said to have a tin roof. The awe which these reflections inspired was attested by the impressive silence and the ranks of staring eyes. This was the great Judge Thatcher, brother of their own lawyer. Jeff Thatcher immediately went forward, to be familiar with the great man and be envied by the school. It would have been music to his soul to hear the whisperings:

"Look at him, Jim! He's a going up there. Say—look! he's a going to shake hands with him—he *is* shaking hands with him! By jings, don't you wish you was Jeff?"

Mr. Walters fell to "showing off," with all sorts of official bustlings and activities, giving orders, delivering judgments, discharging directions here, there, everywhere that he could find a target. The librarian "showed off"—running hither and thither with his arms full of books and making a deal of the splutter and fuss that insect authority delights in. The young lady teachers "showed off"—bending sweetly over pupils that were lately being boxed, lifting pretty warning fingers at bad little boys and patting good ones lovingly. The young gentlemen teachers "showed off" with small scoldings and other little displays of authority and fine attention to discipline—and most of the teachers, of both sexes, found business up at the library, by the pulpit; and it was business that frequently had to be done over again two or three times (with much seeming vexation). The little girls "showed off" in various ways, and the little boys "showed off" with such diligence that the air was thick with paper wads and the murmur of scufflings. And above it all the great man sat and beamed a majestic judicial smile upon all the house, and warmed himself in the sun of his own grandeur—for he was "showing off," too.

There was only one thing wanting, to make Mr. Walters' ecstasy complete, and that was a chance to deliver a Bible-prize and exhibit a prodigy. Several pupils had a few yellow tickets, but none had enough—he had been around among the star pupils inquiring. He would have given worlds, now, to have that German lad back again with a sound mind.

And now at this moment, when hope was dead, Tom Sawyer came forward with nine yellow tickets, nine red tickets, and ten blue ones, and demanded a Bible. This was a thunderbolt out of a clear sky. Walters was not expecting an application from this source for the next ten years. But there was no getting around it—here were the certified checks, and they were good for their face. Tom was therefore elevated to a place with the Judge and the other elect, and the great news was announced from headquarters. It was the most stunning surprise of the decade, and so profound was the sensation that it lifted the new hero up to the judicial one's altitude, and the school had two marvels to gaze upon in place of one. The boys were all eaten up with envy—but those that suffered the bitterest pangs were those who perceived too late that they themselves had contributed to this hated splendor by trading tickets to Tom for the wealth he had amassed in selling whitewashing privileges. These despised themselves, as being the dupes of a wily fraud, a guileful snake in the grass.

The prize was delivered to Tom with as much effusion as the superintendent could pump up under the circumstances; but it lacked somewhat of the true gush, for the poor fellow's instinct taught him that there was a mystery here that could not well bear the light, perhaps; it was simply preposterous that *this* boy had warehoused two thousand sheaves of Scriptural wisdom on his premises—a dozen would strain his capacity, without a doubt.

Amy Lawrence was proud and glad, and she tried to make Tom see it in her face—but he wouldn't look. She wondered; then she was just a grain troubled; next a dim suspicion came and went—came again; she watched; a furtive glance told her worlds—and then her heart broke, and she was jealous, and angry, and the tears came and she hated everybody. Tom most of all (she thought).

Tom was introduced to the Judge; but his tongue was tied, his breath would hardly come, his heart quaked—partly because of the awful greatness of the man, but mainly because he was *her* parent. He would have liked to fall down and worship him, if it were in the dark. The Judge put his hand on Tom's head and called him a fine little man, and asked him what his name was. The boy stammered, gasped, and got it out:

"Tom."

"Oh, no, not Tom—it is—"

"Thomas."

"Ah, that's it. I thought there was more to it, maybe. That's very well. But you've another one, I daresay, and you'll tell it to me, won't you?"

"Tell the gentleman your other name, Thomas," said Walters, "and say *sir*. You mustn't forget your manners."

"Thomas Sawyer—sir."

"That's it! That's a good boy. Fine boy. Fine, manly little fellow. Two thousand verses is a great many—very, very great many. And you never can be sorry for the trouble you took to learn them; for knowledge is worth more than anything there is in the world; it's what makes great men and good men; you'll be a great man and a good man yourself, some day, Thomas, and then you'll look back and say, it's all owing to the precious Sunday-school privileges of my boyhood—it's all owing to my dear teachers that taught me to learn—it's all owing to the good superintendent, who encouraged me, and watched over me, and gave me a beautiful Bible—a splendid elegant Bible, to keep and have it all for my own, always—it's all owing to right bringing up! That is what you will say, Thomas—and you wouldn't take any money for those two thousand verses—no, indeed, you wouldn't. And now you wouldn't mind telling me and this lady some of the things you've learned—no, I know you wouldn't—for we are proud of little boys that learn. Now, no doubt, you know the names of all the twelve disciples. Won't you tell us the names of the first two that were appointed?"

Tom was tugging at a button hole and looking sheepish. He blushed, now, and his eyes fell. Mr. Walters' heart sank within him. He said to himself, it is not possible that the boy can answer the simplest question—why *did* the Judge ask him? Yet he felt obliged to speak up and say:

"Answer the gentleman, Thomas—don't be afraid."

Tom still hung fire.

"Now I know you'll tell *me*," said the lady. "The names of the first two disciples were—"

"DAVID AND GOLIAH!"

Let us draw the curtain of charity over the rest of the scene.

FROM
Pippi Longstocking

ASTRID LINDGREN

Pippi is the most remarkable child in all of Sweden. She lives by herself, with her horse and her pet monkey, Mr. Nilsson, and without benefit of grownups. She doesn't go to school, she just has fun all day long. Some policemen are sent to her home to correct this situation. But Pippi is terribly strong too, a sort of super-child, who can even lift horses. So she finds it no trouble at all to handle the policemen.

Pippi Plays Tag with Some Policemen

IT SOON became known throughout the little town that a nine-year-old girl was living all by herself in Villa Villekulla, and all the ladies and gentlemen in the town thought this would never do. All children must have someone to advise them, and all children must go to school to learn the multiplication tables. So the ladies and gentlemen decided that the little girl in Villa Villekulla must immediately be placed in a children's home.

One lovely afternoon Pippi had invited Tommy and Annika over for afternoon coffee and *pepparkakor* [little spice cakes]. She had spread the party out on the front steps. It was so sunny and beautiful there, and the air was filled with the fragrance of the flowers in Pippi's garden. Mr. Nilsson climbed around on the porch railing, and every now and then the horse stuck out his head so that he'd be invited to have a cooky.

"Oh, isn't it glorious to be alive?" said Pippi, stretching out her legs as far as she could reach.

Just at that moment two police officers in full uniform came in through the gate.

"Hurray," said Pippi, "this must be my lucky day too! Police-men are the very best things I know. Next to rhubarb pudding." And with her face beaming she went to meet them.

"Is this the girl who has moved into Villa Villekulla?" asked one of the policemen.

"Quite the contrary," said Pippi. "This is a tiny little auntie who lives on the third floor at the other end of the town."

She said that only because she wanted to have a little fun with the policemen, but they didn't think it was funny at all.

They said she shouldn't be such a smarty. And then they went on to tell her that some nice people in the town were arranging for her to get into a children's home.

"I already have a place in a children's home," said Pippi.

"What?" asked one of the policemen. "Has it been arranged already then? What children's home?"

"This one," said Pippi haughtily. "I am a child and this is my home; therefore it is a children's home, and I have room enough here, plenty of room."

"Dear child," said the policeman, smiling, "you don't under-stand. You must get into a real children's home and have some-one look after you."

"Is one allowed to bring horses to your children's home?" asked Pippi.

"No, of course not," said the policeman.

"That's what I thought," said Pippi sadly. "Well, what about monkeys?"

"Of course not. You ought to realize that."

"Well then," said Pippi, "you'll have to get kids for your chil-dren's home somewhere else. I certainly don't intend to move there."

"But don't you understand that you must go to school?"

"Why?"

"To learn things, of course."

"What sort of things?" asked Pippi.

"All sorts," said the policeman. "Lots of useful things—the multiplication tables, for instance."

"I have got along fine without any pluttifikation tables for nine years," said Pippi, "and I guess I'll get along without it from now on, too."

"Yes, but just think how embarrassing it will be for you to be so ignorant. Imagine when you grow up and somebody asks you what the capital of Portugal is, and you can't answer!"

"Oh, I can answer all right," said Pippi. "I'll answer like this: 'If you are so bound and determined to find out what the capital of Portugal is, then, for goodness' sakes, write directly to Portugal and ask.'"

"Yes, but don't you think that you would be sorry not to know it yourself?"

"Oh, probably," said Pippi. "No doubt I should lie awake nights and wonder and wonder, 'What in the world is the capital of Portugal?' But one can't be having fun all the time," she continued, bending over and standing on her hands for a change. "For that matter, I've been in Lisbon with my papa," she added, still standing upside down, for she could talk that way too.

But then one of the policemen said that Pippi certainly didn't need to think she could do just as she pleased. She must come to the children's home, and immediately. He went up to her and took hold of her arm, but Pippi freed herself quickly, touched him lightly, and said, "Tag!" Before he could wink an eye she had climbed up on the porch railing and from there onto the balcony above the porch. The policemen couldn't quite see themselves getting up the same way, and so they rushed into the house and up the stairs, but by the time they had reached the balcony Pippi was halfway up the roof. She climbed up the shingles almost as if she were a little monkey herself. In a moment she was up on the ridgepole and from there jumped easily to the chimney. Down on the balcony stood the two policemen, scratching their heads, and on the lawn stood Tommy and Annika, staring at Pippi.

"Isn't it fun to play tag?" cried Pippi. "And weren't you nice to come over. It certainly *is* my lucky day today too."

When the policemen had stood there a while wondering what to do, they went and got a ladder, leaned it against one of the gables of the house and then climbed up, first one policeman and then the other, to get Pippi down. They looked a little scared when they climbed out on the ridgepole and, carefully balancing themselves, went step by step, toward Pippi.

"Don't be scared," cried Pippi. "There's nothing to be afraid of. It's just fun."

When the policemen were a few steps away from Pippi, down she jumped from the chimney and, screeching and laughing, ran along the ridgepole to the opposite gable. A few feet from the house stood a tree.

"Now I'm going to dive," she cried and jumped right down into the green crown of the tree, caught fast hold of a branch, swung back and forth a while, and then let herself fall to the ground. Quick as a wink she dashed around to the other side of the house and took away the ladder.

The policemen had looked a little foolish when Pippi jumped, but they looked even more so when they had balanced themselves backward along the ridgepole and were about to climb down the ladder. At first they were very angry at Pippi, who stood on the ground looking up at them, and they told her in no uncertain terms to get the ladder and be quick about it, or she would soon get something she wasn't looking for.

"Why are you so cross at me?" asked Pippi reproachfully. "We're just playing tag, aren't we?"

The policemen thought a while, and at last one of them said, "Oh, come on, won't you be a good girl and put the ladder back so that we can get down?"

"Of course I will," said Pippi and put the ladder back instantly. "And when you get down we can all drink coffee and have a happy time."

But the policemen were certainly tricky, because the minute they were down on the ground again they pounced on Pippi and cried, "Now you'll get it, you little brat!"

"Oh, no, I'm sorry. I haven't time to play any longer," said Pippi. "But it was fun."

Then she took hold of the policemen by their belts and carried them down the garden path, out through the gate, and onto the street. There she set them down, and it was quite some time before they were ready to get up again.

"Wait a minute," she cried and ran into the kitchen and came

back with two cooky hearts. "Would you like a taste?" she asked. "It doesn't matter that they are a little burned, does it?"

Then she went back to Tommy and Annika, who stood there wide-eyed and just couldn't get over what they had seen. And the policemen hurried back to the town and told all the ladies and gentlemen that Pippi wasn't quite fit for an orphanage. (They didn't tell that they had been up on the roof.) And the ladies and gentlemen decided that it would be best after all to let Pippi remain in Villa Villekulla, and if she wanted to go to school she could make the arrangements herself.

But Pippi and Tommy and Annika had a very pleasant afternoon. They went back to their interrupted coffee party. Pippi stuffed herself with fourteen cookies and then she said, "They weren't what I mean by real policemen. No sirree! Altogether too much talk about children's home and pluttifikation and Lisbon."

Afterward she lifted the horse down on the ground and they rode on him, all three. At first Annika was afraid and didn't want to, but when she saw what fun Tommy and Pippi were having, she let Pippi lift her up on the horse's back. The horse trotted round and round in the garden, and Tommy sang, "Here come the Swedes with a clang and a bang."

When Tommy and Annika had gone to bed that night Tommy said, "Annika, don't you think it's good that Pippi moved here?"

"Oh, yes," said Annika.

"I don't even remember what we used to play before she came, do you?"

"Oh, sure, we played croquet and things like that," said Annika. "But it's lots more fun with Pippi around, I think. And with horses and things."

The Talking Cat

NATALIE SAVAGE CARLSON

Once in another time, my friends, a great change came into Tante Odette's life although she was already an old woman who thought she had finished with such nonsense as changing one's habits.

It all happened because of a great change that came over Chouchou. The gray cat was a good companion because he seemed quite content to live on bread crusts and cabbage soup. Tante Odette kept a pot of soup boiling on the back of the stove. She added a little more water and a few more cabbage leaves to it each day. In this way, she always had soup on hand and she never had to throw any of it away.

She baked her own bread in her outdoor oven once a week, on Tuesday. If the bread grew stale by Saturday or Sunday, she softened it in the cabbage soup. So nothing was wasted.

As Tante Odette worked at her loom every evening, Chouchou would lie on the little rug by the stove and steadily stare at her with his big green eyes.

"If only you could talk," Tante Odette would say, "what company you would be for me."

One fall evening, Tante Odette was busy at her loom. Her stubby fingers flew among the threads like pigeons. Thump, thump went the loom.

Suddenly there was a thump, thump that didn't come from the loom. It came from the door.

The old woman took the lamp from the low table and went to the door. She opened it slowly. The light from the lamp shone on a queer old man who had the unmistakable look of the woods.

He wore a bright red sash around his waist and a black crow feather in his woolen cap. He had a bushy moustache like a homemade broom and a brown crinkled face.

"Pierre Leblanc at your service," said the old man, making a deep bow.

"What do you want?" asked Tante Odette sharply. "I can't stand here all night with the door open. It wastes heat and firewood."

"I seek shelter and work," answered Pierre Leblanc. "I am getting too old to trap for furs or work in the lumber camps. I would like a job on just such a cozy little place as this."

"I don't need any help," snapped Tante Odette. "I am quite able to do everything by myself. And I have my cat."

She was beginning to close the door, but the man put his gnarled hand against it. He was staring at Chouchou.

"A very smart cat he looks to be," he said. "Why don't you ask him if you should take me in? After all, you need pay me nothing but a roof over my head and a little food."

Tante Odette's eyes grew bigger.

"How ridiculous!" she said. "A cat can't talk. I only wish—"

To her great surprise, Chouchou started to talk.

"Oh, indeed I can," he told her, "if the matter is important enough. This Pierre Leblanc looks to me like a very fine man and a good worker. You should take him in."

Tante Odette stood with her mouth open for two minutes before she could make any sound come out of it. At last she said, "Then come in. It is so rare for a cat to be able to talk that I'm sure one should listen to him when he does."

The old man walked close to the stove and stretched his fingers toward it. He looked at the pot of soup bubbling on the back. Chouchou spoke again.

"Pierre looks hungry," he said. "Offer him some soup—a big, deep bowl of it."

"Oh, dear," sighed Tante Odette, "at this rate, our soup won't last out the week. But if you say so, Chouchou."

Pierre sat at the wooden table and gulped down the soup like a starved wolf. When he had finished, Tante Odette pointed to

the loft where he would sleep. Then she took the big gray cat on her lap.

"This is a most amazing thing that you should begin talking after all these years. Whatever came over you?"

But Chouchou had nothing more to say. He covered his nose with the tip of his tail, and there was not another word out of him all night.

Tante Odette decided that the cat's advice had been good. No longer did she have to go to the barn and feed the beasts. And no more skunks crawled into her oven because Pierre saw to it that the door was kept closed. He was indeed a good worker. He seemed quite satisfied with his bed in the loft and his bowls of cabbage soup and chunks of bread.

Only Chouchou seemed to have grown dissatisfied since his arrival.

"Why do you feed Pierre nothing but cabbage soup and bread?" he asked one day. "A workingman needs more food than that. How about some headcheese and pork pie?"

Tante Odette was startled, but Pierre went on drinking his soup.

"But meat is scarce and costs money," she told the cat.

"Pouf!" said the cat. "It is well worth it. Even I am getting a little tired of cabbage soup. A nice pork pie for dinner tomorrow would fill all the empty cracks inside me."

So when Pierre went out to the barn to water the beasts, Tante Odette stealthily lifted the lid of the chest, fished out a torn woolen sock and pulled a few coins out of it. She jumped in surprise when she raised her head and saw Pierre standing in the open doorway watching her.

"I forgot the pail," said Pierre. "I will draw some water from the well while I am about it."

The old woman hastily dropped the lid of the chest and got the pail from behind the stove.

"After Pierre has done his chores," said Chouchou, "he will be glad to go to the store and buy the meat for you."

Tante Odette frowned at the cat.

"But I am the thriftiest shopper in the parish," she said. "I can bring old Henri Dupuis down a few pennies on everything I buy."

"Pierre is a good shopper, too," said Chouchou. "In all Canada, there is not a better judge of meat. Perhaps he will even see something that you would not have thought to buy. Send him to the store."

It turned out that the old man was just as good a shopper as Chouchou had said. He returned from the village with a pinkish piece of pork, a freshly dressed pig's head, a bag of candy and some tobacco for himself.

"But my money," said Tante Odette. "Did you spend all of it?"

"What is money for but to spend?" asked Chouchou from his rug by the stove. "Can you eat money or smoke it in a pipe?"

"No," said Tante Odette.

"Can you put it over your shoulders to keep you warm?"

"No."

"Would it burn in the stove to cook your food?"

"Oh, no, indeed!"

Chouchou closed his eyes.

"Then what good is money?" he asked. "The sooner one gets rid of it, the better."

Tante Odette's troubled face smoothed.

"I never saw it that way before," she agreed. "Of course, you are right, Chouchou. And you are right, too, Pierre, for choosing such fine food."

But when Pierre went out to get a cabbage from the shed, Tante Odette walked to the chest again and counted her coins.

"I have a small fortune, Chouchou," she said. "Now explain to me again why these coins are no good."

But Chouchou had nothing more to say about the matter.

One Tuesday when Pierre Leblanc was cutting trees in the woods and Tante Odette was baking her loaves of bread in the outdoor oven, a stranger came galloping down the road on a one-eyed horse. He stopped in front of the white fence. He politely dismounted and went over to Tante Odette.

The old woman saw at a glance that he was a man of the woods. His blouse was checked and his cap red. Matching it was the red sash tied around his waist. He looked very much like Pierre Leblanc.

"Can you tell me, madame," he asked, "if a man named Pierre Leblanc works here?"

"Yes, he does," answered Tante Odette, "and a very good worker he is."

The stranger did not look satisfied.

"Of course, Canada is full of Pierre Leblancs," he said. "It is a very common name. Does this Pierre Leblanc wear a red sash like mine?"

"So he does," said Tante Odette.

"On the other hand," said the man, "many Pierre Leblancs wear red sashes. Does he have a moustache like a homemade broom?"

"Yes, indeed," said the woman.

"But there must be many Pierre Leblancs with red sashes and moustaches like brooms," continued the stranger. "This Pierre Leblanc who now works for you, can he throw his voice?"

"Throw his voice!" cried Tante Odette. "What witchcraft is that?"

"Haven't you heard of such a gift?" asked the man. "But of course only a few have it—probably only one Pierre Leblanc in a thousand. This Pierre with you, can he throw his voice behind trees and in boxes and up on the roof so it sounds as if someone else is talking?"

"My faith, no!" cried the woman in horror. "I wouldn't have such a one in my house. He would be better company for the loup-garou [devil-wolf], that evil one who can change into many shapes."

The man laughed heartily.

"My Pierre Leblanc could catch the loup-garou in a wolf trap and lead him around by the chain. He is that clever. That is why I am trying to find him. I want him to go trapping with me in the woods this winter. One says that never have there been so many foxes. I need Pierre, for he is smarter than any fox."

The creak of wheels caused them both to turn around. Pierre Leblanc was driving the ox team in from the woods. He stared at the man standing beside Tante Odette. The man stared back at Pierre. Then both men began bouncing on their feet and whooping in their throats. They hugged each other. They kissed each other on the cheek.

"Good old Pierre!"

"Georges, my friend, where have you kept yourself all summer? How did you find me?"

Tante Odette left them whooping and hugging. She walked into the house with a worried look on her face. She sat down at her loom. Finally she stopped weaving and turned to Chouchou.

"I am a little dizzy, Chouchou," she said. "This *loup-garou* voice has upset me. What do you make of it all?"

Chouchou said nothing.

"Please tell me what to do," pleaded Tante Odette. "Shall we let him stay here? It would be very uncomfortable to have voices coming from the roof and the trees."

Chouchou said nothing.

"Is he maybe in league with the *loup-garou?*"

Chouchou said nothing. Tante Odette angrily threw the shuttle at him.

"Where is your tongue?" she demanded. "Have you no words for me when I need them most?"

But if a cat will not speak, who has got his tongue?

Pierre Leblanc came walking in.

"Such a man!" he roared gleefully. "Only the woods are big enough for him."

"Are you going away with him?" asked the woman, not knowing whether she wanted him to say "yes" or "no." If only Chouchou hadn't been so stubborn.

"That makes a problem," said Pierre. "If I go into the woods this winter, it will be cold and I will work like an ox. But there will be much money in my pocket after the furs are sold. If I stay here, I will be warm and comfortable but—"

He pulled his pockets inside out. Nothing fell from them.

"What is this business about your being able to throw your voice to other places?" asked Tante Odette.

"Did Georges say I could do that?"

Tante Odette nodded.

"Ha! Ha!" laughed Pierre. "What a joker Georges is!"

"But perhaps it is true," insisted the woman.

"If you really want to know," said Pierre, "ask Chouchou. He would not lie. Can I throw my voice, Chouchou?"

Chouchou sank down on his haunches and purred.

"Of course not!" he answered. "Whoever heard of such nonsense?"

Tante Odette sighed in relief. Then she remembered that this did not fix everything.

"Will you go with him?" she asked Pierre. "I have made it very comfortable for you here. And now it is only for supper that we have cabbage soup."

Chouchou spoke up.

"Tante Odette, how can you expect such a good man as Pierre Leblanc to work for only food and shelter? If you would pay him a coin from time to time, he would be quite satisfied to stay."

"But I can't afford that," said the woman.

"Of course you can," insisted Chouchou. "You have a small fortune in the old sock in your chest. Remember what I told you about money?"

"Tell me again," said Tante Odette. "It is hard to hold on to such a thought for long."

"Money is to spend," repeated the cat. "Can it carry hay and water to the beasts? Can it cut down trees for firewood? Can it dig paths through the snow when winter comes?"

"I have caught it again," said Tante Odette. "If you will stay with me, Pierre, I will pay you a coin from time to time."

Pierre smiled and bowed.

"Then I shall be very happy to stay here with you and your wise cat," he decided. "Now I will unload my wood and pile it into a neat stack by the door."

He briskly stamped out. Tante Odette sat down at her loom again.

"We have made a good bargain, haven't we, Chouchou?" She smiled contentedly.

But Chouchou tickled his nose with his tail and said nothing.

That is the way it was, my friends. It would have been a different story if Pierre had not been such a good worker. So remember this: If you must follow the advice of a talking cat, be sure you know who is doing the talking for him.

Young Sammy Watkins

AUTHOR UNKNOWN

Young Sammy Watkins jumped out of bed;
He ran to his sister and cut off her head.
This gave his dear mother a great deal of pain;
She hopes that he never will do it again.

A Penrod Story:
The New Pup

BOOTH TARKINGTON

I

On a Friday in April, Penrod Schofield, having returned from school at noon promptly, on account of an earnest appetite, found lunch considerably delayed and himself (after a bit of simple technique) alone in the pantry with a large, open, metal receptacle containing about two-thirds of a peck of perfect doughnuts just come into the world.

The history of catastrophe is merely the history of irresistible juxtapositions. When Penrod left the pantry he walked slowly. In the large metal receptacle were left a small number of untouched doughnuts; while upon the shelf beside it were two further doughnuts, each with a small bite experimentally removed—and one of these bites, itself, lay, little mangled, beside the parent doughnut.

Nothing having been discovered, he seated himself gently at the lunch-table, and, making no attempt to take part in the family conversation, avoided rather than sought attention. This decorum on his part was so unusual as to be the means of defeating its object, for his mother and father and Margaret naturally began to stare at him. Nevertheless, his presence continued to be unobtrusive and his manner preoccupied. Rallied by Margaret, he offered for reply only a smile, faint, courteous and strange, followed, upon further badinage, by an almost imperceptible shake of the head, which he seemed to fear might come off if more decisively agitated.

"But, Penrod dear," his mother insisted, "you must eat a little something or other."

For the sake of appearances, Penrod made a terrible effort to eat a little something or other.

When they had got him to his bed, he said, with what resentful strength remained to him, that it was all the fault of his mother, and she was indeed convinced that her insistence had been a mistake. For several hours the consequences continued to be more or less demonstrative; then they verged from physical to mental, as the thoughts of Penrod and the thoughts of his insides merged into one. Their decision was unanimous—a conclusive horror of doughnuts. Throughout ghastly durations of time there was no thought possible to him but the intolerable thought

of doughnuts. There was no past but doughnuts; there was no future but doughnuts. He descended into the bottommost pit of an abyss of doughnuts; he lay suffocating in a universe of doughnuts. He looked back over his dreadful life to that time, before lunch, when he had been alone with the doughnuts in the pantry, and it seemed to him that he must have been out of his mind.

How could he have endured even the noxious smell of the things? It was incredible to him that any human being could ever become hardy enough to bear the mere sight of a doughnut.

Not until the next morning did Penrod Schofield quit his bed and come out into the fair ways of mankind again, and then his step was cautious; there was upon his brow the trace of an experience. For a little while after his emergence to the air he had the look of one who has discovered something alarming in the pleasant places of life, the look of one who has found a scorpion hiding under a violet. He went out into the yard through the front door, and, even with his eyes, avoided the kitchen.

"Yay, Penrod!" a shout greeted him. "Look! Looky here! Look what *I* got!"

Upon the sidewalk was Sam Williams in a state of unmistakable elation. His right hand grasped one end of a taut piece of clothesline; the other end had been tied round the neck of a pup; but, owing to the pup's reluctance, the makeshift collar was now just behind his ears, so that his brow was furrowed, his throat elongated and his head horizontal. As a matter of fact, he was sitting down; nevertheless, Sam evidently held that the pup was being led.

"This good ole dog o' mine not so easy to *lead*, I can tell you!"

These were Sam's words, in spite of the pup's seated attitude. On the other hand, to support the use of "lead," the pup was certainly moving along at a fair rate of speed. In regard to his state of mind, any beholder must have hesitated between two guesses: his expression denoted either resignation or profound obstinacy, and, by maintaining silence throughout what could not possibly have been other than a spiritual and bodily trial, he produced an impression of reserve altogether deceptive. There do exist reserved pups, of course; but this was not one of them.

Sam brought him into the yard. "How's *that* for high, Penrod?" he cried.

Penrod forgot doughnuts temporarily. "Where'd you get him?" he asked. "Where'd you get that fellow, Sam?"

"Yay!" shouted Master Williams. "He belongs to me."

"Where'd you *get* him? Didn't you hear me?"

"You just look him over," Sam said importantly. "Take a good ole look at him and see what you got to say. He's a full-blooded dog, all right! You just look this good ole dog over."

With warm interest, Penrod complied. He looked the good ole dog over. The pup, released from the stress of the rope, lay placidly upon the grass. He was tan-colored over most of him, though interspersed with black; and the fact that he had nearly attained his adolescence was demonstrated by the cumbersomeness of his feet and the half-knowing look of his eye. He was large; already he was much taller and heavier than Duke.

"How do you know he's full-blooded?" asked Penrod cautiously, before expressing any opinion.

"My goodness!" Sam exclaimed. "Can't you look at him? Don't you know a full-blooded dog when you see one?"

Penrod frowned. "Well, who told you he was?"

"John Carmichael."

"Who's John Carmichael?"

"He's the man works on my uncle's farm. John Carmichael owns the mother o' this dog here; and he said he took a fancy to me and he was goin' to give me this dog's mother and all the other pups besides this one, too, only my fam'ly wouldn't let me. John says they were all pretty full-blooded, except the runt; but this one was the best. This one is the most full-blooded of the whole kitamaboodle."

For the moment Penrod's attention was distracted from the pup. "Of the whole what?" he inquired.

"Of the whole kitamaboodle," Sam repeated carelessly.

"Oh," said Penrod, and he again considered the pup. "I bet he isn't as full-blooded as Duke. I bet he isn't anywhere *near* as full-blooded as Duke."

Sam hooted. "Duke!" he cried. "Why, I bet Duke isn't a *quarter* full-blooded! I bet Duke hasn't got any full blood in him at all! All you'd haf to do'd be look at Duke and this dog together; then you'd see in a minute. I bet you, when this dog grows up, he could whip Duke four times out o' five. I bet he could whip Duke now, only pups won't fight. All I ast is, you go get Duke and just *look* which is the most full-blooded."

"All right," said Penrod. "I'll get him, and I guess maybe you'll have sense enough to see yourself which is: Duke's got more full blood in his hind feet than that dog's got all over him."

He departed hotly, calling and whistling for his own, and Duke, roused from a nap on the back porch, loyally obeyed the summons. A moment or two later, he made his appearance, following his master to the front yard, where Sam and the new pup were waiting. However, upon his first sight of this conjuncture, Duke paused at the corner of the house, then quietly turned to withdraw. Penrod was obliged to take him by the collar.

"Well, *now* you're satisfied, I guess!" said Sam Williams, when Penrod had dragged Duke to a spot about five feet from the pup. "I expect you can tell which is the full-bloodedest now, can't you?"

"Yes; I guess I can!" Penrod retorted. "Look at that ole cur beside good ole Dukie, and anybody can see he isn't full-blooded a-*tall!*"

"He isn't?" Sam cried indignantly, and, as a conclusive test, he gathered in both hands a large, apparently unoccupied area of the pup's back, lifting it and displaying it proudly, much as a clerk shows goods upon a counter. "Look at that!" he shouted. "Look how loose his hide is! You never saw a looser-hided dog in your life, and you can't any more do that with Duke'n you could with a potato-bug! Just try it once; that's all I ast."

"That's nothing. Any pup can do that. When Duke was a pup——"

"Just try it once, I said. That's all I ast."

"I got a right to talk, haven't I?" Penrod demanded bitterly. "I guess this is my own father's yard, and I got a ri——"

"Just try it, once," Sam repeated, perhaps a little irritatingly. "That's all I ast."

"My goodness HEAVENS!" Penrod bellowed. "I never heard such a crazy racket as you're makin'! Haven't you got enough sense to——"

"Just try it once. That's all I——"

"Dry UP!" Penrod was furious.

Sam relapsed into indignant silence. Penrod similarly relapsed. Each felt that the other knew nothing whatever about full-blooded dogs.

"Well," Sam said finally, "what you want to keep aholt o' Duke for? My dog ain't goin' to hurt him."

"I guess not! You said yourself he couldn't fight."

"I did not! I said no pup will——"

"All right then," said Penrod. "I was only holdin' him to keep him from chewin' up that poor cur. Better let him loose so's he can get away if good ole Dukie takes after him."

"Let's let 'em both loose," Sam said, forgetting animosity. "Let's see what they'll do."

"All right," Penrod, likewise suddenly amiable, agreed. "I expeck they kind of like each other, anyways."

Released, both animals shook themselves. Then Duke approached the pup and sniffed carelessly and without much interest at the back of his neck. Duke was so bored by the information thus obtained that he yawned and once more made evident his intention to retire to the backyard. The new pup, however, after having presented up to this moment an appearance uninterruptedly lethargic, suddenly took it into his head to play the jolly rogue. At a pup's gallop, he proceeded to a point directly in Duke's line of march, and halted. Then he placed his muzzle flat upon the ground between his widespread paws and showed the whites of his eyes in a waggish manner. Duke also halted, confronting the joker and emitting low sounds of warning and detestation.

Then, for the sake of peace, he decided to go round the house the other way; in fact, he was in the act of turning to do so when the pup rushed upon him and frolicsomely upset him. Thereupon, Duke swore, cursing all the pups in the world and claiming blasphemously to be a dangerous person whom it were safer not again to jostle. For a moment, the pup was startled by the elderly dog's intensive oratory; then he decided that Duke was joking, too, and returned to his clowning. Again and again he charged ponderously upon, into and over Duke, whose words and actions now grew wild indeed. But he was helpless. The pup's humor expressed itself in a fever of physical badinage, and Duke no sooner rose than he was upset again. When he lay upon his back, raving and snapping, the disregardful pup's large feet would flop weightily upon the pit of his stomach or upon his very face with

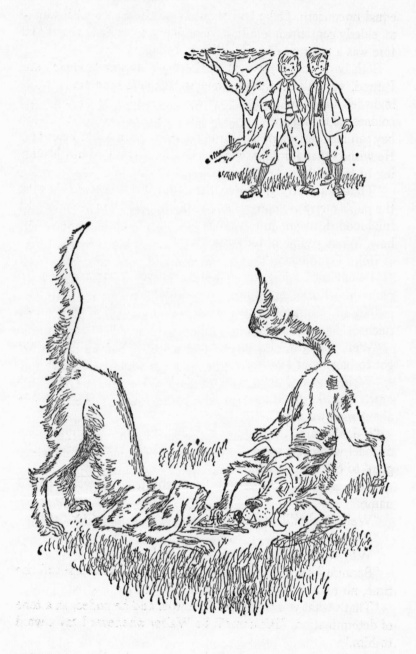

equal unconcern. Duke had about as much chance with him as an elderly gentleman would have with a jocular horse. Never before was a creature of settled life so badgered.

Both boys were captivated by the pup's display of gaiety, and Penrod, naturally prejudiced against the blithe animal, unwillingly felt his heart warming. It was impossible to preserve any coldness of feeling toward so engaging a creature, and, besides, no boy can long resist a pup. Penrod began to yearn toward this one. He wished that John Carmichael had worked on a farm belonging to *his* uncle.

"That *is* a pretty good dog, Sam," he said, his eyes following the pup's merry violence. "I guess you're right—he's proba'ly *part* full-blooded, maybe not as much as Duke, but a good deal, anyhow. What you goin' to name him?"

"John Carmichael."

"I wouldn't," said Penrod. "I'd name him sumpthing nice. I'd name him Frank, or Walter or sumpthing."

"No, sir," Sam said firmly. "I'm goin' to name him John Carmichael. I told John Carmichael I would."

"Well, all right," Penrod returned, a little peevishly. "Always got to have your own way!"

"Well, haven't I got a right to?" Sam inquired, with justifiable heat. "I'd like to know why I oughtn't to have my own way about my own dog!"

"I don't care," said Penrod. "You can call him John Carmichael when you speak to him; but, when *I* speak to him, I'm goin' to call him Walter."

"You can if you want to," Sam returned. "It won't be his name."

"Well, Walter'll be his name long as I'm talkin' to him."

"It won't, either!"

"Why won't it? Just answer me, why."

"Because," said Sam, "his name'll be John Carmichael all the time, no matter who's talkin' to him."

"That's what you think," said Penrod, and he added, in a tone of determination, "His name'll be Walter whenever I say a word to him."

Sam began to wear a baffled expression, for the controversy

was unusual and confusing. "It won't," he said. "Do you s'pose
Duke's name'd be Walter, if you called him Walter while you
were talkin' to him, and then change back to Duke the rest o'
the time when you aren't talkin' to him?"

"What?"

"I said—well, suppose Duke's name was Walter"—Sam paused,
finding himself unable to recall the details of the argumentative
illustration he had offered.

"What's all that stuff you were talkin' about?" Penrod insisted.

"His name's John Carmichael," Sam said curtly. "Hyuh,
John!"

"Hyuh, Walter!" cried Penrod.

"Hyuh, John! Hyuh, John Carmichael!"

"Hyuh, Walter, Walter! *Come* here, good ole Walter, Walter,
Walter!"

"Hyuh, John! *Good* ole Johnny!"

The pup paid no attention to either of the rival godfathers, but
continued to clown it over Duke, whose mood was beginning to
change. His bad temper had exhausted itself, and, little by little,
the pup's antics began to stir the elderly dog's memory of his
own puphood. He remembered the glad unconventionality, the
long days of irresponsible romping, and he wished that he might
live those days again. By imperceptible degrees, his indignation
diminished; he grew milder and milder until, finally, he found
himself actually collaborating in the pup's hoydenish assaults.
Duke's tone of voice became whimsical; he lay upon his back
and pretended to swear and snap; but the swearing and snapping
were now burlesque and meant to be understood as such. Duke
ended by taking a decided fancy to Walter-John Carmichael.

The moral influence of dogs upon one another is profound—a
matter seldom estimated at its value. People are often mystified
by a change of character in a known and tried dog; they should
seek to discover with whom he has been associating himself.
Sometimes the change in a dog's character is permanent; sometimes it is merely temporary. In the latter case, when the animal
returns to his former habit of mind, it is usually a sign that the
source of influence has vanished—the other dog has moved away.
Or it may be merely that the influenced dog has concluded that

his new manner does not pay. One thing, however, is certain: When a dog goes wrong late in life, it is almost invariably due to the influence and example of some other dog—usually a younger one, odd as that may seem.

Walter-John Carmichael proved his light-headedness by forgetting Duke abruptly and galloping off after a sparrow that had flown near the ground. The sparrow betook himself to the limb of a tree, while the pup continued to career and zigzag over the grass in the lunatic belief that he was still chasing the sparrow. Duke thereupon scampered upon an imaginary track, shaped like a large figure eight, and then made a jovial rush at Walter-John, bowling him over and over. Finding that the thing could be done, Duke knocked Walter-John over as often as the latter rose to his feet. Duke had caught the infection of youth; he had been lifted out of himself by Walter-John's simple happiness, and the little old dog was in great spirits. Of course, he did not weigh the question of his conduct carefully; later events proved that he acted on the spur of emotion and paused neither to reason nor to estimate consequences. His promptings were, indeed, physical rather than mental—simply, he felt like a pup once more and in all things behaved like one.

Meanwhile, the two boys sat upon the grass and watched the friendly battle. "I'm goin' to train John to be a trick dog," Sam said.

"What you goin' to train him?"

"Oh, like dogs in the dog show," Sam replied, with careless ease. "I'm goin' to make him do all those tricks."

"Yes, you are!"

"I am, too!"

"Well, *how* are you?" asked the skeptical Penrod. "How you goin' to train him?"

"Lots o' ways."

"Well, what are they?"

"Why, it's the easiest thing in the world to train a pup," said Sam. "Take an ole dog like Duke, and 'course you can't train him. First thing I'm goin' to train John is to catch a ball when I throw it to him."

"You mean catch it in his mouth the same as a baseball player does with his hands?"

"Yes, sir!"

Penrod laughed scornfully.

"You wait and see!" Sam cried.

"Well, how are you goin' to? Just answer me that!"

"You'll *see* how."

"Well, why can't you answer how you're goin' to do so much? Just answer me that; that's all I——"

"Well, I'll tell you how," Sam began, speaking thoughtfully.

"Well, why'n't you *tell* me, then, instead o' talkin' so mu——"

"How can *I*, when you won't let me? You talk yourself all the ti——"

"You don't *know* how! That's the reason you talk so much," Penrod asserted. "You couldn't any more teach a dog to catch a ball than——"

"I could, too! I'd put sumpthing on it."

Penrod's loud laugh was again scornful. " 'Put sumpthing on it!' " he mocked. "*That'd* teach a dog to catch a ball, wouldn't it? What you goin' to put on it? Tar? So it'd stick in his mouth?" And overcome by the humor of this satire, Penrod rolled in the grass, shouting derisively.

Not at all disconcerted, his friend explained: "No; I wouldn't put any ole tar on it. I'd take a ball and rub sumpthing that tastes good to him on the ball."

"What for?"

"Then I'd throw it to him, and he'd catch it just like he would a piece o' beefsteak. Haven't you ever seen a dog catch meat?"

Penrod's laughter ceased; the idea fascinated him at once. "Look here, Sam," he said. "Let's teach both our dogs to do that. Let's go round to the barn and start gettin' 'em all trained up so's we can have a dog show."

"*That's* the ticket!" cried Sam.

Within five minutes, the unfortunate Duke and Walter-John, interrupted in their gambols, were beginning to undergo a course of instruction. The two trainers agreed to avoid all harshness; the new method of teaching by attractive deceptions was to be followed throughout the course, and, for a while, they were consistently persuasive and diplomatic. Penrod brought a bit of raw meat and a solid-rubber ball from the house. The meat was rubbed on the ball, which was then presented to the two dogs for inspection and sniffing. Both took some interest in it, and Duke licked it casually.

The ball was tossed first to Duke, who moved aside and would have taken his unobtrusive departure had he not been detained. Next, Sam tossed the ball to Walter-John, who, without budging, placidly watched its approach through the air, and yet seemed surprised and troubled when it concluded its flight upon his right eye. Meat was freshly rubbed upon the ball and the experiment repeated again and again, so that after a little experience Walter-John learned to watch the ball and to move as soon as he saw it coming toward him. After half an hour, he was almost as able to dodge as Duke.

It may not be denied that by this the trainers were irritated. Their theory was so plausible—it had sounded so simple, so in-evitable—that the illogical conduct of the two dogs could not fail to get more and more upon the theorists' nerves. Naturally, then, in spite of all agreements never to resort to harshness, there were times when, instead of tossing, Penrod threw the ball to Duke, and Sam to Walter-John. In fact, to an observer who had no knowledge of dog-training, the instruction finally might have seemed to be a contest in accuracy between the two trainers, especially as they had found it necessary to tie both Walter-John and Duke rather closely to the stable wall. Indeed, that was the view of the matter ignorantly taken by Della.

"I niver see th' beat!" she exclaimed, coming out upon the back porch from the kitchen. "Chainin' thim two poor dogs ag'inst the wall and throwin' big rocks at 'em to see which can hit 'em the most times and——"

"Rocks!" Penrod interrupted angrily. "Who's throwin' rocks? You tell me who's throwin' any rocks!"

"I'll tell you to come to lunch," Della retorted. "And Mrs. Wil-liams has been telephonin' a quawter'v an hour. They're waitin' lunch at the Williamses; so you let thim two poor dogs go—if they still got the strenk to walk. Are you comin' to yer lunch, Musther Penrod, or not? Come in and try to eat like a human person and not like a rhinoceros the way you did yesterday, and you know what you got fer it, too—I'm glad, praise hiven!" She returned into the house, slamming the door.

"What's she mean, Penrod?" Sam inquired, as he released Walter-John from the wall. "What did you get for what, that she says she was so glad about?"

"Nothin'," said Penrod, though his expression had become momentarily unpleasant. "Those Irish always got to be sayin' sumpthing or other."

"Yey," Sam agreed. "Let's go ahead and train our dogs some more this afternoon. You bring Duke over to our yard, Penrod, and let's get started early."

II

Penrod assented, and, at a little after one o'clock, the training began again in the Williams's yard. Duke and Walter-John passed two hours comparable to hours human beings pass at the dentist's, and both the trainers gradually became hoarse, though they still maintained that their method continued to be humane and persuasive. Experiments with the ball were finally postponed to another day, as both dogs persisted in their dodging and each refused to grasp the idea of a ball's purpose—even when it was forcibly placed in his mouth and held there for minutes at a time.

Duke had long ago mastered the art of "sitting-up," and to-day, upon command, he "sat up" till he was ready to drop, while Walter-John was held up in a similar position and bidden to learn from the example of Duke, but would not even look at him. No progress being perceptible in this, a barrel-hoop was procured, and one trainer held the hoop, while the other accustomed the dogs to passing through it. Patiently, until his back ached, Penrod again and again threw Duke and the cumbersome Walter-John in turn through the hoop; then held it while Sam manipulated the dogs.

"Now I expeck they unnerstand what we want 'em to do," said Sam, at last, straightening up with a gasp. "Anyways, they cert'nly ought to!"

"Jump, Dukie!" Penrod urged. "Jump through the hoop just
like you been doin'! *Come* on, old Dukie—*jump!*"

Again the patience of the instructors was strained. Both Duke
and Walter-John could be coaxed to pass under the hoop or
upon either side of it; but each refused to pass through it of his
free will. Manifestly, they had, for inexplicable reasons, conceived
a prejudice against hoop-jumping, and nothing served to remove
their aversion.

"I'll tell you what we can train 'em," Penrod suggested, after a
long pause of discouragement. "We can train 'em to walk the
tight-rope. We could do that, anyway!"

After the setbacks received in processes apparently so much
simpler (especially for dogs) than tight-rope walking, Penrod's
proposal naturally produced a feeling of surprise in Sam. "What
on earth you talkin' about now?"

"Why, look!" said Penrod. "Listen, Sam—you listen here a
minute! We can teach 'em to walk the tight-rope *easy!* it won't
be anything at all, the way I got fixed up to do it. *Then* just look
where we'll be, when our good ole dogs get so's all we got to do'll
just be to say, 'Hyuh, Dukie, jump up on that clo'esline and walk
it!' And then you can say, 'Hyuh, Walter, jump up——'"

"I wouldn't, neither!" Sam interrupted. "His name's John!"

"Well, anyway," Penrod continued evasively, "you could tell
him to jump up on a clo'esline and walk it just like Duke, and
he'd do it. *Oh, oh!*" Penrod's eyes sparkled; he gesticulated joy-
ously—to his mind, the gorgeous performance was already taking place. "*Oh, oh!* That wouldn't be any good ole show—I guess
not! Why, we could charge a *dollar* for anybody to come in! *Oh,
oh!* Laydeez and gentlemun, the big show is about to commence!
Get up on that tight-rope now, you good ole Duke! Laydeez
and gentlemun, you now see before your very eyes the only two
tight-rope-walking dogs ever trained to——"

"Well, can't you wait a minute?" Sam cried. "I'd like to know
how we're goin' to train 'em to walk any tight-rope when they
don't show any more sense'n they did about that hoop and
catchin' a ball and——"

"*Listen,* I told you, didn't I?" said Penrod. "Look, Sam! First,
we'll train 'em to walk the fence-rail here in your yard. We'll

take one of 'em at a time and put him on the rail. Then one of us'll hold him from jumpin' off while the other pushes him along from behind so's he's got to keep goin'. Well, if he *can't* get off, and if he's *got* to keep goin'—so, well, if we do that enough, say so often a day for so many weeks—well, he can't *help* himself from learning how to walk a fence-rail, can he?"

"No. But how——"

"*Listen*—didn't I tell you? Well, when he's got that much good and learned, all we do is get a board half the size of the fence-rail and do the same thing with him on *it*—and then get another one half the size of that one, and so on till we get him trained to walk on a board that's just the same size as a rope. I'd like to know *then* if he couldn't walk just as well on a rope as on a board he couldn't tell the *difference* from a rope from."

"Well, I don't care," Sam said. "I bet it'll take pretty near forever."

"It would if we just sit around here and never do anything."

"Oh, I'm willing to give it a *try*," Sam said.

Sam's mother, coming out into the yard, half an hour later, preserved her composure, though given cause for abandoning it. Walter-John was seated upon the fence-rail but moving steadily. Sam distrained him from leaving the rail, while Penrod's two extended hands, applying serious and constant pressure at the base of Walter-John's spine, compelled Walter-John to progress along the fence-rail. Walter-John's expression was concerned and inquiring, and Duke, tied to a tree, near by, stood in an attitude of depression.

"Let the dogs go now, boys," Mrs. Williams called. "I've got something for you, and then Sam has to come in and get dressed to go and spend an hour or so at his grandmother's. It's after three o'clock."

"What you got for us?" Sam asked.

She displayed a plate covered with a napkin.

"*Oh*, oh!" Both boys trotted to Mrs. Williams.

"What's under that napkin?" cried the eager Sam.

"Look!" and she withdrew the napkin, while Sam shouted. "Doughnuts!"

He dashed at them; but his mother fended him off. "Wait,

Sam!" she said. "Shame on you! See how polite Penrod is! *He* doesn't grab and——"

"That's only because he's company," Sam interrupted. "Gimme those doughnuts!"

"No," she said. "There are five apiece, and you'll divide evenly. Here, Penrod; you take your five first."

"Ma'am?" said Penrod, his face flushing painfully.

"Don't be bashful." Mrs. Williams laughed, and she extended the plate toward him. "You're Sam's guest and you must choose your five first."

Penrod was anxious to prevent his recent misfortune from becoming known, and he felt that to decline these doughnuts would arouse suspicion. Yet he was uncertain whether or not he could, with physical security, hold five doughnuts even in his hands.

"Hurry, Penrod! I know you want them."

At arm's length he took five doughnuts, two in one hand and three in the other. Then his arms fell at his sides, and he stood very straight, holding his head high and his nose to the clouds.

"There!" said Mrs. Williams, departing. "All right, Sammy! As soon as you've finished them, you must come to dress. Not more than ten minutes."

Sam carolled and capered with his doughnuts, stuffing his mouth full, so that he carolled no more, but capered still, in greater ecstasy. No pleasures of contemplation for Sam, or dwelling long and delicately upon morsels! What was sweet to his flesh he took, and consumed as he took. The five doughnuts sped to the interior almost *en masse*. Within four minutes there remained of them but impalpable tokens upon Sam's cheeks.

"Hah!" he shouted. "Those were *good!*" Then, his eye falling upon Penrod's drooping hands, "Well, for gray*shus* sakes!" he exclaimed. "Aren't you goin' to *eat* 'em?"

Penrod's voice was lifeless. He responded: "Well, some days I kind o' like to save mine up and eat 'em when I feel like it." He swallowed twice, coughed twice.

"I wish I'd saved mine," Sam said. "Come on, John, ole doggie!" he added, beginning to drag the pup toward the house.

"What you goin' to do with him?" Penrod asked.

"I'm goin' to lock him up in the cellar while I'm gone. That's where they said I could keep him."

"What for? Let me have him till you get back. I'll bring him over here before dinner time."

Sam thought this request outrageous. "No, sir!" he cried. "Haven't you got a dog o' your own? You want to go and get mine so's he knows you better'n he would me? I guess not! John Carmichael's goin' to stay right in our cellar every minute I'm not here to be trainin' him!"

"Oh, come on, Sam!" Penrod urged, for he had become more and more fascinated by Walter-John throughout the day. "It isn't goin' to *hurt* him any, is it?"

"I won't do it."

"Oh, come on, Sam! What's the use actin' that way to a poor dog—lockin' him up in a dark ole cellar when he ought to be out in the fresh air so's he could keep strong? He likes Duke, and he ought to be allowed to stay with him. I call it mighty mean, lockin' him up in that ole ugly cellar just because *you* want to go and have a good time at your grandmother's."

"I don't care what you call it; he's goin' to be locked up," Sam said. "And I don't either want to go and have a good time at my grandmother's. I *got* to go."

Whereupon, having thus uttered his final decision in the matter, and defended his character against the charge of selfishness, Sam towed Walter-John as far as the cellar door.

"Wait a minute, Sam," Penrod urged. "If you'll let me have him till you get back, I'll give you some o' these doughnuts."

"How many?"

"I'll give you," said Penrod, "the whole kitamaboodle!"

"Yay!"

Blithely the doughnuts passed from Penrod's hands to Sam's, and the end of the bit of clothesline from Sam's to Penrod's.

"Come on, Walter!" Penrod cried.

Though his utterance was already thick, Sam protested instantly. "Stop that!" he commanded. "His name's John Carmichael, and you got to call him John. You can't have him if you're going to call him Walter."

Penrod began to argue rather bitterly. "My goodness, gracious heavens! He's just the same as *my* dog till you get back, isn't he?"

"He is not!"

"Didn't I just pay you for him? It's just the same as buyin' him till you get back from your grandmother's, and whatever time he's my dog, he's got to be named Walter. If you don't like it, you can give me back my doughnuts!"

"Oh, goodness!" Sam groaned. "Well, you got to quit callin' him Walter after today, anyways. The poor dog's got to learn his name *some* time."

Penrod, wearing an unassuming air of triumph, released Duke from the tree to which he had been tied, and, leading both dogs, proceeded toward the back gate; but before he went out into the alley Sam was amazed to see him pause at the hydrant and wash his hands exhaustively. Then Penrod opened the alley gate and passed from sight with his two charges, leaving Sam staring, open-mouthed.

Duke trotted obediently after his master; but Walter-John still misconceived the purposes of a leash and progressed for the most part in his seated or semi-seated attitude. However, Penrod reached his own yard—the front yard, away from the kitchen— without much difficulty, and paused there, regarding Walter-John with pleasure and affection.

He sat down on the grass, a dog under each arm. His imagination stepped quietly out of the present into the gold-clouded future. He saw himself in the filtered light of a great tent, addressing in a magnificent bass voice the fanning multitude.

"Laydeez and gentlemun, allow me to interdoos to your attainshon, the great tight-rope-walking dog, Walter!" And straightway, from the "Dressing-room tent," Walter-John came hopping on hind legs, white ruff about his neck. Then Penrod proclaimed: "And now, laydeez and gentlemun, let me interdoos to your attainshon, Walter's little boy, Duke, the greatest tight-rope dog on EARTH!" Whereupon, Duke, similarly hopping and similarly beruffed, came forward to the side of the ringmaster in the ring, and the three bowed low, to twenty-thousand plaudits. Anxious attendants in uniform ran to their posts to support the tight-rope, and Penrod, smiling negligently——

His bubble broke. The clatter of a brazen gong and a staccato of iron-shod hoofs—sounds increasing, coming nearer—startled him from the proud daydream. A hose-cart, then a fire-engine, then a hook-and-ladder wagon careened in turn round the corner, passed furiously and roared up the street, followed by panting boys with faces alight.

Penrod leaped to his feet. The stable was too far. He dragged Duke and Walter-John up the front steps and across the verandah; he tried the front door, found it unlocked, opened it, thrust Walter-John and Duke into the hall, slammed the door and made off to the fire.

In the cool hall, Duke and Walter-John looked at each other vaguely; then discovered that they were free. A frolicsome look bloomed upon the fertile face of Walter-John. With no motive, he dashed into a large room that opened from the hall, and knocked over a tall silver vase of lilies that somebody had set upon the floor directly in his way. Then he charged upon Duke, upset him, left him kicking at the air, and scampered to and fro for the love of motion. Duke was instantly infected; his puphood of the morning returned in full flood, and he, in his turn, charged upon Walter-John.

Both dogs had been through a great deal that day; in fact, their trainers had shown them a poor time, and nothing could have been more natural than that Duke and Walter-John should wish to liven things up after their protracted experience as apprentices in baseball, sitting-up, hoop-jumping and tight-rope-walking. They made it an orgy. The house was empty of human life, upstairs and down, as far as the kitchen door, which was closed. Walter-John and Duke engaged in mimic battle all over this empty house, and wherever there was anything that could be upset, they upset it, for Walter-John was undoubtedly cumbersome.

Exhausting for a time this pleasure, Walter-John found matter of interest on a low table in the library. This consisted of a new encyclopedia, limp-leather covers, gilt tops, thin paper, seven volumes, purchased by Mr. Schofield the week before. Walter-John dragged down two volumes, one labelled "Ala-Con," the other, "Mon-Pyx." Walter-John began to eat "Ala-Con," and Duke—all culture fallen from him now in his rejuvenation—Duke

began to eat "Mon-Pyx." That is, they did not eat except acci-
dentally, for neither of them actually swallowed much of the
paper; but the effect upon "Ala-Con" and "Mon-Pyx" was none
the less radical.

Growing tired of this learned work, they found some semi-
edible slippers in Margaret's room upstairs, also a table-cover—
which frightened Walter-John on account of the noise the things
made when he dragged the cover from the table. Next, he discovered, hanging in an open closet in the same room, a beady
substance that proved enjoyable. In this, as in everything, the
senile Duke joined him with gusto. The orgy continued.

Penrod found the fire an unusually satisfactory one. In fact, a
large warehouse, almost full of hides and leather, burned all up,
and dusk was falling when Penrod, smelling intensely, again
reached his place of residence. As he opened the gate, he saw
Duke coming round a corner of the house with a peculiar air.
There was something regretful and haunted about the little old
dog; he advanced hesitatingly, seeming to be without confidence,
and when Penrod spoke to him, he disappeared instantly. In the
darkness, his young master could not see where or even in which
direction he went. Suddenly a chill struck upon Penrod's spine.
He remembered. Where, oh, where, was Walter-John?

Penrod entered the front hall impetuously; but paused there at
once—and more cold chills touched his young spine. A sound of
lamentation—his mother's voice—came from the library, and evidently she was addressing Mr. Schofield.

"You never *saw* such a house! *Oh*, if I'd only followed my
instinct and not let Margaret persuade me to go to that reception
with her! We had Della give Duke a whipping, because he had a
shred of Margaret's best party dress sticking to his nose, and he
must have helped that horrible pup! Della threw lumps of coal
at *him* when she chased him out, and I do hope she hit him. It
seems utterly impossible that there were only *two* dogs in the
house. Look at that encyclopedia—why anybody would think it
must have taken two of them all afternoon to do just *that* much
damage, let alone all the other awful things! Della says she's
sure Penrod let them into the house, and this time I certainly

don't intend to say one word against it if you think you ought
to——"

"Yes, of course I ought to," Mr. Schofield said; and, to the dismayed ears listening in the hallway, his voice was the execu-
tioner's.

With infinite precaution, Penrod returned to the front door,
let himself out, and no one could have heard a footfall as he
crossed the verandah.

He found Sam closing the door of the Williams's cellar upon
Walter-John. "Where'd you come across him?" Penrod asked, in
a preoccupied tone. He was not much interested.

"*Nice* way to bring him home like you promised, wasn't it?"
Sam returned indignantly. "I found him out in the alley, 'way up
by the corner, and he acted like he was scared to death. He didn't
even act like he knew me."

"See here a minute, Sam," Penrod said, in a friendly though
still preoccupied tone. "On account of all those doughnuts I
gave you, and everything, I don't s'pose your mother would mind
if I stayed over here for dinner much, would she?"

The 13th Is Magic

JOAN HOWARD

Jill and her brother Ronnie acquire a black cat which they call Merlin. It turns out to be a most appropriate name, because Merlin is a magician-cat and magic things begin to happen to them—but only on the 13th day of each month. When they meet the mysterious high-bounding Mrs. Wallaby-Jones near the Central Park Zoo, it is the 13th of the month.

Mrs. Wallaby-Jones

NEARLY every day, even in weather that was not fit for ducks, Jill and Ronnie played in the park. But this December afternoon, with the sun shimmering on the first light snowfall of the season, was the only time they had met Mrs. Wallaby-Jones there.

They were used to nice old ladies stopping them to talk and to ask questions, so they chattered with that mixture of open friendliness and polite caution that all sensible children maintain till they are sure of a stranger.

"Are you English?" Jill asked politely.

The lady's speech was rather different from their own, and Jill had heard her mother say once the English went in for hyphenated names. Mrs. Wallaby-Jones had mentioned *her* hyphen when she introduced herself, as if she considered it a mark of distinction.

"No, not English, my dear," Mrs. Wallaby-Jones replied, "though belonging to the British Empire, of course. We Wallaby-Joneses—with the hyphen—are from Australia. New South

Wales, to be more precise. We are a cadet branch of the Macropus family. Surely, even in New York, you have heard of the
Macropuses? Australia could hardly be said to have a history at
all without the Macropuses—or the Wallabies, if it comes to
that. Why, we—"

Ronnie and Jill sighed deeply and wondered if they had not
better be going now. Even the nicest grown-ups were bores when
they got started on the subject of Family. Their own mother—
and she *was* the nicest—went on and on sometimes about her
family who had come over from England on a boat called the
"Mayflower," and then kept on getting into one bit after another
of American history.

"I'm pretty good at the standing broad jump," Ronnie said.
He was not so much boasting as trying to change the subject
tactfully. "I can do five-feet-ten-and-a-half-inches. Jill can't come
anywhere near that, but then girls are never much good at that
sort of thing."

"Are they not?" asked Mrs. Wallaby-Jones.

She sounded distinctly huffy, and as they watched she seemed
to grow about two feet taller. Maybe she was swelling with rage
about something—they had heard about that, though they had
never seen it happen. They wondered anxiously what could have
upset her. She surely could not be angry about jumping, since
jumping was something ladies never went in for, so it must be
because they had interrupted her story about the Macropuses
and the Wallaby-Joneses.

Suddenly, without any warning at all, she flew through the air
in the most spectacular broad jump either of the young Saun-
derses had ever witnessed. She cleared two park benches, three
laurels and two bayberry bushes, and the bridle path; and then
there she stood waiting, as primly respectable as ever, but a good
twenty-five feet away from them.

"That was a beaut!" Ronnie yelled excitedly.

"You are perfectly wonderful!" his sister called, and both of
them ran to catch up to her.

A grown-up who did not let dignity stand in the way of a
broad jump like that was a real friend to cultivate. But they were
soon reminded not to let her get back to the subject of Family.

"If you think that was good," she said smugly, with her pointed little nose high in the air, "you should have seen my Uncle Hubert Macropus in his younger days. For thirteen years straight he won first prize for the broad jump in the Caledonian Games they hold in Australia on Robert Burns's birthday. He was made an honorary Scot to be eligible and his name was printed in the program as Hubert *Mac*Ropus—to go with MacDuff and MacGregor and MacDonald and all the rest of the Macs, you see."

Jill and Ronnie did not see, quite, and fascinating as broad jumps are when you are making them yourself or even watching them, the illustrious history of Mr. Hubert Macropus, or *Mac*-Ropus, did not hold their interest very long.

"Shall we go over to the lake and feed the ducks?" Jill suggested. "I have a bun in my pocket we can crumble up for them."

"A splendid idea, my dear," agreed Mrs. Wallaby-Jones with enthusiasm. "Rules or no rules, I like to see children remember their furred and feathered friends. For myself, I always fancy a nice bit of greens, but I have heard that ducks relish crumbs. There is no accounting for tastes, I always say."

The children were puzzled. "There isn't any rule against feeding the ducks," Ronnie said.

"Is there not? Well, I do call that unfair when there are stupid notices posted on the cages of all the quadrupeds."

Mrs. Wallaby-Jones sounded highly indignant and off she went in another great leap.

"I wish I could do that," Ronnie said wistfully when they had almost caught up with her again.

"Maybe having big feet is a help," his sister suggested, and she pointed to Mrs. Wallaby-Jones's footprints in the light snow. They certainly were enormous for a lady. "I never saw any like that before, and her hands are smaller than mine."

Mrs. Wallaby-Jones was waiting for them, with her tiny gloved hands demurely folded, so Ronnie could see that Jill was quite right.

Just then he caught sight of a policeman friend of theirs. "Hi, Mr. Harrigan," he called. "Do you want to see something that really *is* something? This lady here can do a broad jump that—"

"Hush now, children, don't talk such nonsense," said Mrs. Wallaby-Jones.

She was in a great hurry suddenly, and she had leaped almost out of sight before Ronnie could finish his sentence.

Mr. Harrigan blinked twice and swallowed hard. He pushed his cap back on his head. "Holy Moses, what is your friend, a kangaroo?" he demanded.

"Well, I told you she was a wonderful broad jumper," Ronnie reminded him.

"She's all of that," agreed the policeman. He looked as if he were thinking up some more questions to ask, but Jill and Ronnie had to leave him to catch up with Mrs. Wallaby-Jones.

Their trip across the park was really wonderful, with their new and already dear friend walking in a series of wild leaps, clearing drinking fountains and perambulators and startling some elderly gentlemen who were sunning themselves on the benches. It was such fun that the children hoped they might meet the lady every day after this.

"Look!" Ronnie called. "There are still boats out. Will you come for a row on the lake with us? Our treat!"

"Thank you, I should love to. We Wallaby-Joneses are very fond of water sports. Why, my Great-Aunt Emmeline was the talk of New South Wales when she paddled her own canoe. That was when she was quite a young girl and people had old-fashioned notions about what was ladylike and what was not."

"We'll have to hurry," Jill broke in quickly. "There is Mr. Murphy bringing in his rowboats."

During the summer the children were always coaxing some grown-up or other to take them rowing on the lake. They did the rowing themselves, rather badly, but they had to have an older person with them or they were not allowed out in a boat. There was a printed notice about that rule tacked up on the side of the boathouse where Mr. Murphy took the money.

Mr. Murphy was unusually late storing his boats for the winter this year. Indian summer had continued all through November, and then he had decided to paint up some of them ready for next season. The snow had reminded him that it was near the middle of December, though, so he was working hard today getting them out of the water and stowing them away in a shed. He was closing up shop till next spring.

It took considerable coaxing before he agreed to let them take out a boat for one last hour, but since the lady was with them . . . Jill and Ronnie pooled their allowances to pay the thirty-five cents and two pennies tax.

In the rowboat, Jill and Ronnie sat side by side, each with an oar, while Mrs. Wallaby-Jones settled herself in the stern, an entirely dignified passenger.

Mr. Murphy shoved them off and they started out all right, but as soon as they got really out in the lake their rowing was the kind that always made their father laugh at them. Because Ronnie pulled on his oar so much harder than his sister could, they had a way of going round and round in circles—on their good days in quite large circles, but more often as if they were caught in a small whirlpool.

This promised to be one of their worst days and they were pretty embarrassed about it all until they suddenly straightened out and cut across the ripples in as clean a line as you please.

"Hey!" Ronnie shouted. "Look at us!"

But Jill could not stop to look at them. She was far too intent upon looking at something else. She nudged her brother to watch too. Their eyes got bigger and bigger as they stared at the queerest thing they had ever seen in all their lives.

There was Mrs. Wallaby-Jones, sitting as prim as ever in her sleek fur coat and her fur hat and tippet, her gloved hands folded in her lap. But she had pulled up her skirt just a trifle, probably to keep it dry. And underneath, hanging over the back of the little rowboat and acting as a rudder, was something—something —Jill and Ronnie were not sure *what* it was, but it certainly did look like the tip of a kangaroo's tail.

They were so astonished they could not say a single word. Not even when, encouraged by their fixed attention, Mrs. Wallaby-Jones told them practically *all* about her family. Not until she got to second-cousins-once-removed did Jill find her voice.

"We have a cat," she announced. "A black cat."

"I am not surprised to hear it, my dear," Mrs. Wallaby-Jones said amiably. "That would be Merlin, would it not?"

Jill's mouth dropped open and Ronnie's oar hung dripping in midair. But there was no time for questions. Mr. Murphy was waving his arms at them from the shore to signal that their hour was up, so they had to row back quickly.

Ronnie helped their guest out of the rowboat like a perfect gentleman. He could not see anything peculiar about her then, though his sister noticed that Mrs. Wallaby-Jones wore her skirts just a shade longer than was the fashion this year.

"I must get back now, dears," Mrs. Wallaby-Jones said politely. "It has been a most enjoyable outing."

"When can we see you again?" both children wanted to know. "Can we meet you tomorrow? Or next day? Please . . ."

They had never met a grown-up they were more anxious to see again, as much and as often as possible. They were even willing now to let her talk Family in order that they might enjoy her other charms.

"Well, I cannot be sure just when I shall be free again," Mrs. Wallaby-Jones answered. "I would not want to make a promise and not be able to keep it. It is not always easy to get away, and you never know ahead of time when there is going to be a large audience—it depends upon the weather and so forth. I must not disappoint my public, you know, but one of these days we shall meet again."

It was not till they got home and found Merlin waiting for them to give him his catnip mouse from the toy cupboard that either Jill or Ronnie remembered that this was the thirteenth of the month.

At dinner they could talk of nothing but their new friend. They tried to keep the account as matter-of-fact as possible, knowing from past experiences that anything unusual was apt to be regarded with suspicion, if not actually disbelieved. Sometimes grown-up skepticism is really discouraging.

"When she walked, it was sort of in hops," Ronnie said. He remembered just in time not to mention the length of those hops.

"She had a pointed face and bright brown eyes," Jill put in eagerly. "Her clothes were a little bit old-fashioned but they exactly suited her."

"What do you suppose she meant about not disappointing her public?" Ronnie asked.

"Why, it sounds as though she might be an actress," their mother decided.

It was when Mr. Saunders wanted to know if their rowing had improved that Ronnie forgot to be careful.

"I don't know that we're so much better alone," he confessed, "but we're fine when Mrs. Wallaby-Jones is with us. She sort of steers for us. With her tail."

Mr. Saunders choked on a bread crumb and hastily gulped a whole glass of water. Mrs. Saunders was very much upset.

"It is all very well," she said sternly, "to make up stories now and again. I hope I enjoy a bit of fantasy as well as the next person. But it is *not* nice to be rude when the lady was so kind to you. . . ."

The lecture went on all through the chocolate pudding dessert and for quite a long time afterward, with many remarks of a to-think-that-any-child-of-mine nature. Mr. Saunders got tired of listening and left the table to read his evening paper. He finished the front page and the sports page and then turned back to page two. Presently he looked up from it and changed the subject.

"You children didn't happen to meet a kangaroo in the park today, I suppose? It seems one got loose from the menagerie. Just listen to this. . . ." He began to read and the whole family listened.

REMARKABLE OCCURRENCE IN CENTRAL PARK ZOO

The strange disappearance of a large female wallaby (macropus giganteus) more commonly known as a kangaroo, for two hours today caused considerable excitement at the local menagerie. The animal, who is known to be very friendly and who answers to the name of Jones when called by her keeper, was missing from her cage for that period. At time of going to press, it had not been determined how she got away, nor when and how she was returned. Until her reappearance, her grieving keeper was certain that she had been abducted by a kidnapper disguised as a Miss Smithers, assistant to the curator of the zoo. Their theory was strengthened by the fact that Miss Smithers, an elderly woman, had reported the theft of her outdoor garments—a fur coat, fur hat and tippet—from the closet adjacent to her office. The clothing later reappeared as mysteriously as the missing wallaby, but it was some time before the excitement died down in the zoo.

There was silence for a moment when Mr. Saunders finished reading this extraordinary news item. Then Jill forgot all discretion and burst out in an excited burble of words.

"Why, our Mrs. Wallaby-Jones wore a fur coat and a fur hat an—"

She was stopped short by Ronnie's sharp elbow in her ribs. She yelped, and then the children looked at each other. They both remembered other times when silence had been considerably better than speech.

"Well, I've got some arithmetic homework to do," Ronnie said carelessly. "I expect I'd better get at it. You coming, Jill?"

Jill and Ronnie went off to their own room, followed by a sedate Merlin and the incredulous stares of their parents. Perhaps it was only because it had never before occurred to Ronnie to do his arithmetic homework without being reminded at least three times. Or perhaps . . .

"*What* did they say that woman's name was?" Mrs. Sidney P. Saunders demanded abruptly. "I thought—"

"So did I," admitted her husband. "But it could *not* be that."

A Rootabaga Story

How Hot Balloons and His Pigeon Daughters
Crossed Over into the Rootabaga Country

CARL SANDBURG

Hot Balloons was a man who lived all alone among people who sell slips, flips, flicks and chicks by the dozen, by the box, by the box car job lot, back and forth to each other.

Hot Balloons used to open the window in the morning and say to the rag pickers and the rag handlers, "Far, far away the pigeons are calling; far, far away the white wings are dipping in the blue, in the sky blue."

And the rag pickers and the rag handlers looked up from their rag bags and said, "Far, far away the rags are flying; far, far away the rags are whistling in the wind, in the sky wind."

Now two pigeons came walking up to the door, the door knob and the door bell under the window of Hot Balloons. One of the pigeons rang the bell. The other pigeon, too, stepped up to the bell and gave it a ring.

Then they waited, tying the shoe strings on their shoes and the bonnet strings under their chins, while they waited.

Hot Balloons opened the door. And they flew into his hands, one pigeon apiece in each of his hands, flipping and fluttering their wings, calling, "Ka loo, ka loo, ka lo, ka lo," leaving a letter in his hands and then flying away fast.

Hot Balloons stepped out on the front steps to read the letter where the light was good in the daylight because it was so early in the morning. The letter was on paper scribbled over in pigeon foot blue handwriting with many secrets and syllables.

After Hot Balloons read the letter, he said to himself, "I won-

der if those two pigeons are my two runaway daughters, Dippy the Wisp and Slip Me Liz. When they ran away they said they would cross the Shampoo river and go away into the Rootabaga country to live. And I have heard it is a law of the Rootabaga country whenever a girl crosses the Shampoo river to come back where she used to be, she changes into a pigeon—and she stays a pigeon till she crosses back over the Shampoo river into the Rootabaga country again."

And he shaded his eyes with his hands and looked far, far away in the blue, in the sky blue. And by looking long and hard he saw far, far away in the sky blue, the two white pigeons dipping their wings in the blue, flying fast, circling and circling higher and higher, toward the Shampoo river, toward the Rootabaga country.

"I wonder, I guess, I think so," he said to himself, "I wonder, I think so, it must be those two pigeons are my two runaway daughters, my two girls, Dippy the Wisp and Slip Me Liz."

He took out the letter and read it again right side up, upside down, back and forth. "It is the first time I ever read pigeon foot blue handwriting," he said to himself. And the way he read the letter, it said to him:

Daddy, daddy, daddy, come home to us in the Rootabaga country where the pigeons call ka loo, ka loo, ka lo, ka lo, where the squirrels carry ladders and the wildcats ask riddles and the fish jump out of the rivers and speak to the frying pans, where the baboons take care of the babies and the black cats come and go in orange and gold stockings, where the birds wear rose and purple hats on Monday afternoons up in the skylights in the evening.

(Signed)   Dippy the Wisp,
Slip Me Liz

And reading the letter a second time, Hot Balloons said to himself, "No wonder it is scribbled over the paper in pigeon foot blue handwriting. No wonder it is full of secrets and syllables."

So he jumped into a shirt and a necktie, he jumped into a hat and a vest, and he jumped into a steel car, starting with a snizz and a snoof till it began running smooth and even as a catfoot.

"I will ride to the Shampoo river faster than two pigeons fly," he said. "I will be there."

Which he was. He got there before the two pigeons. But it was no use. For the rain and the rainstorm was working—and the rain and the rainstorm tore down and took and washed away the steel bridge over the Shampoo river.

"Now there is only an air bridge to cross on, and a *steel* car drops down, falls off, falls through, if it runs on an *air* bridge," he said.

So he was all alone with the rain and the rainstorm all around him—and far as he could see by shading his eyes and looking, there was only the rain and the rainstorm across the river—and the *air* bridge.

While he waited for the rain and the rainstorm to go down, two pigeons came flying into his hands, one apiece into each hand, flipping and fluttering their wings and calling, "Ka loo, ka loo, ka lo, ka lo." And he could tell by the way they began tying the shoe strings on their shoes and the bonnet strings under their chins, they were the same two pigeons ringing the door bell that morning.

They wrote on his thumb-nails in pigeon foot blue handwriting, and he read their handwriting asking him why he didn't cross over the Shampoo river. And he explained, "There is only an *air* bridge to cross on. A *steel* car drops down, falls off, falls through, if it runs on an *air* bridge. Change my *steel* car to an *air* car. Then I can cross the *air* bridge."

The pigeons flipped and fluttered, dipped their wings and called, "Ka loo, ka loo, ka lo, ka lo." And they scribbled their pigeon feet on his thumb-nail—telling him to wait. So the pigeons went flying across the Shampoo river.

They came back with a basket. In the basket was a snoox and a gringo. And the snoox and the gringo took hammers, jacks, flanges, nuts, screws, bearings, ball bearings, axles, axle grease, ax handles, spits, spitters, spitballs and spitfires, and worked.

"It's a hot job," said the snoox to the gringo. "I'll say it's a hot job," said the gringo answering the snoox.

"We'll give this one the merry razoo," said the snoox to the gringo, working overtime and double time. "Yes, we'll put her to the cleaners and shoot her into high," said the gringo, answering the snoox, working overtime and double time.

They changed the steel to air, made an *air* car out of the *steel* car, put Hot Balloons and the two pigeons into the air car and *drove the air car across the air bridge.*

And nowadays when people talk about it in the Rootabaga country, they say, "The snoox and the gringo drove the air car across the air bridge clean and cool as a whistle in the wind. As soon as the car got off the bridge and over into the Rootabaga country, the two pigeons changed in a flash. And Hot Balloons saw they were his two daughters, his two runaway girls, Dippy the Wisp and Slip Me Liz, standing and smiling at him and looking fresh and free as two fresh fish in a free river, fresh and free as two fresh bimbos in a bamboo tree.

He kissed them both, two long kisses, and while he was kissing them the snoox and the gringo worked double time and overtime and changed the *air* car back into a *steel* car.

And Dippy the Wisp and Slip Me Liz rode in that car—starting with a snizz and a snoof till it began running smooth and even as a catfoot—showing their father, Hot Balloons, where the squirrels carry ladders and the wildcats ask riddles and the fish jump out of the rivers and speak to the frying pans, where the baboons take care of the babies and the black cats come and go in orange and gold stockings, where the birds wear rose and purple hats on Monday afternoons up in the skylights in the evening.

And often on a Saturday night or a New Year Eve or a Christmas morning, Hot Balloons remembers back how things used to be, and he tells his two girls about the rag pickers and the rag handlers back among the people who sell slips, flips, flicks, and chicks, by the dozen, by the box, by the box car job lot, back and forth to each other.

A Meal with a Magician

J. B. S. HALDANE

I HAVE had some very odd meals in my time, and if I liked I could tell you about a meal in a mine, or a meal in Moscow, or a meal with a millionaire. But I think you will be more interested to hear about a meal I had one evening with a magician, because it is more unusual. People don't often have a meal of that sort, for rather few people know a magician at all well, because there aren't very many in England. Of course I am talking about real magicians. Some conjurors call themselves magicians, and they are very clever men. But they can't do the sort of things that real magicians do. I mean, a conjuror can turn a rabbit into a bowl of goldfish, but it's always done under cover or behind something, so that you can't see just what is happening. But a real magician can turn a cow into a grandfather clock with people looking on all the time. Only it is very much harder work, and no one could do it twice a day, and six days a week, like the conjurors do with rabbits.

When I first met Mr. Leakey I never guessed he was a magician. I met him like this. I was going across the Haymarket about five o'clock one afternoon. When I got to the refuge by a lamp-post in the middle I stopped, but a little man who had crossed so far with me went on. Then he saw a motor-bus going down the hill and jumped back, which is always a silly thing to do. He jumped right in front of a car, and if I hadn't grabbed his overcoat collar and pulled him back on to the refuge, I think the car would have knocked him down. For it was wet weather, and the road was very greasy, so it only skidded when the driver put the brakes on.

The little man was very grateful, but dreadfully frightened, so I gave him my arm across the street, and saw him back to his home, which was quite near. I won't tell you where it was, because if I did you might go there and bother him, and if he got really grumpy it might be very awkward indeed for you. I mean, he might make one of your ears as big as a cabbage-leaf, or turn your hair green, or exchange your right and left feet, or something like that. And then everyone who saw you would burst out laughing, and say, "Here comes wonky Willie, or lopsided Lissie," or whatever your name is.

"I can't bear modern traffic," he said, "the motor-buses make me so frightened. If it wasn't for my work in London I should like to live on a little island where there are no roads, or on the top of a mountain, or somewhere like that." The little man was sure I had saved his life, and insisted on my having dinner with him, so I said I would come to dinner on Wednesday week. I didn't notice anything specially odd about him then, except that his ears were rather large and that he had a little tuft of hair on the top of each of them, rather like the lynx at the Zoo. I remember I thought if I had hair there I would shave it off. He told me that his name was Leakey, and that he lived on the first floor.

Well, on Wednesday week I went to dinner with him. I went upstairs in a block of flats and knocked at a quite ordinary door, and the little hall of the flat was quite ordinary too, but when I got inside it was one of the oddest rooms I have ever seen. Instead of wallpaper there were curtains round it, embroidered with pictures of people and animals. There was a picture of two men building a house, and another of a man with a dog and a cross-blow hunting rabbits. I know they were made of embroidery, because I touched them, but it must have been a very funny sort of embroidery, because the pictures were always changing. As long as you looked at them they stayed still, but if you looked away and back again they had altered. During dinner the builders had put a fresh storey on the house, the hunter had shot a bird with his cross-bow, and his dog had caught two rabbits.

The furniture was very funny too. There was a bookcase made out of what looked like glass with the largest books in it that I ever saw, none of them less than a foot high, and bound in leather. There were cupboards running along the tops of the bookshelves. The chairs were beautifully carved, with high wooden backs, and there were two tables. One was made of copper, and had a huge crystal globe on it. The other was a solid lump of wood about ten feet long, four feet wide, and three feet high, with holes cut in it so that you could get your knees under it. There were various odd things hanging from the ceiling. At first I couldn't make out how the room was lit. Then I saw that the light came from plants of a sort I had never seen before, growing in pots. They had red, yellow and blue fruits about as big as tomatoes, which shone. They weren't disguised electric lamps, for I touched one and it was quite cold, and soft like a fruit.

"Well," said Mr. Leakey, "what would you like for dinner?"

"Oh, whatever you've got," I said.

"You can have whatever you like," he said. "Please choose a soup."

So I thought he probably got his dinner from a restaurant, and I said, "I'll have Bortsch," which is a red Russian soup with cream in it.

"Right," he said, "I'll get it ready. Look here, do you mind if we have dinner served the way mine usually is? You aren't easily frightened, are you?"

"Not very easily," I said.

"All right, then, I'll call my servant, but I warn you he's rather odd."

At that Mr. Leakey flapped the tops and lobes of his ears against his head. It made a noise like when one claps one's hands, but not so loud. Out of a large copper pot about as big as the copper you wash clothes in, which was standing in one corner, came what at first I thought was a large wet snake. Then I saw it had suckers all down one side, and was really the arm of an octopus. This arm opened a cupboard and pulled out a large towel with which it wiped the next arm that came out. The dry arm then clung on to the wall with its suckers, and gradually the whole beast came out, dried itself, and crawled up the wall. It was the biggest octopus I have ever seen; each arm was about eight feet long, and its body was as big as a sack. It crawled up the wall, and then along the ceiling, holding on by its suckers like a fly. When it got above the table it held on by one arm only, and with the other seven got plates and knives and forks out of the cupboards above the bookshelves and laid the table with them.

"That's my servant Oliver," said Mr. Leakey. "He's much better than a person, because he has more arms to work with, and he can hold on to a plate with about ten suckers, so he never drops one."

When Oliver the octopus had laid the table we sat down and he offered me a choice of water, lemonade, beer, and four different kinds of wine with his seven free arms, each of which held a different bottle. I chose some water and some very good red wine from Burgundy.

All this was so odd that I was not surprised to notice that my host was wearing a top hat, but I certainly did think it a little queer when he took it off and poured two platefuls of soup out of it.

"Ah, we want some cream," he added. "Come here, Phyllis." At this a small green cow, about the size of a rabbit, ran out of a hutch, jumped on to the table, and stood in front of Mr. Leakey, who milked her into a silver cream jug which Oliver had handed down for the purpose. The cream was excellent, and I enjoyed the soup very much.

"What would you like next?" said Mr. Leakey.

"I leave it to you," I answered.

"All right," he said, "we'll have grilled turbot, and turkey to follow. Catch us a turbot, please, Oliver, and be ready to grill it, Pompey."

At this Oliver picked up a fishhook with the end of one of his arms and began making casts in the air like a fly-fisher. Meanwhile I heard a noise in the fireplace, and Pompey came out. He was a small dragon about a foot long, not counting his tail, which measured another foot. He had been lying on the burning coals, and was red-hot. So I was glad to see that as soon as he got out of the fire he put a pair of asbestos boots which were lying in the fender on to his hind feet.

"Now, Pompey," said Mr. Leakey, "hold your tail up properly.

If you burn the carpet again, I'll pour a bucket of cold water over you. (Of course I wouldn't really do that, it's very cruel to pour cold water onto a dragon, especially a little one with a thin skin)," he added in a low voice, which only I could hear. But poor Pompey took the threat quite seriously. He wimpered, and the yellow flames which were coming out of his nose turned a dull blue. He waddled along rather clumsily on his hind legs, holding up his tail and the front part of his body. I think the asbestos boots made walking rather difficult for him, though they saved the carpet, and no doubt kept his hind feet warm. But of course dragons generally walk on all four feet and seldom wear boots, so I was surprised that Pompey walked as well as he did.

I was so busy watching Pompey that I never saw how Oliver caught the turbot, and by the time I looked up at him again he had just finished cleaning it, and threw it down to Pompey. Pompey caught it in his front paws, which had cooled down a bit, and were just about the right temperature for grilling things. He had long thin fingers with claws on the ends; and held the fish on each hand alternately, holding the other against his red-hot chest to warm it. By the time he had finished and put the grilled fish on to a plate which Oliver handed down Pompey was clearly feeling the cold, for his teeth were chattering, and he scampered back to the fire with evident joy.

"Yes," said Mr. Leakey, "I know some people say it is cruel to let a young dragon cool down like that, and liable to give it a bad cold. But I say a dragon can't begin to learn too soon that life isn't all fire and flames, and the world is a colder place than he'd like it to be. And they don't get colds if you give them plenty of sulphur to eat. Of course a dragon with a cold is an awful nuisance to itself and everyone else. I've known one throw flames for a hundred yards when it sneezed. But that was a full-grown one, of course. It burned down one of the Emperor of China's palaces. Besides, I really couldn't afford to keep a dragon if I didn't make use of him. Last week, for example, I used his breath to burn the old paint off the door, and his tail makes quite a good soldering iron. Then he's really much more reliable than a dog for dealing with burglars. They might shoot a dog, but leaden bullets just melt the moment they touch Pompey. Anyway, I think dragons were meant for use, not ornament. Don't you?"

"Well, do you know," I answered, "I am ashamed to say that Pompey is the first live dragon I've ever seen."

"Of course," said Mr. Leakey, "how stupid of me. I have so few guests here except professional colleagues that I forgot you were a layman. By the way," he went on, as he poured sauce out of his hat over the fish, "I don't know if you've noticed anything queer about this dinner. Of course some people are more observant than others."

"Well," I answered, "I've never seen anything like it before."

For example at that moment I was admiring an enormous rainbow-coloured beetle which was crawling towards me over the table with a salt-cellar strapped on its back.

"Ah well then," said my host, "perhaps you have guessed that I'm a magician. Pompey, of course, is a real dragon, but most of the other animals here were people before I made them what they are now. Take Oliver, for example. When he was a man he had his legs cut off by a railway train. I couldn't stick them on again because my magic doesn't work against machinery. Poor Oliver was bleeding to death, so I thought the only way to save his life was to turn him into some animal with no legs. Then he wouldn't have any legs to have been cut off. I turned him into a snail, and took him home in my pocket. But whenever I tried to turn him back into something more interesting, like a dog, it had no hind legs. But an octopus has really got no legs. Those eight tentacles grow out of its head. So when I turned him into an octopus, he was all right. And he had been a waiter when he was a man, so he soon learnt his job. I think he's much better than a maid because he can lift the plates from above, and doesn't stand behind one and breathe down one's neck. You may have the rest of the fish, Oliver, and a bottle of beer. I know that's what you like."

Oliver seized the fish in one of his arms and put it into an immense beak like a parrot's but much bigger, which lay in the centre of the eight arms. Then he took a bottle of beer out of a cupboard, unscrewed the cork with his beak, hoisted himself up to the ceiling with two of his other arms, and turned over so that his mouth was upwards. As he emptied the bottle he winked one of his enormous eyes. Then I felt sure he must be really a man, for I never saw an ordinary octopus wink.

The turkey came in a more ordinary way. Oliver let down a large hot plate, and then a dish cover on to it. There was nothing in the cover, as I could see. Mr. Leakey got up, took a large wand out of the umbrella stand, pointed it at the dish cover, said a few words, and there was the turkey steaming hot when Oliver lifted the cover off it.

"Of course that's easy," said Mr. Leakey, "any good conjuror could do it, but you can never be sure the food you get in that way is absolutely fresh. That's why I like to see my fish caught. But birds are all the better for being a few days old. Ah, we shall want some sausages too. That's easy."

He took a small clay pipe out of his pocket and blew into it. A large brown bubble came out of the other end, shaped like a sausage. Oliver picked it off with the end of one of his tentacles, and put it on a hot plate, and it was a sausage, because I ate it. He made six sausages in this way, and while I was watching him Oliver had handed down the vegetables. I don't know where he got them. The sauce and gravy came out of Mr. Leakey's hat, as usual.

Just after this the only accident of the evening happened. The beetle who carried the salt-cellar round tripped over a fold in the tablecloth and spilled the salt just in front of Mr. Leakey, who spoke to him very angrily.

"It's lucky for you, Leopold, that I'm a sensible man. If I were superstitious, which I'm not, I should think I was going to have bad luck. But it's you who are going to have bad luck, if anyone. I've a good mind to turn you back into a man, and if I do, I'll put you straight on to that carpet and send you to the nearest police station; and when the police ask you where you've been hiding, d'you think they'll believe you when you say you've been a beetle for the last year? Are you sorry?"

Leopold, with a great struggle, got out of his harness and rolled on to his back, feebly waving his legs in the air like a dog does when he's ashamed of himself.

"When Leopold was a man," said Mr. Leakey, "he made money by swindling people. When the police found it out and were going to arrest him, he came to me for help, but I thought it served him right. So I said 'If they catch you, you'll get sent to penal servitude for seven years. If you like I'll turn you into a beetle for five years, which isn't so long, and then, if you've been a good beetle, I'll make you into a man with a different sort of face, so the police won't know you.' So now Leopold is a beetle. Well, I see he's sorry for spilling the salt. Now, Leopold, you must pick up all the salt you've spilt."

He turned Leopold over on his front and I watched him begin to pick the salt up. It took him over an hour. First he picked it up a grain at a time in his mouth, lifted himself up on his front legs, and dropped it into the salt-cellar. Then he thought of a better plan. He was a beetle of the kind whose feelers are short and spread out into a fan. He started shovelling the salt with his feelers, and got on much quicker that way. But fairly soon he got uncomfortable. His feelers started to itch or something, and he had to wipe them with his legs. Finally he got a bit of paper, and used it for a shovel, holding it with his front feet.

"That's very clever for a beetle," said my host. "When I turn him back into a man he'll be quite good with his hands, and I expect he'll be able to earn his living at an honest job."

As we were finishing the turkey, Mr. Leakey looked up anxiously from time to time.

"I hope Abdu'l Makkar won't be late with the strawberries," he said.

"Strawberries?" I asked in amazement, for it was the middle of January.

"Oh yes, I've sent Abdu'l Makkar, who is a jinn, to New Zealand for some. Of course it's summer there. He oughtn't to be long now, if he has been good, but you know what jinns are, they have their faults, like the rest of us. Curiosity, especially. When one sends them on long errands they will fly too high. They like to get up quite close to Heaven to overhear what the angels are saying, and then the angels throw shooting stars at them. Then they drop their parcels, or come home half scorched. He ought to be back soon, he's been away over an hour. Meanwhile we'll have some other fruit, in case he's late."

He got up, and tapped the four corners of the table with his wand. At each corner the wood swelled; then it cracked, and a little green shoot came out and started growing. In a minute they were already about a foot high, with several leaves at the top, and the bottom quite woody. I could see from the leaves that one was a cherry, another a pear, and the third a peach, but I didn't know the fourth.

As Oliver was clearing away the remains of the turkey with four of his arms and helping himself to a sausage with a fifth, Abdu'l Makkar came in. He came feet first through the ceiling, which seemed to close behind him like water in the tank of the diving birds' house in the Zoo, when you look at it from underneath while a penguin dives in. It shook a little for a moment afterwards. He narrowly missed one of Oliver's arms, but alighted safely on the floor, bending his knees to break his fall, and bowing deeply to Mr. Leakey. He had a brown face with rather a long nose, and looked quite like a man, except that he had a pair of leathery wings folded on his back, and his nails were of gold. He wore a turban and clothes of green silk.

"Oh peacock of the world and redresser of injustices," he said, "thy unworthy servant comes into the presence with rare and refreshing fruit."

"The presence deigns to express gratification at the result of thy labours."

"The joy of thy negligible slave is as the joy of King Solomon, son of David (on whom be peace, if he has not already obtained peace) when he first beheld Balkis, the queen of Sheba. May the Terminator of delights and Separator of companions be far from this dwelling."

"May the Deluder of Intelligences never trouble the profundity of thine apprehension."

"Oh dominator of demons and governor of gobblins, what egregious enchanter or noble necromancer graces thy board?"

"It is written, oh Abdu'l Makkar, in the book of the sayings of the prophet Shoaib, the apostle of the Midianites, that curiosity slew the cat of Pharaoh, king of Egypt."

"That is a true word."

"Thy departure is permitted. Awaken me at the accustomed hour. But stay! My safety razor hath no more blades and the shops of London are closed. Fly therefore to Montreal, where it is even now high noon, and purchase me a packet thereof."

"I tremble and obey."

"Why dost thou tremble, oh audacious among the Ifreets?"

"Oh Emperor of enchantment, the lower air is full of aeroplanes, flying swifter than a magic carpet,* and each making a din like unto the bursting of the great dam of Sheba, and the upper air is infested with meteorites."

"Fly therefore at a height of five miles and thou shalt avoid both the one peril and the other. And now, oh performer of commands and executor of behests, thou hast my leave to depart."

"May the wisdom of Plato, the longevity of Shiqq, the wealth of Solomon, and the success of Alexander, be thine."

"The like unto thee, with brazen knobs thereon."

The jinn now vanished, this time through the floor. While he and Mr. Leakey had been talking the trees had grown up to about four feet high, and flowered. The flowers were now falling off, and little green fruits were swelling.

"You have to talk like that to a jinn or you lose his respect. I hope you don't mind my not introducing you, but really jinns may be quite awkward at times," said my host. "Of course Abdu'l Makkar is a nice chap and means well, but he might be very embarrassing to you, as you don't know the Word of Power to send him away. For instance if you were playing cricket and went in against a fast bowler, he'd probably turn up and ask you 'Shall I slay thine enemy, oh Defender of the Stumps, or merely convert him into an he-goat of loathsome appearance and afflicted with the mange?' You know, I used to be very fond of watching cricket, but I can't do it now. Quite a little magic will upset a match. Last year I went to see the Australians playing against Gloucester, and just because I felt a little sympathetic with Gloucestershire the Australian wickets went down like ninepins.

---

* This is of course a gross exaggeration.

If I hadn't left before the end they'd have been beaten. And after that I couldn't go to any of the test matches. After all, one wants the best side to win."

We next ate the New Zealand strawberries, which were very good, with Phyllis's cream. While we did so Pompey, who acted as a sort of walking stove, came out again and melted some cheese to make a Welsh rarebit. After this we went on to dessert. The fruit was now quite ripe. The fourth tree bore half a dozen beautiful golden fruits shaped rather like apricots, but much bigger, and my host told me they were mangoes, which of course usually grow in India. In fact you can't make them grow in England except by magic. So I said I would try a mango.

"Aha," said Mr. Leakey, "this is where I have a pull over Lord Melchett or the Duke of Westminster, or any other rich man. They might be able to get mangoes here by aeroplane, but they couldn't give them as dessert at a smart dinner-party."

"Why not?" I asked.

"That shows you've never eaten one. The only proper place to eat a mango is in your bath. You see, it has a tough skin and a squashy inside, so when once you get through the skin all the juice squirts out. And that would make a nasty mess of people's white shirts. D'you ever wear a stiff-fronted shirt?"

"Not often."

"A good thing too. You probably don't know why people wear them. It's a curious story. About a hundred years ago a great Mexican enchanter called Whiztopacoatl came over to Europe. And he got very annoyed with the rich men. He didn't so much mind their being rich, but he thought they spent their money on such ugly things, and were dreadfully stodgy and smug. So he decided to turn them all into turtles. Now to do that somebody has to say two different spells at the same time, which is pretty difficult, I can tell you. So Whiztopacoatl went round to an English sorcerer called Mr. Benedict Barnacle, to borrow a two-headed parrot that belonged to him. It was rather like one of those two-headed eagles they used to have on the Russian and Austrian flags. Then he was going to teach one of the heads one spell, and the other head the second spell; and when the parrot said both at once all the rich men would have turned into turtles.

But Mr. Barnacle persuaded him to be less fierce, so finally they agreed that for a hundred years the rich men in Europe should be made to wear clothes only fit for turtles. Because of course the front of a turtle is stiff and flat, and it is the only sort of animal that would be quite comfortable in a shirt with a stiff flat front. They made a spell to stiffen all the shirts, and of course it worked very well, but it's wearing off now, and soon nobody will wear such silly clothes any more.

"About your mango; you can eat it quite safely, if you just wait a moment while I enchant it so that it won't splash over you."

Quite a short spell and a little wiggling of his wand were enough, and then I ate the mango. It was wonderful. It was the only fruit I have ever eaten that was better than the best strawberries. I can't describe the flavour, which is a mixture of all sorts of things, including a little resin, like the smell of a pine forest in summer. There is a huge flattish stone in the middle, too big to get into your mouth, and all round it a squashy yellow pulp. To test the spell I tried to spill some down my waistcoat, but it merely jumped up into my mouth. Mr. Leakey ate a pear, and gave me the other five mangoes to take home. But I had to eat them in my bath because they weren't enchanted.

While we were having coffee (out of the hat, of course) Mr. Leakey rubbed one corner of the table with his wand and it began to sprout with very fine green grass. When it was about as high as the grass on a lawn, he called Phyllis out of her hutch, and she ate some of it for her dinner. We talked for a while about magic, football, and the odder sorts of dog, such as Bedlington terriers and rough-haired Dachshunds, and then I said I must be getting home.

"I'll take you home," said Mr. Leakey, "but when you have a day to spare you must come round and spend it with me, if you'd care to see the sort of things I generally do, and we might go over to India or Java or somewhere for the afternoon. Let me know when you're free. But now just stand on this carpet, and shut your eyes, because people often get giddy the first two or three times they travel by magic carpet."

We got on to the carpet. I took a last look at the table, where

Leopold had just finished picking up the salt, and was resting, while Phyllis was chewing the cud. Then I shut my eyes, my host told the carpet my address, flapped his ears, and I felt a rush of cold air on my cheeks, and a slight giddiness. Then the air was warm again. Mr. Leakey told me to open my eyes, and I was in my sitting-room at home, five miles away. As the room is small, and there were a number of books and things on the floor, the carpet could not settle down properly, and stayed about a foot up in the air. Luckily it was quite stiff, so I stepped down off it, and turned the light on.

"Good-night," said Mr. Leakey, bending down to shake my hand, and then he flapped his ears and he and the carpet vanished. I was left in my room with nothing but a nice full feeling and a parcel of mangoes to persuade me that I had not been dreaming.

The Duel

EUGENE FIELD

The gingham dog and the calico cat
Side by side on the table sat;
'Twas half-past twelve, and (what do you think!)
Nor one nor t'other had slept a wink!
The old Dutch clock and the Chinese plate
Appeared to know as sure as fate
There was going to be a terrible spat.
(I *wasn't there; I simply state*
What was told to me by the Chinese plate!)

The gingham dog went "bow-wow-wow!"
And the calico cat replied "mee-ow!"
The air was littered, an hour or so,
With bits of gingham and calico,
While the old Dutch clock in the chimneyplace
Up with its hands before its face,
For it always dreaded a family row!
(*Now mind: I'm only telling you*
What the old Dutch clock declares is true!)

The Chinese plate looked very blue.
And wailed, "Oh, dear! what shall we do!"
But the gingham dog and the calico cat
Wallowed this way and tumbled that,
Employing every tooth and claw
In the awfullest way you ever saw—
And, oh! how the gingham and calico flew!
(*Don't fancy I exaggerate!*
I got my news from the Chinese plate!)

Next morning, where the two had sat,
They found no trace of dog or cat;
And some folks think unto this day
That burglars stole that pair away!
But the truth about that cat and pup
Is this: they ate each other up!
Now what do you really think of that!
(*The old Dutch clock it told me so,*
And that is how I came to know.)

The Ransom of Red Chief

O. HENRY

I T LOOKED like a good thing; but wait till I tell you. We were down South, in Alabama—Bill Driscoll and myself—when this kidnaping idea struck us. It was, as Bill afterwards expressed it, "during a moment of temporary mental apparition"; but we didn't find that out till later.

There was a town down there, as flat as a flannel cake, and called Summit, of course. It contained inhabitants of as undeleterious and self-satisfied a class of peasantry as ever clustered around a Maypole.

Bill and me had a joint capital of about six hundred dollars, and we needed just two thousand dollars more to pull off a fraudulent town-lot scheme in western Illinois with. We talked it over on the front steps of the hotel. Philoprogenitiveness, says we, is strong in semi-rural communities; therefore, and for other reasons, a kidnaping project ought to do better there than in the radius of newspapers that send reporters out in plain-clothes to stir up talk about such things. We knew that Summit couldn't get after us with anything stronger than constables and, maybe, some lackadaisical bloodhounds and a diatribe or two in the *Weekly Farmers' Budget*. So, it looked good.

We selected for our victim the only child of a prominent citizen named Ebenezer Dorset. The father was respectable and tight, a mortgage fancier and a stern, upright collection-plate passer and forecloser. The kid was a boy of ten, with bas-relief freckles, and hair the color of the cover of the magazine you buy at the newsstand when you want to catch a train. Bill and me figured that Ebenezer would melt down for a ransom of two thousand dollars to a cent. But wait till I tell you.

About two miles from Summit was a little mountain, covered with a dense cedar brake. On the rear elevation of this mountain was a cave. There we stored provisions.

One evening after sundown, we drove in a buggy past old Dorset's house. The kid was in the street, throwing rocks at a kitten on the opposite fence.

"Hey, little boy!" says Bill, "would you like to have a bag of candy and a nice ride?"

The boy catches Bill neatly in the eye with a piece of brick.

"That will cost the old man an extra five hundred dollars," says Bill, climbing over the wheel.

That boy put up a fight like a welterweight cinnamon bear; but, at last, we got him down in the bottom of the buggy and drove away. We took him up to the cave, and I hitched the horse in the cedar brake. After dark I drove the buggy to the little village, three miles away, where we had hired it, and walked back to the mountain.

Bill was pasting court plaster over the scratches and bruises on his features. There was a fire burning behind the big rock at the entrance of the cave, and the boy was watching a pot of boiling coffee, with two buzzard feathers stuck in his red hair. He points a stick at me when I come up, and says:

"Ha! cursed paleface, do you dare to enter the camp of Red Chief, the terror of the plains?"

"He's all right now," says Bill, rolling up his trousers and examining some bruises on his shins. "We're playing Indian. We're making Buffalo Bill's show look like magic-lantern views of Palestine in the town hall. I'm Old Hank, the Trapper, Red Chief's captive, and I'm to be scalped at daybreak. By Geronimo! that kid can kick hard."

Yes, sir, that boy seemed to be having the time of his life. The fun of camping out in a cave had made him forget that he was a captive himself. He immediately christened me Snake-eye, the Spy, and announced that, when his braves returned from the warpath, I was to be broiled at the stake at the rising of the sun.

Then we had supper; and he filled his mouth full of bacon

and bread and gravy, and began to talk. He made a during-din-
ner speech something like this:

"I like this fine. I never camped out before; but I had a pet
'possum once, and I was nine last birthday. I hate to go to school.
Rats ate up sixteen of Jimmy Talbot's aunt's speckled hen's eggs.
Are there any real Indians in these woods? I want some more
gravy. Does the trees moving make the wind blow? We had five
puppies. What makes your nose so red, Hank? My father has lots
of money. Are the stars hot? I whipped Ed Walker twice, Saturday. I don't like girls. You dassent catch toads unless with a
string. Do oxen make any noise? Why are oranges round? Have
you got beds to sleep on in this cave? Amos Murray has got six
toes. A parrot can talk, but a monkey or a fish can't. How many
does it take to make twelve?"

Every few minutes he would remember that he was a pesky
redskin and pick up his stick rifle and tiptoe to the mouth of the
cave to rubber for the scouts of the hated paleface. Now and
then he would let out a war whoop that made Old Hank, the
Trapper, shiver. That boy had Bill terrorized from the start.

"Red Chief," says I to the kid, "would you like to go home?"

"Aw, what for?" says he. "I don't have any fun at home. I hate
to go to school. I like to camp out. You won't take me back
home again, Snake-eye, will you?"

"Not right away," says I. "We'll stay here in the cave awhile."

"All right!" says he. "That'll be fine. I never had such fun in
all my life."

We went to bed about eleven o'clock. We spread down some
wide blankets and quilts and put Red Chief between us. We
weren't afraid he'd run away. He kept us awake for three hours,
jumping up and reaching for his rifle and screeching: "Hist!
pard," in mine and Bill's ears, as the fancied crackle of a twig or
the rustle of a leaf revealed to his young imagination the
stealthy approach of the outlaw band. At last I fell into a troubled sleep, and dreamed that I had been kidnaped and chained
to a tree by a ferocious pirate with red hair.

Just at daybreak I was awakened by a series of awful screams
from Bill. They weren't yells, or howls, or shouts, or whoops, or
yawps, such as you'd expect from a manly set of vocal organs—

they were simply indecent, terrifying, humiliating screams, such as women emit when they see ghosts or caterpillars. It's an awful thing to hear a strong, desperate, fat man scream incontinently in a cave at daybreak.

I jumped up to see what the matter was. Red Chief was sitting on Bill's chest, with one hand twined in Bill's hair. In the other he had the sharp case knife we used for slicing bacon; and he was industriously and realistically trying to take Bill's scalp, according to the sentence that had been pronounced upon him the evening before.

I got the knife away from the kid and made him lie down again. But, from that moment Bill's spirit was broken. He laid down on his side of the bed, but he never closed an eye again in sleep as long as that boy was with us. I dozed off for a while, but along toward sun-up I remembered that Red Chief had said I was to be burned at the stake at the rising of the sun. I wasn't nervous or afraid; but I sat up and lit my pipe and leaned against a rock.

"What you getting up so soon for, Sam?" asked Bill.

"Me?" says I. "Oh, I got a kind of a pain in my shoulder. I thought sitting up would rest it."

"You're a liar!" says Bill. "You're afraid. You was to be burned at sunrise, and you was afraid he'd do it. And he would, too, if he could find a match. Ain't it awful, Sam? Do you think anybody will pay out money to get a little imp like that back home?"

"Sure," said I. "A rowdy kid like that is just the kind that parents dote on. Now, you and the Chief get up and cook breakfast, while I go up on the top of this mountain and reconnoiter."

I went up on the peak of the little mountain and ran my eye over the contiguous vicinity. Over toward Summit I expected to see the sturdy yeomanry of the village armed with scythes and pitchforks beating the countryside for the dastardly kidnapers. But what I saw was a peaceful landscape dotted with one man plowing with a dun mule. Nobody was dragging the creek; no couriers dashed hither and yon, bringing tidings of no news to the distracted parents. There was a sylvan attitude of somnolent sleepiness pervading that section of the external outward surface of Alabama that lay exposed to my view. "Perhaps," says

I to myself, "it has not yet been discovered that the wolves have borne away the tender lambkin from the fold. Heaven help the wolves!" says I, and I went down the mountain to breakfast.

When I got to the cave, I found Bill backed up against the side of it, breathing hard, and the boy threatening to smash him with a rock half as big as a coconut.

"He put a red-hot boiled potato down my back," explained Bill, "and then mashed it with his foot; and I boxed his ears. Have you got a gun about you, Sam?"

I took the rock away from the boy and kind of patched up the argument.

"I'll fix you," says the kid to Bill. "No man ever yet struck the Red Chief but what he got paid for it. You better beware!"

After breakfast the kid takes a piece of leather with strings wrapped around it out of his pocket and goes outside the cave unwinding it.

"What's he up to now?" says Bill, anxiously. "You don't think he'll run away, do you, Sam?"

"No fear of it," says I. "He don't seem to be much of a home body. But we've got to fix up some plan about the ransom. There don't seem to be much excitement around Summit on account of his disappearance; but maybe they haven't realized yet that he's gone. His folks may think he's spending the night with Aunt Jane or one of the neighbors. Anyhow, he'll be missed today. Tonight we must get a message to his father demanding the two thousand dollars for his return."

Just then we heard a kind of war whoop, such as David might have emitted when he knocked out the champion Goliath. It was a sling that Red Chief had pulled out of his pocket, and he was whirling it around his head.

I dodged, and heard a heavy thud and a kind of sigh from Bill, like a horse gives out when you take his saddle off. A rock the size of an egg had caught Bill just behind his left ear. He loosened himself all over and fell in the fire across the frying pan of hot water for washing the dishes. I dragged him out and poured cold water on his head for half an hour.

By and By, Bill sits up and feels behind his ear and says: "Sam, do you know who my favorite Biblical character is?"

"Take it easy," says I. "You'll come to your senses presently."

"King Herod," says he. "You won't go away and leave me here alone, will you, Sam?"

I went out and caught that boy and shook him until his freckles rattled.

"If you don't behave," says I, "I'll take you straight home. Now, are you going to be good, or not?"

"I was only funning," says he, sullenly. "I didn't mean to hurt Old Hank. But what did he hit me for? I'll behave, Snake-eye, if you won't send me home, and if you'll let me play the Black Scout today."

"I don't know the game," says I. "That's for you and Mr. Bill to decide. He's your playmate. I'm going away for a while, on business. Now, you come in and make friends with him and say you are sorry for hurting him, or home you go, at once."

I made him and Bill shake hands, and then I took Bill aside and told him I was going to Poplar Cove, a little village three miles from the cave, and find out what I could about how the kidnaping had been regarded in Summit. Also, I thought it best to send a peremptory letter to old man Dorset that day, demanding the ransom and dictating how it should be paid.

"You know, Sam," says Bill, "I've stood by you without batting an eye in earthquakes, fire, and flood—in poker games, dynamite outrages, police raids, train robberies, and cyclones. I never lost my nerve yet till we kidnaped that two-legged skyrocket of a kid. He's got me going. You won't leave me long with him, will you, Sam?"

"I'll be back some time this afternoon," says I. "You must keep the boy amused and quiet till I return. And now we'll write the letter to old Dorset."

Bill and I got paper and pencil and worked on the letter while Red Chief, with a blanket wrapped around him, strutted up and down, guarding the mouth of the cave. Bill begged me tearfully to make the ransom fifteen hundred dollars instead of two thousand. "I ain't attempting," says he, "to decry the celebrated moral aspects of parental affection, but we're dealing with humans, and it ain't human for anybody to give up two thousand dollars for that forty-pound chunk of freckled wildcat. I'm willing to take a chance at fifteen hundred dollars. You can charge the difference up to me."

So, to relieve Bill, I acceded, and we collaborated a letter that ran this way:

Ebenezer Dorset, Esq.:
  We have your boy concealed in a place far from Summit. It is useless for you or the most skillful detectives to attempt to find him. Absolutely, the only terms on which you can have him restored to you are these: We demand fifteen hundred dollars in large bills for his return; the money to be left at midnight at the same spot and in the same box as your reply—as hereinafter described. If you agree to these terms, send your answer in writing by a solitary messenger tonight at half-past eight o'clock. After crossing Owl Creek, on the road to Poplar Cove, there are three large trees about a hundred yards apart, close to the fence of the wheat field on the right-hand side. At the bottom of the fence post opposite the third tree will be found a small pasteboard box.

The messenger will place the answer in this box and return immediately to Summit.

If you attempt any treachery or fail to comply with our demand as stated, you will never see your boy again.

If you pay the money as demanded, he will be returned to you safe and well within three hours. These terms are final, and if you do not accede to them, no further communication will be attempted.

Two Desperate Men.

I addressed this letter to Dorset, and put it in my pocket. As I was about to start, the kid comes up to me and says:

"Aw, Snake-eye, you said I could play the Black Scout while you was gone."

"Play it, of course," says I. "Mr. Bill will play with you. What kind of game is it?"

"I'm the Black Scout," says Red Chief, "and I have to ride to the stockade to warn the settlers that the Indians are coming. I'm tired of playing Indian myself. I want to be the Black Scout."

"All right," says I. "It sounds harmless to me. I guess Mr. Bill will help you foil the pesky savages."

"What am I to do?" asks Bill, looking at the kid suspiciously.

"You are the hoss," says Black Scout. "Get down on your hands and knees. How can I ride to the stockade without a hoss?"

"You'd better keep him interested," said I, "till we get the scheme going. Loosen up."

Bill gets down on his all fours, and a look comes in his eye like a rabbit's when you catch it in a trap.

"How far is it to the stockade, kid?" he asks, in a husky manner of voice.

"Ninety miles," says the Black Scout. "And you have to hump yourself to get there on time. Whoa, now!"

The Black Scout jumps on Bill's back and digs his heels in his side.

"For heaven's sake," says Bill, "hurry back, Sam, as soon as you can. I wish we hadn't made the ransom more than a thousand. Say, you quit kicking me, or I'll get up and warm you good."

I walked over to Poplar Cove and sat around the post office and store, talking with the chawbacons that come in to trade. One whiskerando says that he hears Summit is all upset on account of Elder Ebenezer Dorset's boy having been lost or stolen. That was all I wanted to know. I bought some smoking tobacco, referred casually to the price of blackeyed peas, posted my letter surreptitiously, and came away. The postmaster said the mail carrier would come by in an hour to take the mail on to Summit.

When I got back to the cave, Bill and the boy were not to be found. I explored the vicinity of the cave, and risked a yodel or two, but there was no response.

So I lighted my pipe and sat down on a mossy bank to await developments.

In about half an hour I heard the bushes rustle, and Bill wabbled out into the little glade in front of the cave. Behind him was the kid, stepping softly like a scout, with a broad grin on his face. Bill stopped, took off his hat, and wiped his face with a red handkerchief. The kid stopped about eight feet behind him.

"Sam," says Bill, "I suppose you'll think I'm a renegade, but I couldn't help it. I'm a grown person with masculine proclivities and habits of self-defense, but there is a time when all systems of egotism and predominance fail. The boy is gone. I have sent him home. All is off. There was martyrs in old times," goes on Bill, "that suffered death rather than give up the particular graft they enjoyed. None of 'em ever was subjugated to such supernatural tortures as I have been. I tried to be faithful to our articles of depredation; but there came a limit."

"What's the trouble, Bill?" I asks him.

"I was rode," says Bill, "the ninety miles to the stockade, not barring an inch. Then, when the settlers was rescued, I was given oats. Sand ain't a palatable substitute. And then, for an hour I had to try to explain to him why there was nothin' in holes, how a road can run both ways, and what makes the grass green. I tell you, Sam, a human can only stand so much. I takes him by the neck of his clothes and drags him down the mountain. On the way he kicks my legs black-and-blue from the knees down; and

I've got to have two or three bites on my thumb and hand cauterized.

"But he's gone," continues Bill, "gone home. I showed him the road to Summit and kicked him about eight feet nearer there at one kick. I'm sorry we lose the ransom; but it was either that or Bill Driscoll to the madhouse."

Bill is puffing and blowing, but there is a look of ineffable peace and growing content on his rose-pink features.

"Bill," says I, "no heart disease in your family, is there?"

"No," says Bill, "nothing chronic except malaria and accidents. Why?"

"Then you might turn around," says I, "and have a look behind you."

Bill turns and sees the boy, and loses his complexion, and sits down plump on the ground, and begins to pluck aimlessly at grass and little sticks. For an hour I was afraid of his mind. And then I told him that my scheme was to put the whole job through immediately and that we would get the ransom and be off with it by midnight if old Dorset fell in with our proposition. So Bill braced up enough to give the kid a weak sort of smile and a promise to play the Russian in a Japanese war with him as soon as he felt a little better.

I had a scheme for collecting that ransom without danger of being caught by counterplots that ought to commend itself to professional kidnapers. The tree under which the answer was to be left—and the money later on—was close to the road fence with big, bare fields on all sides. If a gang of constables should be watching for anyone to come for the note they could see him a long way off crossing the fields or in the road. But no, sirree! At half-past eight I was up in that tree as well hidden as a tree toad, waiting for the messenger to arrive.

Exactly on time, a half-grown boy rides up the road on a bicycle, locates the pasteboard box at the foot of the fence post, slips a folded piece of paper into it, and pedals away again back toward Summit.

I waited an hour and then concluded the thing was square. I slid down the tree, got the note, slipped along the fence till I struck the woods, and was back at the cave in another half an hour. I opened the note, got near the lantern, and read it to Bill. It was written with a pen in a crabbed hand, and the sum and substance of it was this:

Two Desperate Men.

Gentlemen: I received your letter today by post, in regard to the ransom you ask for the return of my son. I think you are a little high in your demands, and I hereby make you a counter proposition, which I am inclined to believe you will accept. You bring Johnny home and pay me two hundred and fifty dollars in cash, and I agree to take him off your hands. You had better come at night, for the neighbors believe he is lost, and I couldn't be responsible for what they would do to anybody they saw bringing him back.

Very respectfully,

Ebenezer Dorset.

"Great pirates of Penzance!" says I; "of all the impudent——"

But I glanced at Bill, and hesitated. He had the most appealing look in his eyes I ever saw on the face of a dumb or a talking brute.

"Sam," says he, "what's two hundred and fifty dollars, after all? We've got the money. One more night of this kid will send me to a bed in Bedlam. Besides being a thorough gentleman, I think Mr. Dorset is a spendthrift for making us such a liberal offer. You ain't going to let the chance go, are you?"

"Tell the truth, Bill," says I, "this little he ewe lamb has somewhat got on my nerves, too. We'll take him home, pay the ransom, and make our get-away."

We took him home that night. We got him to go by telling him that his father had bought a silver-mounted rifle and a pair of moccasins for him, and we were going to hunt bears the next day.

It was just twelve o'clock when we knocked at Ebenezer's front door. Just at the moment when I should have been abstracting the fifteen hundred dollars from the box under the tree, according to the original proposition, Bill was counting out two hundred and fifty dollars into Dorset's hand.

When the kid found out we were going to leave him at home, he started up a howl like a calliope and fastened himself as tight as a leech to Bill's leg. His father peeled him away gradually, like a porous plaster.

"How long can you hold him?" asks Bill.

"I'm not as strong as I used to be," says old Dorset, "but I think I can promise you ten minutes."

"Enough," says Bill. "In ten minutes I shall cross the Central, Southern, and Middle Western States, and be legging it trippingly for the Canadian border."

And, as dark as it was, and as fat as Bill was, and as good a runner as I am, he was a good mile and a half out of Summit before I could catch up with him.